H. J. Bessey.
1966

The Garden House

by the same author
(*for the young*)

*

THE DAFFODIL BIRD
THE SEA MICE

The
Garden House

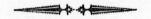

RUTH TOMALIN

FABER AND FABER
24 Russell Square
London

First published in mcmlxiv
by Faber and Faber Limited
24 Russell Square London W.C.1
Printed in Great Britain by
Latimer Trend & Co Ltd Plymouth

To
N. V. L.

Contents

The Garden House   *page* 11

PART ONE

1. Feet-off-the-Ground   23
2. Rabbit   32
3. Vole   37
4. Santa   39

PART TWO

5. School   53
6. Listener   61
7. Governess   67
8. Waif   75
9. Talons   80
10. Bird-field   86

PART THREE

11. Beau Temps   101
12. Dragon's Teeth   113
13. Harvest   117
14. Brownie   128

Contents

15. Dormouse   *page* 132
16. "In Mornigan's Park . . ."   142

PART FOUR

17. Treason and Plot   151
18. Day-boy Prefect   166
19. A Squirrel by Christmas   174
20. Winter Holiday   188
21. Snowdrop   202
22. The First of March   215

PART FIVE

23. Water-hide   223
24. Cuckoo   234
25. Caravan   245
26. "The Bird of Time"   252

Unwatch'd, the garden bough shall sway,
The tender blossom flutter down,
Unloved, that beech will gather brown,
This maple burn itself away;

.   .   .   .   .

Uncared for, gird the windy grove,
And flood the haunts of hern and crake;
Or into silver arrows break
The sailing moon in creek and cove;

Till from the garden and the wild
A fresh association blow,
And year by year the landscape grow
Familiar to the stranger's child.

Alfred, Lord Tennyson—*In Memoriam*

The Garden House

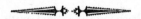

Grandmother called Ralph into her bedroom to see the full moon that had risen over the Wicklow Hills. The moon, swimming above white feathers of mist, was not silver or gold, but red.

The March night was still. Hardly a breath of wind swung the budding sycamores beyond the garden wall. The sheep, with their new-born lambs, were quiet in the fields. The peak of the Sugar-loaf mountain glittered with snow; faint apricot shadows lay on the lower slopes.

Grandmother's bedroom was dark, except for a tiny glow above the window seat. Ralph knew that Aunt Lizard would be sitting there, smoking a cigarette. The moon hung in the eastern sky like a copper gong or a Chinese lantern. Grandmother told Ralph: "You might never see a moon that colour again."

Grandmother had been a schoolmistress; her instinct, when a child came in her way, was to admonish it or to improve its mind. This was natural to her as breathing, whatever she might be doing. Shelling peas, for instance, one summer morning at the kitchen table, her fine contralto had been raised in song:

The Garden House

"Lives of great men all remind us
We can make our lives sublime,
And, departing, leave behind us
Footprints on the sands of time:

Footprints, that perhaps another,
Sailing o'er life's solemn main,
A forlorn and shipwrecked brother,
Seeing, shall take heart again."

—while her blue Irish eye gleamed with laughter, and the
peas went bobble, bobble, into the basin. Though elderly, she
was still handsome, with black hair and a pink-and-white
complexion.

Tonight her hair, uncoiled, streamed down her back, over
her grey silk dressing gown. She had just come upstairs after
feeding the cats—last ritual of her day.

Grandfather Izard's farm was called Nine Wells. The long
white house overlooked a mile of green paddocks, interlaced
with streams. The house had a derelict basement, where once
a bevy of maids had lived like mice in the twilight under the
ground floor. Now their sitting room was an apple store;
even in March, rows of crinkled yellow apples filled one
shelf, and their sweet reek met one at the top of the basement
stairs. In the echoing pantries, among spiders and white-
aproned ghosts, mother cats lay with their kittens, nesting on
copies of *Horse and Hound*. The old kitchen, with its gaunt
cold range, was the cats' refectory. Neither sun nor moon
could penetrate its low, ivy-sealed windows. Each evening
the farm cats prowled up and down at the back door—Tinker,
Tailor, Soldier, Sailor, black, white, tortoiseshell, tabby, with
their many-coloured children—until Grandmother appeared.
She led the flock down the basement stairs, encouraging

them in a high-pitched chant—"P-u-u-u-u-u-ussies! P-u-u-u-u-u-u-ussies!"—to the dishes set ready on newspapers by the last of the maids, old Nan Hanlon.

Shadows—one tall, with Roman nose, candlestick and a knot of hair; smaller ones, with waving tails and mewing profiles—danced around the mistress as she went down into that eerie darkness, holding her candle high. The basement door was shut, and the cats were left to lap and crunch in the dark, eyes glinting over skim milk and rabbit bones. In the night they would squeeze one after another through a broken window pane, and return to their farmyard hunting.

Only one cat did not join this orgy. Cuckoo, a haughty grey tabby belonging to Aunt Lizard, lived apart in the high sunny bedroom she shared with Ralph.

Ralph had not been to sleep. Sent upstairs after supper, he had lingered on the upper landing, within sight of the comforting hall light, hearing the murmur of voices at the distant fireside. At night the loneliness of Ireland haunted him. The house was like a little island in a sea of darkness. The night sounds—a curlew's call, a bleating sheep, a whinny from the paddock—were like sad cries for help. He shivered, pressing against the banisters, until Grandmother's rallying chant told him that his vigil was over. Then he bolted into the bedroom, rushed into pyjamas and was ready to feign sleep, when he heard Grandmother call him. Her quick ear had not missed a scuffle and creak from his room, as she came upstairs. He appeared, wary, expecting reproof; but her thoughts were on the moon.

He leaned over her window sill, gazing first at the moon, as he was told, and then down into the garden where he spent most of his day. The garden seemed more real to him than the home he had left a year ago to come here "from China all the way". He knew every foothold in the apple trees, every

13

den in the thick box hedges and the snowberry patch. Just below, hidden in the dark, was the sundial. (Could you have a moondial? he wondered.) In the distance, he could just make out the white lines of the greenhouse. He thought with a smile of his secret, out there between the plum wall and the greenhouse: the garden house he had built.

It had been the work of weeks: an airy structure of pampas grasses, pea sticks and Jerusalem artichoke stalks, thatched with last year's rusty ferns, and carpeted inside with moss from the orchard wall. The carpet alone had been a day's work. The thick roots of a fig tree made a natural armchair. He had polished it, cushioned it with grass and fern, and dragged a round log from the woodshed for a table. He had searched the garden beds, keen as a mousing owl, for scraps of china, pink, white and blue, to set the table. He had found an old wire geranium basket to serve as a fireplace. A little shelf of jutting brickwork he had set with ornaments: snail-shells from the box roots, palest pink and grey, or striped in brown and yellow like a mint humbug: delicate as the china in Grandmother's cabinet. He had laid a fire ready, with dry grass, tiny sticks, little knobs of coal carried there in his pockets. Tomorrow he could roast an apple; he could bake a potato; he could invite Aunt Lizard to dinner, in his own house . . . tomorrow. . . .

"Fast asleep. Take him to bed, girl," he heard. And then, "Have you told the child yet?"

"Not yet," came Aunt Lizard's voice, gentle as the snuffing of her cigarette in the ash tray.

Ralph's eyelids did not flutter; but his grandmother lowered her voice. "Why not leave him here with us? Surely that would be best?"

"I did promise Rose. . . ."

At the sound of his dead mother's name, Ralph was wide

awake; but still his eyelids were too heavy to lift, his ear not quick enough to catch Aunt Lizard's next words. Now Grandmother was urging, "Yes, if you still had your own little home! But not to be taking him off with you, all round the moon. . . ."

"Next year," Aunt Lizard murmured. "When Rollo comes over . . . and then, I suppose, he'll go to school. . . ." Rollo was Father, another face dimly remembered, left behind with *The North China Daily Post.*

In the silence that followed, Ralph felt himself beginning to drift out of the window, across the garden, towards the brilliant moon. An owl shrieked from the spinney: or was it Grandmother's voice, raised sharply:

"But if you're to go the day after tomorrow! . . ."

Ralph jerked upright.

"Going where?" His teeth began to chatter. "Told me *what?*"

"Only that we're going to England, chicken. To Uncle Laurie's. Come on to bed, now you're awake."

"I was awake. Going away where? I *am* awake."

Aunt Lizard wrapped him in a rug that prickled his legs, like climbing the juniper tree. He could hear her smile as she said slowly:

"In England . . . there's a forest. In that forest is a park. In that park there is a garden. In that garden is a cottage . . . the garden house. You'll like it there. We both will."

Grandmother lit a candle. In the flickering light he looked at them, bewildered.

"I *have* a garden house," he stammered. "Not in England. Out there—" Struggling with dismay and with sleep, he began to wail: "I was going to light a fire tomorrow. It was all a secret. I can't go away to England . . . just when it's ready!"

The top stair creaked. Grandfather, appearing in the door-

15

way, said mildly to no one in particular, "Y' should all have more sense." He set down his lamp, picked up the child, carried him over the landing and slid him into bed. The sheets were cold as snow; they folded him, and he was feasting on apples, white-hot and sweeter than honey, in the house by the greenhouse door; a house filled with treasures, carpeted in green velvet, and lit by a low red lamp that he might never see again.

But, next morning, when Ralph ran down the garden, free from lessons because it was "the last day"—when he turned the corner of the greenhouse, ready to duck down and crawl through his front door—the door was gone. His house was gone. Under the wall lay a pile of rubbish, fern, grass, scraps of broken crockery, a handful of twisted wire, an armful of artichoke stalks, and the woodshed chopping block, missing for a week. Old John had cleared away the mess, unlocked the greenhouse door, and was busy inside with seed boxes and flower pots. He looked at Ralph sourly, because this, he felt, was not his proper work; he was here to see to the horses, not to be philandering with flower pots. To the boy he seemed more savage than he guessed; he had played the Wolf: *I'll huff, and I'll puff, and I'll blow your house down.* Ralph stood for a moment, shivering in the bitter air, and then quickly went away.

In the kitchen, the blind tabby Sailor sat before the range, gazing between the bars at the glowing cinders. His purr had dried to a rattle in his throat. He swayed, drunk with sleep. Nan Hanlon sat at a corner of the table, drinking red tea. Grandmother was ironing.

Ralph hovered in the doorway, making the hinge creak annoyingly. Their placid calm mocked him. He fought his tears.

"Come in, or go out," Grandmother advised him.

Playing for time, he asked, "Can I take one of the kittens to England?"

"You can, but you may not."

"I do want to see that garden house."

"Well, it won't run away before tomorrow, child."

"It could fall down!" Ralph hurled his squib. "Don't you know that? It could get burnt! *You* could get struck by lightning, anyone could! The ship could sink, tomorrow!"

Afraid he had gone too far, he added in a different, frivolous tone, "Would they have a special lifebelt for the cat?"

A cinder fell from the range, and Sailor backed a pace.

"Sure, we're all in the hand of God," said Nan Hanlon pensively, stirring her tea with the sugar spoon and placing it back in her sugar pot. The red stain spread through the white sugar like moonlight on snow.

Grandmother set down her iron on a stand carved like an ebony fern. She turned the shirt on the table, and again the iron went to work. Unresting, unhasting, upright as a bamboo stalk, she began to recite,

> "*The state of man does change and vary,*
> *Now sound, now sick, now blithe, now sary,*
> *Now dancing merry, now like to die:*
> *Timor mortis conturbat me.*"

She went through seven verses. Ralph caught the drift of the dirge, and it was strangely comforting. It put into words what he knew to be true; and the truth could be faced. What he had feared was the mocking grown-up quip—*It's all your silly imagination!*

At the seventh verse, Aunt Lizard appeared from behind him, saying, "Would you like to come and help me pack?"

He answered meekly, "I should like a piece of seed cake."

Upstairs, kneeling by an open trunk, Aunt Lizard asked, "What were you shouting for? Or, doesn't it matter now?"

"Oh . . . no. It doesn't matter."

He sprawled in a patch of sunlight, eating his cake. Cuckoo, the grey cat, stirred in the rocking chair, sniffed, caught the whiff of caraway seeds and went to sleep again. Watching Aunt Lizard pack her painting things, Ralph asked:

"What will you paint, in England?"

"Well. First, I'm going to draw fifty wild flowers. In pen and ink, for a new book."

"What will you do, when you're not drawing?"

"Look after the house. And Uncle Laurie—he's the head gardener—and Fergus, and you. Fergus will be at school all day. *His* mother's dead, too. Uncle Laurie isn't there all the year round."

She was deftly wrapping and stowing as she spoke.

"Where else will Uncle Laurie be?"

"At another garden, over here in Ireland."

"Is he my Uncle Laurie?"

"No, nor mine. He's Grandfather's cousin. But if you like," said Aunt Lizard briskly, "you may call him 'Cousin Laurie twice removed'."

"No, I don't think so . . . Aunt Lizard!"

"Well?"

"Could we keep some of your pictures, this time?"

She looked up in surprise. Ralph explained:

"We never keep them, do we? Or—could I take one from here? Could I take two?"

He ran to the wardrobe, slid out a shelf and brought two small framed pictures, wrapped in green baize. Quickly he unwrapped them. One showed a lion, pale honey-green, faintly smiling, lying in a cave among green weeds and shadows. In the other, a forest path led to a little bridge over a stream. Each had her signature, L. Izard, like a black twig in the corner. Ralph had found the two pictures one wet day, while exploring the dark cavern of the wardrobe: it was usually kept locked.

Aunt Lizard did not glance twice at them. She looked thoughtfully into the trunk, and said:

"But—those are put away."

"Oh, *why*? I like them. I like the lion's face, and the other one, with that peacock——"

"Pheasant——"

"I think they're quite the best you've done," Ralph said, in unconscious echo of Grandfather's serious, critical approval. "Don't laugh!" he added, laughing himself. "Can—may we take them?"

"Yes! You may have them for your own." Aunt Lizard covered the pictures again, and fitted them into the trunk.

Ralph played hopscotch in a patch of sunlight. He would take something of his own choice from Nine Wells; as he had brought away something from China—his mother's green leather-covered diary, with the writing on the flyleaf: "Rose Izard, from Ralph Oliver. Christmas 1926." He was glad, too, that Aunt Lizard was packing her Swiss inkstand, with the carved cat's-head lids set with golden eyes, like the eyes of the lion in her painting.

Out in the paddock a magpie chattered. Ralph strolled to the window and waited to see the flash of black-and-white wings. Two magpies fluttered up into the walnut tree; quarrelling, perhaps, over a last year's walnut found under the violet leaves there. Ralph thought of the walnut, with its beautiful bitter smell, and the green rind that would be black now, like a forest in winter; enclosing the walls of shell, that enclosed the sweet nut. He thought of tomorrow's journey. What had Aunt Lizard said, last night? "In a forest—in a park —in a garden. . . ." He was torn between romantic hopes of shipwreck and his eagerness to see the next garden house.

PART ONE

1

Feet-off-the-Ground

The clanging of a bell woke Ralph. He could not think where he was. The bedroom was dark, except for a square of light reflected on the ceiling. The bell seemed to be ringing out of doors. He jumped out of bed. Another bed stood by the wall. He ran his hands over the pillow; empty, and the bedclothes folded neatly back. Was it morning, then? Below the uncurtained window he made out a gabled roof, with a lamplit skylight. Beyond, chimneys and high peaked trees rose against a dark blue sky. Ralph pushed up the window. Icy air streamed over him, and he heard a roaring like the sea. The bell stopped ringing; not far off, he heard footsteps, a bicycle bell, men's voices and a tuneful whistling.

Leaning out, he realized that the roaring came, not from the sea, but from a high grove of trees swaying in the wind. Memories of yesterday began to tease him. He stood with one cold foot crossed over the other, trying to sort them out.

Yesterday had begun with a cart horse, and ended with a pony. It was still dark when Grandfather and Grandmother stood on the steps at Nine Wells to wave goodbye. The luggage had been loaded on the car; inside were two baskets, one holding a docile broody hen named Black Lady, the other holding Cuckoo, stiff with dismay. The car would not start; and then John had led out Prince, the farm horse, and hitched him on to the front. Ralph, pleased and surprised, thought Prince would pull the car to the station five miles away; but after a few yards the engine hummed, Prince was unhitched, and they drove away under the budding sycamores.

There was no shipwreck that morning. They landed at Holyhead, and the long afternoon in the train went by, as Ralph sat watching the endless dip and soar of telegraph wires, and the little dark objects like mice scurrying along them. Aunt Lizard held Cuckoo on her knee; he was quiet, except for the darting of his wild green eyes. Then they were in London, having a late tea at aunt Emmy's house, where he had stayed last year when he came from China. But soon they were in another train, and night and sleep closed over him, until he woke at a country station with the name Hurst Castle painted on hanging lamps. He felt certain he had woken then; surely he could not have dreamed the drive that followed?

Aunt Lizard and the luggage disappeared into a taxi. A tall boy lifted Ralph into a trap behind a black pony. They drove away under a high echoing archway, into a forest. Grey tree trunks loomed on either side of the white road, like church pillars; boughs met overhead like a church aisle. They moved through a funnel of windy darkness; Ralph remembered the smell of oil from the square carriage lamps, the click of the pony's hooves, the creak of harness. A white owl hovered once in the lamplight, startling the pony to a gallop. The driver—Fergus?—stood up, tightening the reins. The pony's ears flicked back, listening with brief interest to his shouted curses; it continued to bolt in the direction of its stable. The trap rocked, and one of the lamps began to flare. Then something appeared in the roadway ahead. The pony saw it first, and dropped into a trot, ears pricked forward. The driver blew at the flaring lamp. Before the flame went out, Ralph saw a creature standing still to gaze at them, its antlered head high, ready to spring away. The pony snorted and pulled up with a frightening plunge, ready to bolt backwards, trap and all, in alarm that was only half pretence. Then, with a leap, the stag was gone. The driver turned excitedly to Ralph, but his words were blown away. They trotted on fast through the swaying trees, past a stone house with pillars like tree trunks. The forest gave way to open country; the gale swept over them, spattering their faces with rain, and the tired pony trudged with head down, dragging its hooves through shingle, like a child on the beach. Then they were sheltered again by a belt of trees; lights shone, and suddenly they had arrived. Ralph remembered a lighted doorway; a room with a huge log fire; a new, delectable smell which he could not place; and a bowl of bread and milk which he was too sleepy to eat. He remembered nothing else, until the bell began to ring.

Behind him the door was opened a crack, and Aunt Lizard put her head through. The wind redoubled its pace, and she hurried to put down the tray she carried, to pull down the window and hustle Ralph back to bed. She disappeared, and returned with a hot water bag under one arm, and Cuckoo under the other. The hot water bag went under Ralph's feet, and the tray on his knees. Cuckoo, offered a nest in the eider-down, sprang to the floor and began irritably to wash. Aunt Lizard took a white net from her trunk, and fastened it across the open window, hammering in half a dozen little staples.

"He mustn't go out yet," she warned Ralph. "Not alone, on any account. He might get lost."

"May *I* go out?"

"Not now. A good rest, while I'm getting straight. Don't come down till I tell you." She clicked the door shut on his protest.

Ralph finished bread and butter, boiled egg and cocoa, and slid the tray to the floor. An electric light switch, like a smooth walnut, dangled over his pillow. He clicked off the light, and lay listening to the sounds outside: birds, a man singing, loud creaking and sliding noises which he did not know, and a sound that was either a cart horse walking or a pony trotting. He closed his eyes to listen better.

Again the bell woke him. Now the room was yellow with midday light. He sprang to the window. Just below the sill was a blue slate roof; beyond was another roof of mossy tiles, and, at right angles, a flat stone coping a hundred yards long. At either end rose a massive glasshouse, high, white and sparkling as the Sugar-loaf peak. From each mountain, a grey wall stretched into the distance.

Ralph pushed the window up again. Cedar branches hung down close to the blue roof. A little green bird was fluttering among the needles; its head was crested as if with a tiny flame. Gazing at it, he did not hear the soft pad of Cuckoo's paws on the carpet. The next moment the cat had sprung through the open window, dashed across the roof and disappeared behind a high chimney.

Appalled, Ralph swung his bare feet over the sill and slid after him. He landed softly on the roof. Through the skylight he caught an intriguing glimpse of the top of Aunt Lizard's head. She was standing at a table; behind her he saw a narrow kitchen, and the glow of a kitchen fire. Should he call to her that Cuckoo had escaped? As he hesitated, Cuckoo came from behind the chimney and crossed the next roof, moving with his belly close to the ground, as though hunting; but he was not hunting—he was trying to take his bearings in a new place. If he moved too far away, he would be lost, as Aunt Lizard had said; and then he might try to find his way back to Ireland, trotting with blistered paws across England and Wales, struggling in the stormy Irish Sea. . . . Ralph groaned with misery at this picture. He must catch Cuckoo at once. He hitched his pyjama trousers, knotted the string and started in pursuit.

The cat ran over the tiled roof. Rose thorns grabbed at Ralph as he followed. At the end was a small cold chimney. Ralph looked down it, and a bird flew out with a shriek. Cuckoo looked round, then sprang on to the high flat wall, and from there to the glass mountain.

Ralph stood on the high flat wall. Before him lay what seemed like miles of gardens; windless, walled in like the inner courtyards of an old castle. "Joyous Gard," he thought; and then—"Aunt Lizard said, *Don't come down*. But I shan't."

Cuckoo was stalking along a wooden catwalk on the mountain. Supposing he ran down the wall? Inside, he would be safe in the garden; but outside lay lawns, trees and open parkland. Ralph thought, I *must* catch him on the wall. . . .

"Feet-off-the-ground!" he called to Cuckoo. They had often played this game together in their bedroom at Nine Wells—from bed to chair, from chair to tallboy, from tallboy to window sill, over the fender, round the slippery base of the wardrobe.

He edged gingerly along the catwalk, clinging to a wooden ridge above his head. Below was a sheer drop through a lower greenhouse. Pausing to rest, trembling with excitement, he looked for the first time through the glass. Green leaves pressed against the panes; he saw a cluster of creamy flowers, and pale yellow fruits. Oranges: growing under the glacier, on the slopes of the mountain!

Smiling at this discovery, he paced confidently along the

cliff. Suddenly it ended. He wriggled round a stone urn, over a green door—an ice bridge, he thought, over a crevasse—and round another urn. It rocked dangerously, and he gasped. He stood still, his heart stood still, the urn stood still. He was safe, on the long wall. Far ahead, he saw Cuckoo still snaking rapidly along. Turning at the angle of the wall, Cuckoo hesitated and glanced back, then darted away again. Ralph rested, watching him.

Close to the wall was a clump of trees with long, pearl-grey catkins. Running his fingers down them, Ralph thought they felt silky, like the cord on Grandmother's fur. What would Grandmother say if she could see him now, out in the March wind, in his pyjamas, chasing the cat along a wall? He grinned, and crawled on. Cuckoo, a dozen yards along the cross-wall, had stopped and was sniffing the air suspiciously.

A moment later, Ralph knew why. An acrid, choking whiff came up from a greenhouse below; through the glass he saw a swirling white fog. He held his breath, scurrying sideways like a crab. The cat was crossing an archway over a garden path. Ralph followed quickly. The smell died to windward. Looking down through another glass roof, he saw a jungle of orchids, green, amber and cream-coloured; he remembered orchids in his mother's house. Now he was looking at a high shelf set with pots, and in the pots, among fresh leaves, were strawberries, half ripe, pale green, pink and white. Below he saw masses of flowers, daffodils, lilies of the valley and blue irises. He took a deep breath; but the strawberries and flowers kept their sweetness to themselves, sealed under the glass, out of the keen wind.

Looking far down the wall enclosing the lower garden, Ralph saw Cuckoo standing on his hind legs, peering through a window. As Ralph looked, the cat crouched low, then reared up again, dancing from one hind paw to another.

28

Something had made him forget his disquiet. Now was the time to catch him!

"I'll double back," Ralph thought, "and come up the wall from the other end." He turned and scurried past the gas-filled house without drawing breath, then started down the parallel wall, painfully wriggling on hands and knees. He turned the corner, and stopped short with a gasp. In a glasshouse behind the lower wall there was an orchard of peach trees in full blossom, pale pink against walls painted pale blue. Brown bees flew from three white hives under the trees. The sun broke through the grey sky and sparkled in a barrel of water; a tap dripped, sending rings of brightness across its surface. Planted beside the barrel, Ralph saw a long yellow cane, topped by a wisp of white fur. He stared. He had made wands of that kind himself, in the garden at Nine Wells, playing at magic. Did some other child play here? But the glass orchard was deserted as the garden. Since he started after Cuckoo, he had not seen a living soul. He was alone, except for rooks in the treetops, and Cuckoo, still prancing at the window.

Ralph turned the corner and started up the other wall. Shed roofs sloped downward to his left; then came the brick wall where Cuckoo had found the window under the eaves. He came to the window; but Cuckoo was gone.

Through dusty glass, dim with cobwebs, he saw a dark little room below—a narrow box between wooden walls, hung with black leathers. He made out a lantern, hanging on a nail, and a shelf with brushes and curry combs, and another with tins and bottles. A harness room. On either side, he heard a stamping of hooves, champing of oats, the rattle of a halter ring; then the whirring sneeze of a horse blowing an oat from its nostril.

But what had so excited Cuckoo? And where had he gone?

His face pressed to the glass, Ralph saw the answers. Under

29

the far window was a bin, with a round measure that gleamed like dull silver; a scatter of oats had been left inside. As he watched, something moved in a crack in the wall. First, a whisker, then a nose, then with a spring a mouse jumped on to the bin and scrambled into the measure. Another mouse followed, and a third. Ralph could imagine the squeak of claws on metal as they fled. Then, above the bin, he saw something else. Cuckoo dropped with a soft flump from the roof to the window sill, and then, with hardly a pause, from the sill to the top of the open window. He was inside the harness room. The mice were gone. Ralph saw Cuckoo sniff at the measure, then settle down, front paws folded under, to watch the crack in the wall where the three tails had vanished.

Ralph sat back on his heels. He need not worry now. Cuckoo would not try to walk to Holyhead, to swim to Ireland—he had found a new hunting ground. Ralph left the window and crawled on. He passed a cart shed where, on a bale of straw, a man sat eating bread and cheese and reading a newspaper. Ralph smiled at the thought of the three dining-rooms, side by side—for the man, the horses and the mice: all unaware of each other as they ate. Only the poor cat was still hungry—and *himself*. A sudden wave of hunger swept over him. He was famished. He stood up and boldly took the long wall at a trot. He reached the second glass mountain, and climbed around it; again through the glass he saw blossoming fruit trees, and a tank of goldfish; but he could not stop. He dropped on to the upper wall, and in the distance, for the first time, he saw the garden house—square, and grey, with a blue slate roof, and sash windows painted white, and cedars towering behind.

He ran, monkey-wise, on all fours; as he drew level with his bedroom window, the bell clanged out from the yard behind him, and he heard men's voices again. He scrambled across the roofs, and skinned his knees as he rolled back over the window sill. He was rubbing them when Aunt Lizard opened the door, a covered plate in her hand. The plate held three smoking pancakes. He tasted fried chicken, bacon, mushroom, as he bit and swallowed and bit again. Aunt Lizard thoughtfully picked bits of cobweb from his hair, then a scrap of dead leaf and a green needle. She looked at his pyjamas, covered with shreds of moss, then suddenly caught her breath and cried:

"*Where's Cuckoo?*"

Not waiting to swallow, he tilted his head towards the stables, and nodded, like a duck, to help his mouthful down and to reassure her.

"He's all right! He's mousing, in a harness room. I went after him—we played feet-off-the-ground. He's got a mouse-hole down there. . . ." Watching her, he knew when it was safe to grin and take another pancake.

Aunt Lizard sat on her bed.

"Fergus said to tell you: you may go wherever you like, but *not* in the stokeholds, and *not* in the glasshouses, till he takes you."

"I don't——" he bit the pancake. Aunt Lizard took it away and brought his shorts and jersey.

Rapidly dressing, he thought of glaciers, oranges, poison gas, strawberries, orchids, peach blossom: they might all stay out of bounds. He did not want them. A pancake in each hand, he ran down the steep staircase, out of the front door, and paused to take his bearings. Then, like a homing cat, he darted away to find the harness room.

2

Rabbit

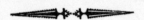

I n the west park, a hundred yards from the harness room,
a clump of beeches drew Ralph out to climb and swing
on their trailing boughs. One bough was polished like a
saddle by generations of riders. Cantering gently, Ralph
noticed earth flying up from a bramble patch near by. He
put his right foot to the ground, and watched. Then he saw
the flick of a white tail. He sat still. A rabbit backed out,
glanced round with twitching nose, laid its ears back and
began to nibble grass. For a long time Ralph sat motionless,
while the rabbit hopped to and fro, a few feet away, in the
thin afternoon sunlight. Then the garden bell rang. The
rabbit skipped into its burrow, and Ralph limped home, his
left foot stiff with pins and needles.

In the kitchen, he found Aunt Lizard cutting bread and
butter at a table shaped like half a mushroom, set against the
wall. Cuckoo scratched at a table leg that was almost worn
through from the claws of many cats. A satchel and school
cap lay on the dresser; in the next room, where tea was laid,
Ralph found the boy who had driven him through the forest.

Fergus Metherell was fifteen years old; a tall, thin, Scottish-
looking boy, with bright hair the colour of Grandfather's bay
pony. He silently ate four pancakes, a whole rice pudding

with strawberry jam, an orange and half a new ginger cake. Then he told Ralph, "Come and see my dormouse."

His bedroom lay next door, through a short stone passage. It overlooked a green churchyard to the east, and a chapel to the north; a queer, dim room, Ralph thought; but his eyes went quickly from a bow and arrows, in one corner, to the boy's museum set out on shelves—feathers, fossils, birds' eggs, bones—and down to a trapdoor in the floor beside the fire-place.

"What's *that* for?"

"The trapdoor? Oh, a secret passage," said Fergus care-lessly. He took a chocolate box from a shelf, and parted a covering of moss to show Ralph the sleeping dormouse. It was still as a mouse of pale milk chocolate, and cold to the touch. Ralph asked:

"He's not alive?"

"Listen."

At last Ralph heard a faint whistling snore.

"That's how I found him," Fergus said. "We were having a paper chase through the woods, on bikes, and I stopped to pump up my tyre. I heard a funny little noise, but I thought it was the pump. Then I kept still, and I heard it again, and I thought it was a bird, but I couldn't see one. So I hunted around, and I found this chap, curled up in a rabbit bury. Lucky it was me, not a weasel."

"Where will you keep him, when he wakes up?"

"Oh, I shan't keep him. I'll let him go, in the woods."

"I wish——" said Ralph; and was silent. Fergus looked at him.

"If you want a pet, what about a rabbit? I'll make you a hutch for it."

"Oh, yes!"

"A hutch for what?" Aunt Lizard asked from the door.

"Could he keep a rabbit? I did when I was a child," said Fergus.

"A rabbit? Yes, I expect so, if we can find one."

Ralph stopped himself on the point of crying, "I know where to find one!"

He ran through the archway by the back door, across the paved Dutch garden, across the bell yard, over the west park to the beeches. He lay down and slid one arm inside the rabbit's burrow. The length of his arm inside, a tree root grew across the tunnel. The rabbit must be in a nest down there, beyond his reach. He went back to jog on the saddle branch, keeping watch; and again he saw the rabbit wriggle out backwards, graze for a time, and hop back into its burrow.

Next morning, Ralph was up and dressed before the seven o'clock bell had finished ringing. He tiptoed downstairs. Aunt Lizard was in the kitchen, cooking breakfast for Fergus. He turned the key of the front door with both hands, and ran out into cool starlit twilight. Reaching the burrow, he lay down on the carpet of brown beech leaves, pressed his right hand against the inside wall of the tunnel, and waited; a long, long wait.

Cocks crowed in the distance. He jumped when an owl flew low over his head, with a sharp "Queeep!" A boy passed, swinging two empty milk cans, and stared at him curiously. The sky grew lighter. Suddenly he heard a thump and a scuffle, deep inside the burrow. The rabbit was wriggling round the tree root. Ralph braced himself. Fur brushed the palm of his hand. His fingers closed round two soft hind feet.

The rabbit's frantic kick surprised him, and he almost lost his grip. Thrusting his other hand in, he clasped the furry body and drew it out. He thought the rabbit might bite him, as a young jackdaw had done at Nine Wells; but it huddled

34

in his arms, burying its nose in his jersey, stiff with fear. It did not struggle again. It was a young one, he thought—half-grown perhaps—dark-eyed, with glossy brown fur. He knelt on the beech leaves, rocking it to and fro. He had never had a pet of his own before. He told it, over and over, "You're all right, you're all right, I won't hurt you. . . ." Looking up, he saw the boy with the milk cans; they were full now, and he carried them as though each weighed a ton. He nodded at the rabbit and said with respect:

"Nice pie you've got, then."

"It's not a *pie*," Ralph said furiously, "it's a *pet*," and sped away to show Aunt Lizard and Fergus.

He burst into the warm kitchen, where Fergus was drinking coffee and buckling his satchel.

"Look! Look! I've got it. When will you make the hutch?"

"What on earth . . . I say, a *rabbit*!"

Surprised at Fergus's surprise, Ralph cried:

"But you said, if I could find a rabbit . . ." He turned to Aunt Lizard. "*You* said . . . and Fergus said he'd make a hutch. . . ." He stopped, out of breath from running.

"Darling . . . not a *wild* rabbit!"

Something was wrong, he saw by their faces. He put the rabbit on a chair. It cowered, pressing its muzzle into the cushion. Cuckoo paused in his washing to stare with disbelief. They all stared. Ralph looked from Fergus to Aunt Lizard, his triumph ebbing. He repeated stubbornly, "It's my rabbit."

"Where did you find it?"

"Over in the park. By some trees."

He explained how he had caught it. Fergus gave a shout of laughter.

"Catching a wild one! Wait till I tell the keeper!" He swallowed the coffee and ran for his bicycle, calling back:

"We'll make the hutch tonight!"

Aunt Lizard said slowly, "Ralph . . . it was clever of you. But it wouldn't be happy in a hutch."

"Then *why* did you say I could?" He stroked the rabbit. "Look how soft it is . . . and it only eats grass. . . ." His voice trailed away.

"You see . . . we meant a tame rabbit."

"But I'll tame it! And look how quiet it is."

"It's so frightened. It would die of misery. Poor little thing."

He stroked the rabbit's ears. It started and gave a grunt of terror, pressing its nose against the chair back. Ralph sighed. Defeated, he picked it up and trailed out.

His sandals made black patches in the grey dew as he crossed the park. Cuckoo trotted after him, devoured by curiosity, shaking his wet paws absently, while with pricked ears and critical nose he took note of this new hunting ground.

3

Vole

Cuckoo loved his new home. Each evening he slipped out at dusk to the stable yard, the park or the fir plantation, and presently he would be heard crying *Muuuuuuuuurow!* as he hurried across the Dutch garden, eager to show Aunt Lizard what he had caught. An April kitten, this was his first spring hunting; he was enthralled by the rich variety of game outside the garden house.

Rolling proudly on his back in the yard, showing his handsome stomach with its pale fur and twelve black spots—a six of dominoes—he taunted his prey: a wretched mouse, it might be, a young rat, or a baby rabbit. He found a doe's nest in the elm grove and caught the weaned litter, one after another, eating them down to the waist and leaving the furry hind part among the primroses by the back door. Ralph watched him fiercely, determined that Cuckoo should not eat *one* rabbit; he was sure he would know his pet again. Then Cuckoo seemed to tire of rabbiting. He brought in several long-tailed field mice, and once a shrew, which he would not eat: a pathetic morsel of dark fur, with a nose like a single cowslip pip.

One evening, Aunt Lizard was out when Cuckoo's call came from the Dutch garden. Fergus was doing homework at the table in the breakfast room. Ralph slipped out. A moment later he was back, with a little brown object in his palm.

"Is it dead?" he asked Fergus. "What is it, a mouse?"

"It's a little vole."

Ralph tried to warm it in his hands. "Cuckoo wasn't even there. He just left it on the path. I think it's *dazed*."

"It's alive all right," said Fergus. The vole had opened its bright eyes. It lifted its nose and sniffed the air.

"Oh, Vole!" cried Ralph, dancing with pleasure at the prick of its feet. He found an empty goldfish bowl on the scullery shelf. Holding the vole carefully in one hand, he picked grass and leaves with the other, to make a nest. He told Aunt Lizard anxiously:

"I'm nursing it back to health."

Safe from the cat, the vole seemed to make a rapid recovery. It frisked on Ralph's sleeve and nuzzled his jersey, as though puzzled by wool and skin. In the glass cage, it sucked a raindrop from a leaf, and burrowed a tunnel through the grasses. Fergus offered it a withered hazel nut; but it would not eat. It ran to and fro in Ralph's hand, brief whiskers tickling his wrists. He put the glass bowl on a chair by his bed, covered it with wire netting, and lay awake listening to the patter and rustling.

In the morning, he woke with a throb of excitement. All was quiet in the glass cage. He parted the grasses, and found Vole curled in a ball, like the dormouse, nose drooping between cold paws. It was dead. Ralph was stricken by something meek and helpless about the little corpse, so busily alive at nightfall, and tears ran down his fingers into the goldfish bowl.

He dug a grave the size of an egg cup in the churchyard grass. Aunt Lizard gave him a white forget-me-not to plant there, and Fergus carved on a flower pot label: "Vole. *Vale*."

4

Santa

Woodsmoke: this was the unfamiliar smell which Ralph had noticed when he first came into the garden house. A log fire burned all day on one hearth or another, lit by Fergus before he dressed for school. As soon as the seven o'clock bell had rung, a garden boy brought a barrow load of sticks, then another of logs, to replenish the woodshed by the back door. The woodshed had once been a bakehouse, and at one end there was still a rusty stove and oven; above was the chimney in which Ralph had surprised a starling, on that first morning's climb. Coals were heaped in front of the old oven, and logs and kindling neatly stacked.

Now the house was filled with another thrilling smell: whitewash. Uncle Laurie was still away at the estate in Ireland, and Aunt Lizard decided to spring clean the kitchen and scullery before his return. Ralph helped her to stack china, pots and pans out of the way, to roll mats and spread dust sheets. The sweep came first, and they breakfasted upstairs at dawn on tea and porridge made on an oil stove; a picnic which only Ralph enjoyed, as he enjoyed all that week. He could not understand why Aunt Lizard should be short-tempered, Fergus so glum and Cuckoo distracted. He roamed about the house, envying the workmen, and was sorry to see

39

them depart with their ladders, brushes and buckets. The weather had changed while they were at work; the sky was blue, the air soft, the sun shone through the kitchen window on to the fresh cream-coloured walls, with their pungent new-painted smell which would remain for Ralph the authentic smell of springtime.

Now Ralph had a daily task of his own. In the long low shed at the end of the yard—an old brewhouse, with a vast round copper—the broody hen, Black Lady, was sitting on twelve duck eggs. A superb mother, Black Lady had to be prised off her eggs each morning to peck at a saucer of grain, drink from her water dish and take a short stroll in the yard before fussing back to her coop. Ralph acted as henwife. The whole performance took only ten minutes, but he was always thankful when the lid of the coop could be lowered over her beady, dedicated stare, leaving him free until next morning.

Free: to explore the gardens, the frame yard, the rubbish yard, the fir plantation, the sheds and outhouses; to watch Frank grooming the horse and the pony, or Harry oiling the motor mower on which he would ride, day after day, through the summer; to gallop at full speed across the west park to the oak tree knoll, and then lie, perhaps, for an hour on the grass under the maple tree, watching the bees come to the flower clusters hanging like little bunches of pale green grapes. He liked to steal into the harness room, to surprise a mouse at play on the corn bin. The mice, at home inside the wooden wall, sometimes sat with their tails dangling care-lessly through a crack in the boards. Ralph played a game with them, tiptoeing in to touch the tails and see them vanish.

Cuckoo no longer troubled the stable mice, preferring to hunt outdoors; but he still brought in his prey to be admired. Often he left it, unhurt, to return to the chase. He was drunk with power.

One evening, Ralph dashed into the room where Fergus was at work.

"Fergus! Here, quick!"

"Go away."

"No, no——"

"How can I do algebra? Well, what?"

"Cuckoo's got a baby rabbit. It's *tiny*. He's gone off and left it. It's not hurt. But it's lost its mother——"

Fergus, with a patient grown-up sigh, threw down his pen and followed Ralph.

It was not a rabbit. It was a baby hare; small, glossy, golden-brown, flecked with black. Its head was round as a kitten's; its eye black and intelligent. Set down on the kitchen rug, it did not cower, as the rabbit had done, but raised its head to gaze alertly round. Ralph murmured:

"Isn't it *awake*?"

"I don't think it's hurt," Fergus murmured. "But it's awfully young——"

Their eyes met in the firelight. Ralph said:

"We can't set it free without its mother."

A pair of Ralph's socks hung by the fire. Fergus took one and slipped the little hare inside. Its bold small face peered over the top, soft ears laid back. Ralph cried:

"It looks—like Christmas morning. Fancy getting a hare in your stocking!"

Fergus did not answer. He handed the squirming sock to Ralph. He said, "Look. We've got to feed it somehow."

"In books," Ralph said, "they always use a fountain pen filler. What *is* a fountain pen filler?"

"*I* don't know. Perhaps it's that rubber tube the ink goes in?" Fergus began to rummage through a dresser drawer; then another. Then he shook out a jar that stood on the dresser shelf. Rubber bands, pencil stubs, safety pins, farthings,

41

knobs of sealing wax, beads, paper clips, cascaded over the dresser. Fergus muttered, "I know there was an old one here. To hell with spring cleaning!"

"An old *what*?"

"Fountain pen. It's no use. I'll have to use my own."

He took his school pen to pieces. Blue-black ink streamed down the scullery sink as he washed the rubber tube under the tap, washed and blew and washed until the water ran almost clear. Ralph squatted by the fire, tilting a saucepan of milk over the coals. The pan turned dark brown where the milk did not reach. The boys crouched on the mat, Ralph still clasping the sock, while Fergus with infinite care tested the warmth of the milk. The little creature took no notice of the rubber tube at its lips. Fergus squeezed. It shook its head, and drops of milk flew about. Fergus shook more drops between its lips. It wriggled. Quite suddenly, it blinked, sniffed and tasted. A pink tongue flickered. Fergus and Ralph hung over the sock, hardly breathing. There was more wriggling and more spilt milk.

"He licked that drop. He swallowed it. I saw."

"He's supposed to suck. He isn't."

"Let's try soaking a bit of bread, shall we?"

Aunt Lizard, coming in from her walk, stopped short in the doorway, too surprised to speak. Her kitchen might have been ransacked by thieves. The two boys lay full length on the mat, their nurseling between them. At her gasp, two faces looked up, sharp with reproach.

"Sh! Sh! He's asleep!"

Cuckoo brought in a mouse and crunched it loudly under the kitchen table. Ralph sat with the sock on his knees. Fergus said:

"He'd better sleep in my room."

"Oh, no!" Ralph prepared to grizzle and beg; but Fergus

cut him short. "Cuckoo comes in your window, doesn't he?"

The cat-net had long been taken down. Ralph nodded. Cuckoo came in and out of the bedroom window as he pleased. The hare would not be safe in the same room. Resigned, Ralph went upstairs, leaving Fergus to finish his algebra in pencil, while he nursed the sock in the crook of his left arm.

But, in the dark, Ralph suddenly thought of Vole. It had seemed so well and sprightly; but it had died in the night.

"I won't go to sleep," Ralph thought. "I'll creep down to Fergus's room and look after the hare. If I'd stayed awake, perhaps Vole wouldn't have died. Perhaps it was hungry. I'll go down at midnight."

But midnight struck, and Ralph slept. It was Fergus who lay awake. The little hare scuffled and scampered about his room half the night, refreshed every hour by drops of milk which Fergus warmed for him in a tin over a candle.

"Isn't he *racy*?" Ralph said admiringly next morning, watching his pet dash to and fro in the kitchen; and Racy he was called.

Now began a strenuous time for Ralph. The little hare thrived. Ralph was his nursemaid. No one else had time. Aunt Lizard was busy all day with housework, or drawing in the high light garret which Fergus called "the Sky". After tea she went out to find colt's-foot, or cuckoo-pints, or cowslips, for her drawings. Her table under the skylight was ranged with little glass pots, each holding a single flower. There were pots of indian ink, too, and all kinds of painting gear; but now the Sky was out of bounds to Ralph, because of his mischievous charge.

The hare grew quickly. He was beautiful, long-legged, long-eared, graceful, restless and inquisitive; he took up all

Ralph's time. Ralph loved him devotedly, but sometimes he looked fagged. Racy was not like patient Black Lady. He would not be shut in anywhere. If Ralph were free for ten minutes at once, he might think himself lucky.

Racy had learned to suck from a rubber teat; then, quickly outgrowing it, he sucked for a day or two at a milky crust; then he was drinking from a saucer, splashing eagerly, so that Aunt Lizard said he must be fed in the woodshed.

Fergus brought a hurdle of split hazel sticks, and fitted it across the open door of the woodshed. Shut in, Racy butted at the hurdle, but could not move it. He was still too young to jump over it. His saucer empty, he amused himself by knocking down the neat piles of sticks, scrabbling in the coal and scattering tins of shoe polish from the shoe cleaning bench. A lid fell off, and Racy's chest and muzzle were plastered a rich chocolate when Ralph came out to inspect him. Wisps of straw could not clean him. Ralph had to bathe his fur with cotton wool and soapsuds, and to rub him dry in a sack. He looked like a raddled lamb. He was not subdued.

Fergus thought Racy should have a hutch, and learn to stay quietly in it for "rests".

"A big hutch," Fergus said, "not a little hovel."

"A boudoir," Aunt Lizard agreed.

"He might like it," Ralph said hopefully.

Fergus, at home now for the Easter holidays, made the hutch from a roomy crate, and set it on a little platform by the kitchen window. "You won't be lonely," Ralph promised him.

Racy was not lonely; he never lived in the hutch. Shut in for his first "rest", he threw himself against the wire, butted the door, and tried pitifully to squeeze himself between the slats. Growing frantic, he began to race in circles, throwing

out his long hind legs. He was released after ten minutes, and
that was the end of his captivity.

By day, he skipped about the house and yard. Fergus took
the hurdle from the woodshed door, and fastened it across
the archway into the Dutch garden.

Callers had to be warned, for Racy's safety. Some came
daily: the postman first, at six o'clock in the morning, opening the back door with his cheerful cry—*Postyman! Thank
you!*—as he picked up the letters left ready for the post. Then
came the boy with his wood barrow and milk can; and later
a man from the kitchen garden, with a basket of spring cab-
bage, young carrots, an apple-green lettuce from the peach
house or a punnet of mushrooms from the brewhouse pit.
Butcher and grocer came once a week; the baker twice. All
patiently unclipped and reclipped the hurdle. None brought
a dog.

"Dogs," Aunt Lizard warned Ralph—"we'll have to watch
for dogs!" No dog lived near by; but any day, without
warning, a visitor might bring one. At night a stray dog
might come. Racy still spent his nights with Fergus. When
the hare was tired of dozing, Fergus would drop him into
the churchyard, to run about safely inside its lattice work
fence. Sometimes Fergus complained bitterly of his broken
nights: "If it's not Racy, haring about, it's cuckoos making
that filthy din. When *he* stops flouncing, *they* start cuckooing."

Cuckoo the cat was no longer a danger. Racy had even
tried to romp with him; but Cuckoo backed away at his
approach, and fled to the lid of the water-tank outside the
kitchen window. There he sat for hours, watching Racy
with the stern gaze of an older child deploring a toddler's
antics. Racy, in his turn, took over Cuckoo's wicker apple-
basket by the range, and—Ralph declared—would sometimes
sit quietly in it for two minutes by the clock.

Racy was growing up. Instead of bread and milk or porridge, he ate dry oats, apple, carrots, raisins, lettuce, cake, radishes and daffodils.

It was April, and daffodils were everywhere; massed in the shrubberies, under budding thorn trees and horse chestnuts; on the high lawn, in the "pleasure ground", in the wild orchard and the grove of wych elms beyond; daffodils, narcissi and jonquils, single and double, ancient and modern, yellow, deep gold, creamy, lemon-coloured. Aunt Lizard made a drawing of a wild daffodil. Ralph hunted for the little "hooped petticoats", the green-spotted snowflakes, and the rich-coloured polyanthus narcissi which, he said, "smelt like the taste of watercress". He and Racy played hide-and-seek among them. Fergus saw them in a different light.

Fergus wanted a tent for the summer holidays. He wrote to his father, and a bargain was struck. Twice a week, on Sundays and Thursdays, he got up at dawn to pick for the daffodil market. The owner of the estate was abroad, and would not return for two years; so the daffodil fields were stripped, the budding flowers lightly piled in wooden trays, and then bunched in the packing shed by the stables. The flat-backed bunches were laid between layers of tissue paper, and the trays piled on a cart to catch the London train. Fergus and two men from the garden would work at the job all day; Fergus was paid twopence for a dozen bunches. As fast as they picked, new buds seemed to spring up behind them. At night, when Fergus closed his eyes, he saw, like the poet, a host of daffodils; but by day, as he snapped and tied the dripping stems, his feet numb, his fingers chill, he pictured the tent he would have: pale green, with snow-white guy ropes, pitched in some grassy byway, and himself sitting in front of it, beside his evening fire.

In the soft weather, the countryside had a powdered look. A light bloom seemed to lie across the sunlight, like the bloom on the young horse chestnut leaves and cowslip stalks. Cuckoos called at dawn and in the twilight. The mud-lined nest in the laurel hedge had a clutch of blue eggs. Black Lady's ducklings hatched, and pattered to and fro, straw-coloured, on the straw before her coop. If she had misgivings about these broad-billed, web-footed chicks, she still mothered them fondly, keeping them under her eye with ceaseless calls and cluckings. But one stormy afternoon she had a shock. Rain, streaming down the sloping yard, gathered in a deep pool beside the shed wall. The warm drops splashed into great glassy bubbles on the puddle; it was thick and pale as barley water from the chalky soil of the yard. The ducklings rushed from shelter and plunged in. Ralph, hearing Black Lady's shrieks, found her dashing helplessly up and down by the brink. As fast as Ralph caught the ducklings and returned them to the shed, so they eluded him and waddled back to the pool. Black Lady squawked in vain. They had found their element.

Ralph thought of them when, a day or two later, the dormouse awoke in the chocolate box. Fergus, going into his bedroom, heard the mouse rustling and found him bright-eyed and alert. Already he had eaten the nuts left for him in the box. The two boys carried it over the garden paddock to a hazel copse bordering the "old garden"—an orchard with nut plats, rhubarb beds and beehives. Fergus set the box down under a briar. The dormouse scrambled through the briars and ran gaily up a hazel tree. His fur, so drab-looking when he was asleep, was now bright as the hazel bark. He swung down into a bramble, nipped off a young shoot and held it between his front paws while he ate. The boys stood watching. Bats fluttered in the dusk. From the wood came scents of sweet briar, old oak leaves and primroses. The dormouse was at home there, like the ducklings in the water.

Ralph waited anxiously for Aunt Lizard to say, "*Now* we must set Racy free." But the days passed, and she did not say it. Perhaps she thought Racy was too tame, too much of a pet, now, for life in the fields? He was quick; but he had grown trustful. Sometimes it was on the tip of Ralph's tongue to ask, "Could he look after himself, do you think? Could he get away from a dog?" But he kept the questions back; and before they were ever asked, Racy had shown him the answer.

For once, Racy was alone in the yard for a while, that afternoon. Fergus and his friend, Peter Hassall, had set up a row of hurdles in the west park. They were flying the hurdles, and Ralph had gone out to watch.

The Sealyham pack that came with their owner into the Dutch garden had no need of hurdle practice. Their mistress went on to the garden office, on a peaceful errand to buy daffodils. Too late, she found that her dogs had not followed. For all their short legs, the hurdle was no obstacle. Scenting Racy, they bundled over it on wings of glee, and made straight for the clump of balm where the hare was dozing. Pandemonium broke out. Racy uttered one high shriek, like the shriek of a frightened child. The Sealyhams yelped in chorus.

Ralph was gone before Peter and Fergus began to listen. He never remembered climbing the park fence. Perhaps, in his terror, he cleared it like a hurdle. Upstairs, in the Sky, Aunt Lizard dropped her pen and ran. The foreman ran from the garden, the dogs' owner close behind him. Her tweed skirt was ripped to shreds as she gallantly took the hurdle, certain that her rascals had caught a napping cat: but Cuckoo had sprung from the tank to greater safety on the roof. He watched, his eyes blazing.

Aunt Lizard was there first. Poor Racy had gone to ground in the woodshed. The place was littered with sticks, coal, logs, and yelling Sealyhams: she could not see what she dreaded to see. She hurled the little dogs right and left with trembling hands, while she searched for the torn remains of Racy—to hide them quickly, quickly, before Ralph could see them.

She could not find anything. Ralph came; Peter and Fergus came. The dogs, whining with disappointment, were dragged away. Their mistress hoarsely mingled curses and apologies.

There was no sign of Racy—not a wisp of fur, a ginger paw, or a drop of blood. He must have been torn to pieces on that one shriek; and the pieces mercifully veiled in dust. Very white, Aunt Lizard sat down on the shoe bench. At her nod, Fergus took the dogs' owner firmly away. Ralph, his face black with coal dust, was still searching through the debris, whispering to himself. Aunt Lizard could not bear the sound. She and Peter and Fergus went away into the house.

Ralph's screams brought them headlong back. They were shocked to find him in hysterics, shaken by peal after peal of laughter. He pointed to the old chimney, where a sooty object was thrashing its way downward. "A jackdaw," Aunt Lizard thought miserably, and took him by the arm. "Ralph, Ralph, be quiet——"

He jerked away and scooped the object into his arms. Hugging it, he struggled with tears, words, laughter, soot and the squirming creature. He gasped:

"I—I—I—the night he came—I said it was like C-C-C-C-Christmas——"

Fergus suddenly joined in his laughter. Racy, in Ralph's arms, shook cobwebs from his ears and whiskers, blinked soot from his sore eyes, scraped furiously with his strong hind feet, choked, sneezed, and rubbed himself against Ralph's jersey. Tears of laughter made runnels down Ralph's black face. They crowded round to feel the ledge inside the chimney where Racy had taken refuge.

Aunt Lizard broke away at last to put on the kettle for tea and poke the fire for hot baths. Ralph followed her into the kitchen, carrying Racy. He said in his normal voice, very happily:

"*Now* we'd better call him Santa."

PART TWO

5

School

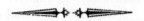

After the smell of woodsmoke, the smell of whitewash; and after whitewash, wistaria. This was the smell of May at the garden house. The grey boughs that lay across the grey front wall were thickly hung with mauve flowers, opening from slim tassels to blowsy festoons. Indoors and out, their heavy sweetness filled the air, drowning the lighter scents of tulips and forget-me-nots in the Dutch garden.

The daffodils were gone, but white pheasant's-eye narcissi were still in bud in the shrubberies, under pink hawthorns and chestnut candles.

Ralph could count fifteen nests in his morning saunter through the fir plantation, the derelict rock garden, the orchard, wych elm grove, and back through the pleasure ground, where red squirrels skipped in the redwood trees. *Pleasure ground*: it was an apt name. He found nest after nest there, in the low boughs of blue spruce, juniper, cedar, pine and cypress trees, and in the half circle of spotted laurels enclosing the rose garden at the lower end. At the top end, overlooked by the back windows of the garden house, high lawns sloped towards the "great house", with its tall, white-shuttered windows. From the terrace one looked down on a broad yew hedge dividing the lawns and gardens from the

east park. The hedge top was clipped so flat and smooth that
Ralph fancied one could run along it, and he thought he
would try some day.

The fifteenth nest had no eggs. Ralph was building it
himself, in a clump of ivy in the fir plantation. It was to be
made partly of moss and horse-hairs, like a chaffinch's; partly
of brown leaves, like a wren's; and, partly, like a long-tailed
tit's, of blue-green lichen from an oak tree. Fergus had named
each nest for him. His own nest he found surprisingly tricky
to build; and it was hard not to cheat—to take something that
a bird could not have found, like woodwool from the fruit
room, or feathers from his pillow. Struggling with eight
fingers and two thumbs, he was filled with respect for the
birds, who had only their beaks. He no longer scorned the
wood pigeon for its casual platform of crossed twigs; and he
greatly admired a pair of swallows building in the brewhouse, using a plaster of mud and wet beech bud scales,
scooped from the gutters.

Cuckoo meanwhile had a problem of his own. Five young
blackbirds had grown up in a nest in the fir plantation; and,
as they began to fly, he could not resist catching them one by
one. But these hardy fledgelings, once caught, did not hang
meekly in his jaws like baby rabbits. They flapped their wings,
fought and shrieked at the tops of their voices, frightening
the hunter out of his wits. Still clutching his prey, he would
bolt wild-eyed for the house, and, finding Aunt Lizard, cast
the blackbird at her feet with a look of appeal—*Take it away
and give me some milk*. Ralph carried the young birds back to
the plantation, often getting pecked in the process; but
Cuckoo would not learn. Half an hour later the shrieks would
be heard again, coming nearer and nearer as he raced for help
with another dangling victim.

A pair of golden-crested wrens had started to build in the

cedar, close to Ralph's bedroom window, but out of Cuckoo's reach. Ralph woke to their lisping chatter, and eyed their nest critically. Like fragile olive-green butterflies, they fluttered in and out of the branches, carrying tiny roots and hairs and feathers.

He was watching them one morning when Aunt Lizard called from the kitchen. He went down, still in pyjamas, and found a girl talking to his aunt: a tall girl, almost grown-up, he thought; but with a school satchel over her shoulder.

Aunt Lizard said calmly, "Here's Ralph. And this is Katy Wood. She's come to ask if you'd like to go to school?"

He looked at them, speechless. Katy said:

"We'll have to hurry. Governess doesn't like it if we're late."

Ralph had never been to school; but now it seemed that he was going. Katy took him in hand, washing his face, helping him to dress, polishing his shoes, deft and kind and firm as an old Nanny. Aunt Lizard poured milk for him to drink, and made him a packet of sandwiches—("Have you got a dinner bag?" Katy asked: "Never mind, it'll go in mine")— and a hot bacon sandwich to eat on the way.

Santa hopped in from the yard, and Ralph stood still with one arm in his coat sleeve. "Oh, I can't go! Who'll look after Santa?"

Aunt Lizard said, "I will."

"But—when you're up in the Sky—?"

"I'll take him with me," she promised; and Ralph had a vision of Santa streaked with indian ink.

He set off, running at Katy's side. They went through a clinking gate, over the north-west park by a narrow path, and out at a crossroads by the head keeper's house, with its grey stone pillars. Here Katy let him pause to eat his sandwich. A mirror four feet high stood at the roadside, opposite the drive. Katy strolled over to finger her curly hair. Ralph tried to read a mossy tablet on the side of the keeper's house. "The New Plantation," he read, and called, "what are all those capital letters? They don't make sense."

"They do," said Katy, "Mrs. Duffel told us. It's a date. More than a hundred years ago. There *is* Mrs. Duffel!" she added, pointing downhill to a figure on a bicycle. She waved; the figure waved back, toiling on towards them. Up the hill, a mile away on the skyline, they could see a row of black ants in silhouette.

"*She's* your teacher," Katy said tersely, "and *those* are the others, nearly up to the Castle Ride." She whisked him into a trot, saying as they ran, "You can have a rest at the yew trees, and one at the top of the bank, and then at the palm tree, and then at the Castle Ride."

The long hill to High Forest ran through a tunnel of oaks and beeches. The children's route to school was a ritual. From the keeper's house to the yew trees, they ran on the tarred road. From the yew trees, they followed a path along a steep mossy bank. For the second mile, they raced on a ribbon of soft turf between the hard road and the forest. Ralph kept watch for a palm tree, but could not see it.

The school, a long high building of polished flint, stood at right angles to the church. The tall windows, diamond-paned, were set so high that the children could see only the tops of the beeches bordering the forest. All day, from their desks, beyond the murmur and hum of the schoolroom, the quiet voice of Mrs. Duffel, and the more strident tones of Governess—the head teacher—they could hear the sound of the wind-blown trees.

Katy led Ralph into a classroom that seemed to him vast as a cathedral, smelling of soapsuds, chalk and cowslips. Mrs. Duffel followed, panting gently from her ride, and set him in a row of urchins at the bottom of the room. Katy had disappeared to some high rank. There was a hush, then a roar: "Good morning, miss; good morning, ma'am; good morning, sir"—the last to the Vicar, who had just come in. Then came a great clatter, as of hobnailed boots, although every boy and girl in sight was wearing plimsolls. The noise died away, and Ralph listened with the rest as the Vicar described the siege and fall of Jericho. The Vicar, once an Army chaplain, had been at the siege of Ladysmith; so for many years Ralph would keep a vivid impression of his first lesson at High Forest, picturing seven priests circling the city of Jericho, "bearing seven trumpets of rams' horns before the ark of the Lord", while "our fine fellows" inside the walls held out on a diet of rats.

Nothing for the rest of the day came up to this; and the day passed like a dream. Once, he found himself reading aloud to Mrs. Duffel, who smiled at him teasingly and said: "Shure, hasn't he the lovely Irish brogue?"

He did not know what to make of this. She asked:

"It *is* Irish, isn't it?"

"Chinese, I think," he ventured, after a moment's doubt. But at break, in the playground, a big boy dubbed him "Frenchy", and this was more puzzling still. He would have to ask Aunt Lizard what they meant. ("'A French mouse', come over with the Huguenots," Aunt Lizard was to tease him in her turn.) He was taken aback, to be a foreigner. Then Katy swooped to his rescue from the girls' playground, and the puzzle was forgotten.

In the classroom again, his neighbours began to nudge each other and to whisper in chorus, "Please, ma'am"—"Please, ma'am—could we *be* something?"—and again Ralph was at sea, but not for long. They wanted to write down some flight of fancy beginning, "I am a horse", or "I am a train"—to

57

escape a grammar lesson. Ralph knew this game of old, from lessons with Grandmother; and beginning over-hastily, "I am a Rabbi", he was soon launched on the story of his captured rabbit. Next to him sat a speechless child who hummed softly as his pen scratched across the page. Leaning over his shoulder, Mrs. Duffel read, "I am an Injun," and laughed. "A Red Indian, Tim?"

"Black," he whispered.

"Oh . . . you mean brown?"

"No, ma'am," breathed Tim. "The black tar injun that butters the road." In a trance, he continued to write.

All at once they were on their feet again, singing a chorus of which Ralph caught only the first line: *Be present at our table, Lord.* Morning school was over.

Their table was a beech stump at the edge of the forest, among bracken fronds and dog-violets. There Katy marshalled her band—three or four "big girls" and a family of young ones. One of the girls, Dora, uncovered a sheaf of cowslips and pale oxlips which she had picked on the way to school and hidden under a bush. She tied a string between two saplings and hung it with cowslip heads, then drew it together into a cowslip ball. She tossed it to Ralph; but, as they ran back to school, a boy snatched it from him and tore it to pieces with a laugh. Katy said, "I'll make you another, Ralph"; but already he was planning to make one for himself that evening; there were cowslips in the ditch beside the wych elm grove.

Nodding over a cardboard model of a fort, in the afternoon warmth and the smell of gum, Ralph suddenly pictured his return home. Would Santa have missed him? Would the chaffinch in the orchard have laid a second egg? Would Aunt Lizard remember that he would need dinner? Three o'clock: at this time, on each school day, she put two plates to warm on the rack above the kitchen range, ready for Fergus. Today it should be four plates: six, if she had made soup. . . . Gazing at the names on a map that covered the end wall—Northumberland, Cumberland, Durham with their dire sound—he thought of asparagus soup, of new potatoes simmering in mint, and of his favourite "pink pudding", made with rhubarb juice. He sighed. He seemed to have been away a week.

Suddenly, it was time to go home.

The low evening sun dappled the west park. Behind the elm grove, the stable yard was in deep shadow. Ralph sat in the harness room, at the end of his day at school, lolling on a horse blanket, watching Santa, and playing with the cowslip ball he had made.

He could hear the mice scampering behind the wooden wall. He and Santa and the mice had the place to themselves; the horse and the pony were grazing in the paddock after their day's work. Sparrows pecked and twittered in the empty loose box, and outside among long rows of pots holding young chrysanthemums. The twilit harness room felt homely. Ralph had spent many hours there on wet days. Frank, the horseman, never seemed to see him; but Ralph noticed that an oil can, and a bottle labelled *Pioson*, had disappeared from the shelf, the day after his arrival.

In the distance, he could hear Black Lady coaxing her ducklings home to their coop under an elm tree. Then he heard another sound—a long blast of the whistle which Aunt Lizard kept on a nail by the back door. There was a pause, then a second blast. Should he wait for the third? But he was really so tired that the thought of bath and bed was almost welcome. He took Santa under his arm, ducked under the bar of the loose box and trudged homeward through the frame yard. The duty-man was sliding glass lights on to

frames filled with boxes of seedlings. He winked at Ralph.
"Hello! Get the cane today?"

Ralph stared. So people knew he had been to school?

He felt a moment's dismay. It had been fun to come home
to five o'clock dinner, running alone across the home park,
greeting Santa and Cuckoo, describing his day to Aunt
Lizard with all the prestige of the traveller. But, ever since,
he had been secretly planning a retreat. It was all very well to
go to school for a day, for the fun of it (he would tell Aunt
Lizard); but he really did not think he could go again. There
was so much to do at home . . . all the time that he was
picking the cowslips, hunting in the packing shed for string,
tying and retying the flower heads that would not go quite
as Dora had shown him . . . all the time, he had had his
verdict ready: "I don't think I want to go there tomorrow."

But the duty-man's joke changed all that. He had not said,
"So you've started, have you?" or "How did you get on?"
or any of the things one might say to a beginner. From his
off hand tone, Ralph might have been going to school for
years; he might have started, with Miss Hazel's "infants", in
the little room behind the big schoolroom, from which came
the sound of voices chanting the alphabet, the faint creak of
a rocking horse.

Suddenly he grinned at the man. His plans turned a complete somersault; he could not cry off now, after all. And he
found, to his surprise, that he was longing for tomorrow.
He must get to bed quickly; he would have another early
start. Katy would be at the keeper's lodge at twenty past
eight, and he meant to be there first, waiting.

6

Listener

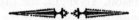

The forest children lived in a world of their own: an old world, far older than the date on the New Plantation plaque. It seemed only yesterday that King Charles had stolen by, disguised as a page, hiding for a night in the next parish. Only a year or so before that, Queen Elizabeth had ridden through the forest with her courtiers, and had christened the stony lane that led through the home farm: "Stumble-mare!" she had cried scornfully to her mount, when it tripped over a stone; and the watchers had given that name to the lane. It was still covered with loose stones, and still called Stubblemare.

Aunt Lizard laughed when Ralph brought home this tale; but a few days later she said, "Ralph, I apologize. I've been reading some local history. Queen Bess did ride this way, and she stayed here, too. Of course the country people would remember."

"After three hundred years!" said Fergus.

"How long is that? Less than five lifetimes. Grandfather would hear about it from his grandfather, and he'd tell his grandson. Imagine the story it would be. And then Stubblemare got into it. Or perhaps she *did* say something like it?"

The children would have jeered at these doubts and concessions. To them, such Royal events were as real as the Coronation just over. Dawdling up and down the long hill,

61

Ralph heard other scraps of history. Katy's grandfather remembered the planting of the Groves, an avenue somewhere in the woods. Dora's uncle had helped to plant the Larches, a spinney beside the Castle Ride that ran from High Forest to Hurst Castle. Several fathers and mothers could remember the great fire; not the fire of London, but the burning of the mansion. To them, the great house was "the new house", although it had stood there over thirty years. There were stories, too, about the ruined tower beyond the east park. Smugglers had hidden there, everyone agreed, and signalled with lights to their friends at sea. Nat Wood had other tales—about a dell in the east park where young men used to ride donkeys, like a circus. The old sexton had said so; and he said there was a ghost in the lane by the tower, a headless lady . . . but Nat, Katy's wild young brother, was not to be trusted.

Ralph learned other things: that you must never dig, or sew, in a thunderstorm, or the lightning would strike your spade—or your needle, if you were a girl; that if a yaffle called, or you saw several weasels hunting, that meant rain; that if a fierce snake happened to chase you, you could baffle it by *running in circles*; that even if you crushed a snake, it would not die until sunset; that olive oil was good for a viper sting; that if gipsies were about, they must all stay together, because gipsies stole children . . . and that if you were mixed up in a fight with Ricky Thrower or Ernie Thrower, you were fighting a whole clan—nine of them, the girls more deadly than the boys. He learned to dodge traps like: "You're *daft*"; "I'm not"; "You *are* daft"; "I'm not"; "*You* are daft!"; "No, I'm not, you are!"; "Oh, oooh, Harry, Lil, Ernie, he's calling names! He said I was daft!"

With Katy and her band, he escaped from the tougher element to share the gentlest of amusements; to hunt for sweetbriar, or "shiver grasses", or for oak apples, with their satin skins, coloured pale green, pink or cream; to pop the seed pods of lady's smocks, suck the honey from cowslip pips or clover, make dandelion whistles or play at "dibs" with white pebbles.

At break the girls often played games of their own, but the smaller boys would scramble up to watch from the playground wall. Years later, Ralph would read in a book of country memoirs that the singing and dancing games of the countryside had died out after the 'eighties. At once he would feel again the warmth of the stone wall through corduroy shorts, the smart of his shins where he had scraped them to reach his perch; and, closing his eyes, would hear the sound of the girls' weaving footsteps, and their voices chanting:

> "*Dan, Dan, thread-the-needle, Dan, Dan, sew*——"

or,

> "*Poor Jenny sits a-weeping, a-weeping, a-weeping,*
> *Poor Jenny sits a-weeping on a bright summer's day.*
> *O, why are you a-weeping, a-weeping, a-weeping?*
> *O, I'm weeping for my true love, on a bright summer's day:*"

or,

> "*Wallflowers, wallflowers, growing up so high,*
> *We are all the little ones, we stand by,*
> *Excepting Irish Ashdown, she's the only one,*
> *She can hop, and she can skip,*
> *And she can turn the candlestick:*"

or,

> "*In and out the windows,*
> *In and out the windows,*
> *In and out the windows*

63

As you have gone before.
Stand and face your lover,
Stand and face your lover,
Stand and face your lover
As you have done before.
Follow him to London . . ."

On two afternoons a week, Mrs. Duffel gave lessons in verse-speaking and acting to the upper forms. Then Mrs. Duffel was no longer the bland, amused, self-effacing assistant teacher, but a spirited actress, highlight of a hundred successful amateur plays. Ralph opened his eyes when he first saw her "tread a measure" with a shadowy Lochinvar:

> *"So stately his form, and so lovely her face,*
> *That never a hall such a galliard did grace"*

—and, a few moments later, as a Shipmaster, hallooing the opening lines of a shipwreck scene: "Boatswain! Good, speak to the mariners: fall to't yarely, or we run ourselves aground: bestir, bestir!"—in a voice that brought an echo—"stir!"—back from the churchyard wall.

Soon Ralph knew this scene by heart; and another in which Dora had to sigh and droop, while Katy rallied her:

> *"Shall we be sundered? Shall we part, sweet maid?*
> *No, let my father seek another heir . . ."*

Eloping daughters seemed to be a favourite theme; but, better than *Lochinvar* or *Lord Ullin's Daughter*, the boys liked a poem called *Going Downhill On A Bicycle*; and another which Ralph chanted at home:

> *"Old Meg she was a gipsy,*
> *And lived upon the Moors:*
> *Her bed it was the brown heath turf,*
> *And her house was out of doors."*

"Well, so is everyone's," said Fergus annoyingly.

With singing lessons, Mrs. Duffel was less ambitious. Two black-eyed brothers could sing. Tim Lamb, Ralph's shy desk mate, could be coaxed to raise his piping treble if Governess were not by; and a poised little girl called Francie had a voice to match her straight bright hair. With the others, Mrs. Duffel did her best. Tuning fork in hand, she drilled them patiently in country songs: *The Cuckoo*, *Strawberry Fair*, *Early One Morning*, and one beginning:

> "*Spring once said to the nightingale,*
> *I mean to give the birds a ball*"

—with a chorus in which the girls trala'd while the boys whistled like blackbirds.

Then they sang rounds: *London's Burning*, *I Hear Thunder*, and *The Chairmender*. This last they were taught to begin almost in a whisper: "because he's still right up at the top of the village, near the Crooked Billet"; then to sing more and more loudly: "now he's nearly at the school gate. Louder, children!"—and then diminuendo: "he's going farther and farther away. Now he's down at the bottom of the hill. Shhhh! He's nearly gone."

Only Ralph hated this round. It was Nat Wood's fault. He told Ralph that the chairmender was the ghost of a murderer, a fearful character who used to steal children away, and stuff chairs with their hair, and sell their clothes to the rag shop and their flesh as dried fish. Did Ralph believe this farrago? He was not sure. But at night the chairmender wandered in and out of his dreams, a plaintive stray, crying his skills and wares through the forest.

Sometimes on gloomy afternoons, as they made their way downhill, some distant sound would make him glance round uneasily, and hurry on with the others; straining forward to

E 65

catch the friendly noise of a woodman's chopper, and backward in terror of a far-off cry:

> *"Chairs to mend?*
> *Old chairs to mend?*
> *Mackerel, fine mackerel!*
> *Any old rags?*
> *Any old rags?"*

7

Governess

Governess, like her title, had remained a Victorian. Her special talents were for needlework and discipline. She was also a skilful teller of tales; and, if these were on the harrowing side, this made them more memorable.

One morning she told the story of the ten lepers. Ralph had imagined that lepers were found only in the Bible, like prophets and virgins and the sick of the palsy; but suddenly Governess began to talk of a young doctor she had known, who went to a fashionable gathering, and danced with a charming lady who chatted gaily to him . . . (the children waited, sensing danger: *Beware, beware, her flashing eyes, her floating hair!*) . . . and then the doctor's glance fell on her throat, and his smile froze; for there, just under her necklace, he saw *a little snow-white spot*. "Leprosy. And he died, children, in a leper colony." Then Governess recalled another poor leper, who tried a fearful cure for his disease: he thought, if he let a rattlesnake bite him, the snake venom might kill the poison in his blood. He was allowed to try, and a lot of doctors came to watch. At first the snake would not bite him. Then he pinched it . . . "he was dead in a few hours. Now get out arithmetic books."

Two days later, Ralph happened to notice something on his

wrist. A small white blister. He licked it idly; and then he gasped. He remembered what Governess had told them. "A little white spot." He glanced sideways at Tim, and pulled down his cuff; yet he knew it was no use trying to hide. Soon it would spread. He tried to go on with his long division sum, but he could not. What else had Governess said? "They had to go away and live with the other lepers. If they moved about, they must ring a bell to warn people." Aunt Lizard will come with me, he thought. But what would become of Santa, and Cuckoo? At break he avoided the others, wandering over the playing field to a patch of yews and fir trees. His wrist tingled. The May sun shone, and it made him feel sadder than ever.

Katy caught up with him at last.

"Where *have* you been? I've looked everywhere. We're playing one-foot-over-the-line, come on!" Then she looked at him, and added, "What's the matter? You hurt yourself?"

He showed her the white mark. She looked puzzled.

"That little nettle sting? That doesn't hurt! I saw you do it, down by the yew trees, and you never even noticed!"

"A nettle sting!" He stared. "Are you *sure*?"

"What did you think it was, a viper?"

"Leprosy," he breathed, and waited to see her turn pale.

Katy's shout of laughter was a reprieve. "Here," she said, "here's a dock leaf, wrap it round your wrist, that's right. And would you like a cheesecake? Come on, there's still time for a game if you make haste!"

The sunshine looked glorious. He bit into the cheesecake —which was not filled with cheese but with lemon curd— and ran and laughed until Katy said, "Leprosy! Hiccups is what you'll get."

Next day was Ascension Day. There would be no school, only a short church service, and then a holiday. The children were to bring flowers to decorate the church—"blue flowers, remember, children, to remind us that Our Lord ascended into heaven."

Running down the hill, they discussed what they could bring. Bluebells, most of them decided; or speedwells—"only they drop off". Katy thought her mother would let her pick the first pale blue grannies'-bonnets from the garden. Nat Wood said he had found a sort of bush, with little blue flowers, growing wild near the Rough Ride—the "wuff wide", he called it, for he had trouble with his r's; but as usual no one believed him. Ralph said nothing, but an idea began to take hold of him. That morning, as he came through the Dutch garden, two men had been pulling up the tulips and forget-me-nots to make room for summer flowers. Great heaps of forget-me-nots, still a mass of blue, had been piled in barrows. What had become of those heaps?

Reaching home, he tore into the Dutch garden. The grey flagstones were tidily swept; the flower beds newly dug, brown and bare, except for a sprinkling of grey forget-me-not seeds. Ralph ran through the bell yard, down the frame yard, past the stables, and on beyond the laurel hedge to the rubbish heaps. There he saw a mountain of blue forget-me-nots.

Joyfully he circled the mountain, seeing it transferred to High Forest church. They could fill the font, hedge in the pulpit, plant a blue mass all along the altar rails. He ran to the garden office to find Uncle Laurie, who had now returned from Ireland. "As many as you can carry," Uncle Laurie promised. Ralph pictured himself staggering uphill under a bushel of blue—"Four pecks or eight gallons, one bushel", as he and his classmates had learned—but Aunt Lizard had a better idea. She would drive him in the pony trap, with the best of the forget-me-nots, and would come to church, and bring him home afterwards, with as many others as the trap would hold.

"You'll get hiccups," Katy had warned; and—"You musn't get so excited," Aunt Lizard said, helping him to sort out the bluest flowers, and to tie them with raffia into great bunches, which would be left overnight with their stems in a tub of water. Ralph lay awake and longed for the night to be over. By his pillow was a matchbox with five ladybirds collected from the forget-me-nots. He counted them every few minutes, and raced them over his hot pillow until two flew away. He slept at last, but woke early and got up at once. By breakfast time he felt hollow with waiting and looking forward. In the stable yard, Sally the pony would be standing in her harness, ready to be backed into the shafts. The mountain of forget-me-nots was fresh as it had been in the Dutch garden. Ralph tried to eat his toast, but he felt sick with suspense. Quite suddenly, to his own astonishment, he was really sick.

Sally was unharnessed. The forget-me-nots were thrown back on to the rubbish-heap. Ralph lay in bed, wan with misery, watching the light ebb and flow across the ceiling with the flapping of the blind. Aunt Lizard brought him a drink of something thick and white and fizzy: like white-wash, he thought. He swallowed it, and swallowed his bitter disappointment, and fell asleep. Aunt Lizard did not say as usual, "You'll be better tomorrow." Tomorrow would be too late.

Tomorrow in fact brought another surprise. When he handed Aunt Lizard's note of explanation to Governess, she said in an odd dry tone: "So you were sick? *I* see. And Stanley was sick, and Winnie had the toothache. What an unlucky day for you all, dear me!"

Vases of bluebells, left over from the church decorations,

stood along the window sills. On the top table stood a jar of branches from Nat Wood's "fir bush"; they had spiky grey foliage and pale blue flowers.

"Rosemary," Governess said, rubbing one of the twigs between finger and thumb. "And who can tell me what rosemary is good for?"

The children were silent, watching her.

"No? Well, it used to be used as a hair tonic. Mothers would boil a little in rainwater to wash their children's hair ... in the old days," with sudden emphasis, "when mothers took a pride in doing things beautifully!"

The older girls looked at her quietly. Several of them had had their hair washed in rosemary since babyhood; but no one spoke.

In the Scripture lesson, Governess told them the story of the Good Samaritan. Speaking of inns, she said:

"There used to be pilgrim inns, and coaching inns, in England, for travellers—for people to stay the night. Inns were never meant"—and again Ralph was puzzled by her sudden look of anger—"just for men to go and get drunk, night after night!"

One or two of the older boys looked sullen and shuffled their feet under the desks. Their fathers went nightly to the Crooked Billet, though not to get drunk, for they could not afford it.

"She's ratty," said Ralph to Katy at break.

"She's *miserable*," Katy agreed; and perhaps in one sense this was true.

"You know why?" Katy asked. "Well, she thinks you stayed away yesterday on purpose, you and Stanley and Winnie, because it was a holiday. Just to miss church, you see?"

Ralph said nothing. There was nothing to say. The gulf

71

was too wide, it could never be bridged. But he wondered why Governess was so different from Grandmother, the only schoolmistress he had known in the past. Grandmother did not really like children either: as any child could tell, she preferred her cats; still, she expected that you would improve, while Governess was sure you would turn out badly. Grandmother would never look for deceit. Ralph could imagine her saying to a deceiver, as she had said when he threw a snowball across the drawing-room, "I am *surprised*!" Sin of any kind would be no surprise to Governess. She thought, as the children sang:

> "*An honest mind . . . but such are rare,*
> *I doubt if I'll find one at Strawberry Fair . . .*"

Poor Governess! She had spent her youth in another part of the country; looking back, she saw a sunlit landscape. At the end of this day, as the children were packing up their sewing and handwork things, she suddenly began to tell them of a summer day long ago, when she was a young teacher. Some church festival had offered itself, but the Vicar had said that the children must not miss two hours' schooling.

"So I said, 'Well, children, what about it?' 'Oh, we'll come to school at seven o'clock in the morning, miss!' And they did, and they were all there at seven, every single one, even the smallest infant!"

She said no more, but dismissed them abruptly, and went away to her solitary evening in the sunless little house behind the school.

If Governess liked any of her children, she liked the small boys; so Ralph might still have returned to favour, but for an unlucky incident. Mrs. Duffel's class was busy with sum books when Governess pounced from the upper end of the room, crying:

"Someone down here is *humming*!"

The children looked up, startled. Mrs. Duffel murmured, "Humming? Oh, I don't think so—" but Governess insisted: "I've heard it all the morning. Quite distinctly. Who *is* it? Hand up, the boy or girl who was humming!"

At this dreadful order, the children sat petrified.

Governess looked them up and down, her eyes alert behind her glasses.

"Very well. Any child who hears his neighbour hum is to put up his hand at once!"

She rapped for silence with a steel knitting needle, and waited optimistically.

In the hush that followed, engulfing the whole room, a bee backed out of a bluebell on the window sill, and began to drum on the pane. Ralph felt a giggle rising inside him. His cheeks turned crimson. He stole a glance at Mrs. Duffel. Catching his eye, she shook her head slightly, bit her lip, and turned away to study a picture of King Canute. Ralph could resist no longer; he felt he must hum or burst. He uttered a low hum. At once a hand shot up from the desk in front, and a fat little boy called Vincent cried gleefully, "Oh, miss, it was *him*! Ralph Oliver, miss!"

"*That* boy! I thought as much!" Governess glared at Ralph, whispered fiercely under her breath to Mrs. Duffel, and marched back to her own classes.

Later, Ralph became aware that his neighbour, Tim, often hummed softly to himself when he was intent on anything. Tim did not know this; and in the stir of the classroom, the tiny contented sound was rarely audible.

So Ralph found himself among the black sheep of the school; but—perhaps because of this—the children had begun to accept him as one of themselves. Big boys no longer shouted, "Hey, Froggie", or galloped up to offer him snails, jeering at the girls' disgust. "Ralphy", they called him now, or "old Ralph"; though not "our Ralph", which was used only by brothers and sisters, to show family solidarity. Ralph sometimes envied the Throwers when they talked of "our Rick" or "our Lil", but he no longer felt an outsider. His Irish accent, picked up in the past year, was quickly lost. He was eager to copy his new friends and learn their idiom, which was pithier among themselves. "Governess doesn't like it if we're late," Katy had said demurely to Aunt Lizard. Alone with Ralph, it was, "Govvy won't half moan." Katy was leader of the girls, and Ralph was her favourite; he could hardly have been better off.

Then quite suddenly he found himself, as Nat Wood called him—a waif.

8

Waif

There were six big girls in the top class; tall, self-confident, with thick shining hair and clever hands. They knitted stockings, made frocks for themselves on the school sewing machine, and fashioned dolls' clothes, beautifully smocked and embroidered, for a show of school work in the county town. They were eleven, twelve, thirteen. Dolls, of course, they had long discarded, and no one looked on them as children. "You big girls don't want a playtime, do you?" smiled Governess, with raised eyebrows, at break one morning. But they were not quite grown up. On the paths bordering the hill, or in the forest at midday, they played at family life with the younger ones, inventing hectic nursery scenes, meals and treats and illnesses, mischief and punishments, parties and disasters. Katy, in her high-handed way, kept Ralph under her thumb, bullying and protecting him, and talking to him with a mixture of endearments and bossiness which offset the ups and downs of the long school day.

But Katy came to school one Friday with a thoughtful look. She was offhand, and did not join in the morning games, but walked by herself, preoccupied, chewing a grass stalk. Ralph pulled a stalk for himself, and skipped behind her. At midday, she went off alone on an errand to the village, and he played with Dora's brood. Going home, Katy was still aloof. At the keeper's lodge, she turned to him.

"You won't be my little boy any more, Ralph. Mrs. Meadows's Ronnie's coming to school Monday, I've got to look after *him*."

Ralph nodded, not understanding a word; but on Monday he began to understand. Katy, ruthless as a mother cat, shook him off without another glance. She devoted herself to Ronnie, whose blue eyes brimmed over with tears all the way to school. At dinner time Ralph trailed after them. Katy had her hands full with Ronnie, who was in tears again. He would not eat his sandwiches—princely sandwiches of thin bread and butter and coddled egg, in equal layers of white, yellow and orange; like the narcissus called "butter-and-eggs", Ralph thought, nibbling his own plain bread and cheese. Ronnie pushed them away and sobbed for home, and Katy led him back to school, saying patiently, "Come along now, it's time to wash your paws, don't cry." It was the same on the way home. Ralph tried to play the elder brother, to carry Ronnie's dinner bag and amuse him with a dandelion clock, but Katy brushed him aside. Ralph was "out", as in "catcher" or cricket: for him the game was over.

On the third evening he still lingered by the school gate, waiting for Katy from habit. She was taking off Ronnie's sandal to shake out a stone, while Ronnie leaned against the wall, sniffing dolefully. Nat Wood came skimming along the path, one foot on the near-side pedal of his bicycle. Handed on the week before from a grown-up brother, the bicycle was rusty, battered and far too large for Nat: he was the envy of all the other boys. The saddle had been let down as far as it would go. Nat steered blithely, ready to mount— by Governess's order—on the other side of the school gate. Nat paused to put on a pair of motor cycling goggles, making a soft noise—*Brrrrrmmmmmm, brrrrrmmmmm*—to represent the revving of an engine. Seeing Ralph, he suddenly asked:

"Coming on my cawwier?"

Taken by surprise, Ralph gasped, "Oh, *yes!*" Then he hesitated, looking back. Katy ignored him. He scrambled on to the carrier. Nat pushed away from the gate, and Ralph clung to him. For a moment they tottered; then found their balance together. The wheels ticked, Nat roared like an engine at full throttle, and they sped away downhill between the whirling cliffs of the beeches.

There was a poem Ralph had heard many times from Mrs. Duffel's classes: *Going Downhill On A Bicycle*. Now the lines came spinning back to him; they sang in his ears like the wind:

> *"Swifter and yet more swift,*
> *Till the heart with a mighty lift*
> *Makes the lungs laugh, the throat cry,*
> *'O bird, see, see, bird, I fly:—*
>
> *'Is this, is this your joy?*
> *O bird then I, though a boy,*
> *For a golden moment share*
> *Your feathery life in air!' . . ."*

The steepest part of the hill was nearly a mile long. Nat drove his cycle at full speed, spurred on by Ralph's gasp as they swerved to miss a stone, his chuckle in Nat's ear as they took the sheer slope, by the bank, faster and faster.

But Nat was not reckless. Far down by the yew trees, he began to brake. The wheels skidded on grit, and then rolled more slowly, until they stopped by the lodge. Ralph slid off, and they parted without a word. Next morning, Ralph was early at the crossroads. Nat was waiting. Turning away from the steep hill, they took a roundabout road; down the drive towards Hurst Castle, then up the Castle Ride through the forest. They passed between young bracken thickets, through a dark tunnel of larches, where Nat shrieked like a train —"They may as well get used to it," he said. "Prob'ly end up as railway sleepers"—and between hedges of birch, hazel and dogwood. Near High Forest they came out on to the road, and clanked past the others without pausing.

At dinner time, Ralph went with Nat and the older boys to roam about the Hurst Castle downs, bird-nesting, cutting sticks and turves, and taking turns to tuck themselves inside an old motor tyre and roll down the slope; an exciting sport, for someone's cousin had nearly broken his neck at it. The other boys—"Kinger", "Pecky", "Randy", and "Hoppy"— treated Ralph as an equal. Morning and evening, he and Nat shared their uphill ride through the dewy forest, and their homeward flight downhill.

One morning about three weeks later, Ralph was surprised to notice Katy watching him at break, while he played cricket with the boys. At midday she waylaid him before he could join Nat. Would he like to come in the woods? Would he like a cake? Why not? Then she came to the point. She was just about sick of young Ronnie. He was a great crybaby, he never played anything properly, he was no good at all. Would Ralph like to come back? He could if he wanted!

Speechless, he stared at her. She smiled, and took his hand. He tore it away and dashed after Nat. The boys rode Nat's bicycle round and round a wall-of-death inside a grassy dell. Ralph laughed and shouted, as reckless as Hoppy, who had lost one foot in a reaper when he was three, but had not lost his nerve.

In fact Ralph was stunned by Katy's offer, racked with indecision, furious with her and with himself. He had suffered, and all for nothing. He had found other, better

78

things to do, and other people to play with. He wanted to go back, but it was too late. He had outgrown the old games; now they seemed babyish. But for a day or two he was wretched. Though he could not have put his feelings into words, he felt that Katy had been cruelly unfair—not in dropping him, but in trying to call him back: as though John, having pulled his little den to pieces, had told him he might go back and play there.

9

Talons

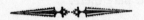

"**G**weat powerful claws, they've got," said Nat Wood. He and Ralph were standing under an old horse chestnut tree, in the shrubbery between the elm grove and the wych elm grove. When Ralph first saw the tree, its grey sloping boughs, signed with five-nailed horse-shoes by last year's leaves, had been covered with sticky brown buds. In April, the buds had swelled into puffs of green and silver. Now each twig had its tender green fan, shivering in the evening breeze.

The tree was very old. All the way up, at intervals, the trunk was hollowed into nesting holes, where rotten boughs had fallen. Every spring, Nat said, some of the holes had tenants—a jackdaw, a starling, a pigeon. This year, he was sure, a pair of tawny owls was living in the top of the tree.

The lowest hole twisted like a human ear from a large outer cavity down to a small passage. Nat beckoned Ralph: "Come and listen!"

Standing on tiptoe, Ralph put his ear to the thick grey rim of the chestnut ear. Deep inside, he heard a faint noise, a bubbling and hissing, like a kettle warming to the boil.

"What *is* it?" he whispered. "Not the owls, is it?"

Nat's smile was innocent. "It's a nest. Put your hand in."

Then, as Ralph hesitated, Nat thrust one finger into the

tree, with a daring sideways grin. The bubbling stopped. Suddenly came a fierce explosive hiss, and Nat snatched his finger away.

"Snakes' nest," Nat said carelessly. "Nearly got me that time!"

"*Snakes?*"

"Yes, there's a lot of little 'uns in there, just hatched, all mixed up like stwing." Spurred on by Ralph's expression, Nat added, "You should see them when they leave the nest, all cweeping and wiggling down the twee."

"Oh . . . where do they go then?"

"Come and see!"

They moved into a belt of rough grass bordering the wych elms. The grass was pitted with little dells, where older trees had died and been grubbed out. Nat went towards one of these hollows, Ralph following uneasily.

"Look, there! Quick, quick!"

Ralph looked, and saw a brown snake coiled round a thistle on the edge of a hollow. It slowly unwound itself, with a dreadful leisurely rippling that sent a cold shiver down Ralph's spine. Then it disappeared into a hole.

Before Ralph could speak, Nat clutched his arm, crying again: "The owl! Look, look!"

A dark shadow swooped over their heads and hovered away. From a distant tree came a sharp cry: "Whit!" and again, "Whit!"

"That's *him*," said Nat, and ran back towards the chestnut. Ralph followed gingerly, on the alert for snakes. Nat was settling his motor cycling goggles over his eyes. He held out another pair to Ralph. Behind the celluloid discs, Ralph felt as though he were at the bottom of a pond. Peering at Nat, he thought the owls might mistake them for two more owls. Nat muttered:

"What are you gwinning for? D'you want your eyes slashed out? Think these are like linnets or bottle-tits? *Gweat powerful claws, they've got.*"

Walking on all fours, Ralph followed him up the lowest bough. They climbed easily, higher and higher; at last Nat paused, listening. He whispered:

"I don't believe she's sitting. I think they're hatched alweady! I think I can hear them . . . baby owls. Listen!"

His ear to the trunk, Ralph thought he could hear a low squawking, crooning noise, like Black Lady complaining when she was turned off her eggs for her morning stroll. Then he caught another sound—a chittering, bickering noise, like two or three nestlings chirping at once. Ralph whispered:

"Oh, come on, let's hurry! I've never seen a baby owl!"

Nat's shocked look was lost under his goggles, but his voice was sharp with scorn. He seemed as wary of owls as Ralph had been of snakes.

"Think I'm going up there, with the old 'uns about? Want to fall all that way down, with *her* slashing at us?"

There was a sound of wings, and again the dark shadow hovered, and the sharp "Whit!" came like a warning. Nat began to climb rapidly down, and Ralph followed, regretfully. But even when he was alone he did not climb to the owls' nest. He did not quite believe Nat's tales of slashing talons; what daunted him was the snakes' nest in the lowest hole. But, watching the tree one Saturday afternoon, he was puzzled to see a small bird, blue and yellow, slipping unharmed in and out of the snakes' nest hole. That morning, he had seen just such another bird—blue-winged, blue-capped, yellow-breasted—fly into a crevice in the wall of the Dutch garden.

Now he wandered thoughtfully back to the garden, and

stood looking at the crevice under a clump of jasmine. Very cautiously, he slipped a finger into it. A moment later he snatched it out at the sound of an angry hiss. A small bird dashed out of the hole with a flurry of feathers, and again Ralph groped with a careful finger. He brought out an egg the size of a cherry petal, looked at it, and slid it back; inside, he could feel other eggs, and a lining of feathers, warm to the touch.

A shout made him look round. Nat Wood came flying along the flagged path.

"Ralph, Ralph, come quick! Come and see!"

"What is it *now*?" Ralph asked. "More baby snakes? Or an elephant's nest?"

Nat stared, then cried impatiently:

"Come down to the chestnut—there's two little owls, sitting in the grass, and they don't fly away. Just sitting there!"

The boys ran to the elm grove. The young owls had not moved; they were sitting in the grass by the chestnut, their soft fawn-coloured plumage ruffled, their expression forlorn. Ralph picked one up; at once its claws were wrapped like steel coils about his finger. He prised it off, claw by claw, and Nat brought a branch for them to perch on. The little owls fluttered awkwardly on to it, and Ralph sucked his finger. They saw no sign of the parent owls.

"We can't just leave them here," Ralph said. "A weasel might get them, or a rat."

They carried the perch between them to the garden house. The owls clung glumly, teetering a little. In the yard they found Fergus, mending a puncture; he was not sympathetic.

"Take them back. They'll be all right."

"But the old birds—they've *deserted* these two!"

"Not they. Look," said Fergus, "how can you feed them?

They need fresh meat, dozens of mice, and how can you catch them?"

"Cuckoo might help."

"And where can we keep two owls? Not in *my* bedroom, not with Santa, no, thank you."

"Oh no . . . in mine," Ralph said quickly.

"There's Cuckoo. Aunt Lizard won't let you."

"Well, in your wabbit hutch," said Nat. Santa's hutch still stood by the water tank, unused.

"We *couldn't* leave them alone in the dark, with foxes and weasels," Ralph persisted.

"But little owls *like* the dark, you silly little owls."

"Where's Aunt Lizard?"

"In the Sky, drawing old-maid's-bedsocks. She won't let you keep them," Fergus warned.

"I'll tell her they're lost."

The Sky smelled of elder flowers and antirrhinums from a tall vase on the bookcase; the flowers were like creamy lace and dark red velvet. Aunt Lizard was drawing at her table; in front of her, in specimen glasses, were lady's-bedstraws and sprays of the greenish yellow hedgerow buds which would turn to the silver fluff of old-man's-beard. She did not look round when Ralph said:

"Can you come?"

"Later," she said absently.

"We want to show you something special. . . ."

"Yes, later! Run away now, chicken."

Ralph virtuously closed the door and ran. He found a raw joint of meat in the larder safe, and hacked off a chunk. He and Nat coaxed the foundlings on to a new perch inside the hutch; they petted them, stroked their feathers and urged them to taste the meat. Fergus and his bicycle had disappeared; Ralph stayed by the hutch long after Nat had gone. When he touched them, the little owls sidled closer together, gazing at him with glassy eyes. He brought Cuckoo and Santa to see them. Santa ignored them; Cuckoo eyed them with deep distrust, and escaped to his watch tower on the tank. Ralph tiptoed up to bed; Aunt Lizard, finding him in pyjamas, reading *Dr. Dolittle*, was surprised but not suspicious. He could not resist asking:

"Do you think Too-too's a good name for an owl?"

No sound came from the hutch below. Whatever tomorrow might bring, he would have them for one night.

Ralph dreamed of owls, and woke with the tawny owl's cry in his ears. He had not dreamed that: it came again, loud and urgent, close to the window. Ralph sprang out of bed. Beyond the roof, in the moonlit churchyard, he saw a dark bird swaying to and fro on the tip of a branch. His face pressed to the glass, he watched it launch itself into the air and hover across the blue night sky. The owl calls sounded over the Dutch garden, and stopped. Ralph sat on in the dark, feeling cold and miserable. Now he longed to reassure the mother owl, to give her back the young ones for whom she was searching. He must creep downstairs and let them out. Thinking this, he fell asleep; when he woke again it was daybreak. He hurried downstairs to the yard, expecting to find the young ones in a frenzy from hearing their mother's wild cries.

Racing out of the back door, he stood still in amazement. The wire on the new hutch was ripped apart, twisted as though a tiger had clawed it. The staples had been dragged out by the roots, as the netting was slashed away. The hutch was empty. The mother owl had taken matters into her own efficient talons.

"See?" Nat said later. "I told you. They've got gweat powerful claws."

10

Bird-field

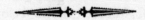

The woodshed roof was covered with a waterfall of roses: little yellow scented roses, growing in clusters. In the morning the new buds were still close-folded; by evening, the full-blown flowers would be pale from the day's sun. Their sweetness filled the air, as the wistaria scent had done in May. Yesterday's petals, brittle as flakes of scorched paper, lay in drifts along the kitchen roof.

Because of the roses, Ralph could no longer scramble over the shed roof to the place he called his summerhouse; a grey slab of stone between the woodshed and the brewhouse roof, screened from the yard by a clump of bushes. The stone, and the shed wall above it, were still warm from the sun when he climbed up after tea. He lay hidden through the long June evenings, nibbling cherries from a tree in the old orchard, or golden-drop gooseberries from a bush in the derelict rock garden, and reading *Tanglewood Tales*. Sometimes he brought Santa there, and watched him making sorties up the brewhouse roof, his nails scratching and sliding on the slates. Sometimes Cuckoo joined him there, and they sat together on the warm stone; the cat's eyes following the flight of swallows in the sky, and their downward swoop through the low door of the brewhouse, where a row of beaks waited. The parent swallows worked until long after sunset, feeding

86

their brood; and sometimes Ralph woke to hear them, before dawn, calling "twit, twit", as they began their new day's work.

Above, in the cedar trees, the goldcrests too were feeding their young. Cuckoo's ears and whiskers twitched at the sound of their notes, *Seeeseeeeseeeeeseee*, like a breeze in a bamboo clump; but their nest was safe in the high cedar bough, among the dark green needles and pale green cones, bedewed with drops of resin clear as honey.

Ralph was glad to rest in the evenings; he and Nat travelled miles through the forest, before and after school. Each morning they made their way down the drive and up the Castle Ride, where wild roses were in flower, and foxgloves grew in the bracken, and ropes of honeysuckle twined among the firs and larches.

Sometimes the boys found rarer flowers; little wild yellow pansies; bee orchids, like bumble bees with pale mauve wings; a brown bird's-nest orchid, and the butterfly orchid, which Nat traced by its heavy scent, as he traced wild garlic or pallid stink-horns. Ralph brought them one by one to Aunt Lizard, who sketched them in black ink and wrote their names underneath in delicate script. "Don't pick more than one," she told Ralph. "Let them grow."

She had finished twenty drawings for the wildflower book when one Sunday the author came to fetch them. A harassed-looking young man, he glanced quickly through the pages, and then smiled and said simply, "Thank God".

Aunt Lizard and Ralph looked at him in surprise. He told them:

"A year or two ago, I did a little monograph on wild orchids. Then I wanted to bring it out quickly, with water colours, and I heard of a man who could do them splendidly, I thought. I went to see him. Yes, he'd be delighted, and he

gave me all sorts of instructions about sending specimens. No
nonsense with the post; they must be packed directly they
were picked, in wet cotton wool, in tin boxes, and put on
express trains to London. Then I was to wire him at once,
and he'd have the trains met."

The author put down his teacup and looked ruefully at
Aunt Lizard.

"Well, I was as keen as anything, and I didn't care how
much trouble I took, if he'd get the illustrations right. I went
to stay at a spot near here—and I got up at dawn and walked
miles, and found what I wanted, green-veined orchids, and
egg, and bee and fly and butterfly. I took two of each, and
packed them the way he wanted, and put them on trains, and
tipped the guards, as though they were my children, and sent
off telegrams. Well, then I had a stroke of luck; someone
promised to show me a green man orchid. Of course I wasn't
going to pick that, but I thought this artist might come and
see it too. I'd heard nothing from him, so I rang him up."

He paused. "He had quite a struggle to remember who I
was. Then he said—he said, 'Oh, yes, your little book. Yes,
I'd love to illustrate. I really would. Now tell me, *what would
you like?*'"

Aunt Lizard uttered a suitable groan. Ralph urged:

"But then . . . what became of all those orchids that went
by train?"

"So far as I know," said the young man bitterly, "they're
still withering at Waterloo. Good-bye."

The railway line to Waterloo ran at the foot of the Hurst
Castle downs. From the edge of the forest, Nat and Ralph
watched the trains go by. It was strange, Ralph sometimes
thought, to see them from the forest, that seemed so wild and
old, as though wolves and wild boars might still be lurking

there. At night, when the sound of the trains seemed louder, he sometimes fancied them as monsters, prowling up the long beech avenue towards the garden house; a serpent, perhaps, or an iron dragon, "with the widest jaws that ever a dragon had, and a vast many rows of horribly sharp teeth". He had the same fairy tale feeling when he and Nat, one rainy afternoon, found themselves riding down the hill through a great army of tiny black frogs, each about the size of a thumb nail, marching in steady hops, a quarter of an inch at a time. Where could they be going? The boys stood and watched; the mass of frogs passed on up the shiny wet road, and out of sight. Next morning they had vanished, except for a few little corpses flattened by cars.

The forest around the Castle Ride had not always been so lonely. One dinner time, searching for wild strawberries, he and Nat came on a clearing with traces of flint walls where a house had stood. A keeper's house, Nat said: his father could remember it. Here, in the forlorn garden was the rosemary bush he had found before Ascension Day. There was one apple tree, and a pink-and-white cottage rose, and a brick well, into which the thirsty boys peered eagerly; but it was dry, and half full of rubble and dead leaves. There were wild cats here, Nat said, left behind by the last inhabitants. Then, swearing Ralph to secrecy, Nat showed him a gooseberry patch, where large green berries were ripening; agreeably sour, like lemon squash. Nat and Ralph filled their pockets to help them through the afternoon.

They had no water to drink at school. The woman who scrubbed the floors drew three extra buckets each morning from a deep well in the schoolhouse yard—spring water, cold and pure; but it was for washing only, one bucket each for boys, girls and infants, poured into wash basins before afternoon school.

The High Forest children could run home to drink with their midday dinner. The children from the valley and the outlying farms brought bottles of water, lemonade or cold tea in their dinner bags; but often this was gone by the time they arrived at school. Ralph had a little flask in a wicker sheath, carried by his Uncle Alfred in the Great War. The flask gave Ralph's water ration a pleasant flavour which he would later recognize as whisky; but there was never enough. The children chewed grass, beech leaves, wild rose petals or sorrel, trying to slake their thirst. Wild strawberries imposed a kind of torture. It was a point of honour to carry the biggest home to mother, and longing glances would be cast at these morsels, wrapped in a dock leaf and hidden under the desk among pens and rulers.

Then came an afternoon when even thirst was forgotten in a new sport. The oaks in the forest bordering the hill had been sold; a gang of woodmen had cut them down, and now horses had come to drag the great trunks along the rides; the trees lay on the road verges awaiting lorry and trailer. Stripped of their branches, the bare trunks were placed end to end on the turf, and the children pulled off shoes and socks to run merrily up and down the grey bridges. As the days passed, they found that they could play feet-off-the-ground over tree trunks and piles of cordwood, from the Castle Ride to the top of the bank. Nat left his bicycle at home, and he and Ralph raced barefoot with the rest.

The days were hot and sunny; then followed a grey, sultry day, with a hint of thunder. When he left Nat by the keeper's lodge, Ralph felt that he did not know how to bear the long trek home over the park; coming from the deep shade, and the scent of white pinks and Madonna lilies in Mrs. Hassall's garden, he was a parched traveller faced with a desert. In the distance he could see a green oasis—beech trees, and near them a cluster of wild raspberry canes—but that was only a mirage. There would be no raspberries today; he and Nat had nibbled too many yesterday, even the sour little yellow ones that they called "rabbits' noses". He would have to hold out to the other side of the desert.

Sandals and socks still slung around his neck, he plodded, skipped and trotted by turns, head down, eyes fixed on the dry field path, because it seemed shorter that way. He reached the shade of the beech clump, and winced as his bare feet met last year's beech nut husks. He was a blind man now: eyes shut, he made his feet find their own way among the tree roots. Beyond the oasis, the path would dip down into a shallow valley; then came a last climb towards the white gate. He tried not to think of the garden house, with its cool scullery, the beautiful chill of the brick floor to bare feet, the cold water running down his throat at last: then the jug of lemon water on the kitchen table, the smell of new sodabread loaves propped against the crock, and dinner laid ready in the breakfast room, so cool and dark after the glare of the sun. There might be cold broiled ham, perhaps, with little broad beans in pale green sauce; or an egg salad, with cos lettuce, crisp to bite as an apple, and slices of pinkish Fircone potatoes, and red French Breakfast radishes. Later, no longer famished, he would join Aunt Lizard and Uncle Laurie in the shady strip of garden under the chapel wall, to sip tea and nibble a crust of sodabread, with salty butter from Nine Wells, and perhaps new raspberry jam . . . *but he still had to get there.* Scuffing through dead leaves, he knew he was only half way through the beeches. He groaned, and quickened his pace.

A shout made him open his eyes. He stopped in surprise. Under the giant beech on the edge of the clump, a black cara-van was drawn up, and a fire burned in a ring of stones. Three men were sitting beside it. For a moment he thought of gipsies, and remembered the tales of kidnapping; then he saw that these were not gipsies but gamekeepers. Mr. Hassall, the head keeper, was holding out something to *him*: a mug of tea.

It was sweet and very hot, and the tin mug burnt his lips, but he gulped and gulped again. The men watched in sympathy.

"You wanted that!" Mr. Hassall said. Ralph nodded, smiling now at the memory of his thirst.

"I know your school," the keeper added. "Parched in summer and shrammed in winter: my boy was just the same." But winter seemed unreal as a dream. The sun, stabbing through the clouds, was hot on Ralph's back as he climbed towards the gate; and now he did not mind it. He sat down by the gate to put on his socks and sandals, and for the first time he noticed how comfortable they felt, after running barefoot. It was like the happiness of drinking, after the day's fast. He wished someone would camp in the beeches every afternoon, to give him a drink as he crossed the desert.

Next morning Ralph had another surprise, for the desert was gone; or rather, it had changed overnight from a waste of grass stubble to a town of little wooden houses. Row after row of hencoops stood there in the morning sunlight. Mother hens—not hen pheasants, but farmyard hens like Black Lady —clucked behind bars, and hundreds of fawn-coloured pheasant chicks ran to and fro. Beyond the beech clump, where the dew was only just off the grass, Ralph found the three keepers striding up and down the rows, taking the lids from the coops. Each lid was thrown backward, with a swift jerk, clear of the chicks as they raced out. With practised eye the keepers counted each brood, sixteen or eighteen to each hen, then scattered grain by the coop.

Ralph thought of a day, a few weeks back, when he and Nat had been lying hidden at noon in deep bracken beside a forest path, and had heard a bicycle approaching. They lay still. The head keeper cycled past—then stopped, sprang from his cycle and came back to investigate: his eye, that missed nothing, had not missed two grey jerseys under the greenery. "Keep to the paths, my lads," he told them, "the birds are laying." If he had said "the wolves are running", Nat could not have been more impressed. *Birds*, he explained to Ralph, were not blackbirds and thrushes, but pheasants and wood-cock; and if the keepers found their nests, they would take the eggs to rear the chicks by hand. Now the eggs had been hatched in the pheasantry behind the keeper's lodge; and the young ones would run about here, in the bird-field, until they were old enough to be taken to the coverts.

More than once, in the weeks that followed, Ralph was late for school. He loved to watch the growing chicks. Almost at once they could fly, and the down on their wings gave place to feathers. Like Aunt Lizard's young ducks, they roamed in widening circles. The ducks came in single file across the park to the bird-field, quacking in a soft com-panionable way as they ran their beaks through the grass in search of chick food. The hens would squawk and fret in their coops, but the ducks remained serene and friendly.

The keepers laughed at the wandering ducks. "They'll march into the fox's mouth some day!" they warned. But other visitors were unwelcome; they came, and they never went home.

The field was never left unguarded. One of the keepers slept at night in the caravan, and by day there was always one man on the watch. Hawks hovered over the field. A vixen, with cubs to feed, might linger in the shade of the forest, watching her chance. The morning the coops were set out, Mr. Hassall had inspected the hollow oak in the middle of the field. One year, he told Ralph, a barn owl had nested there, and whipped up the game on her doorstep. A dozen chicks had disappeared before the nest was spotted. Ralph was glad there was no nest to be destroyed this year. He often thought of the young tawny owls, and wondered where their parents had taken them. Fergus had seen a tawny owl sitting on a low elm bough, making feints at Cuckoo as he sat watching a burrow where there were baby rabbits. Fergus thought the owl wanted the rabbits for itself; and perhaps Cuckoo, frightened away from the burrow by those "great powerful claws", found another hunting ground.

Mr. Hassall paid an evening visit to the garden house. Meeting Aunt Lizard and Ralph in the Dutch garden, he stood chatting for a while. Dittany, a Labrador retriever bitch, sat on the flagged path, watching the gambols of Santa with gentle curiosity. Cuckoo appeared and rubbed round the keeper's stockings. At this, Dittany rose to her feet, waving her feathery tail. "Up, Dittany," said the keeper; and she sank back on her haunches.

The keeper went on telling them about an old cock pheasant that lived, half tame, in the shrubbery.

"He's crafty, you see: won't fly! He lies low when the guns are around, and there he is, year after year, turning up in the bird-field for his bit of feed."

As he talked, he bent down to pick up something from the path, and turned it thoughtfully in his fingers. It was a tiny feather, pale brown, with a darker marking. Suddenly Mr. Hassall broke off his remarks to say:

"Miss Izard, look . . . this is a young bird's feather. A young pheasant," he said softly, and nodded at Cuckoo, who began self-consciously to wash. Aunt Lizard and Ralph looked from the cat to the keeper, startled.

"It's this cat, Miss Izard. I won't deceive you—if he wasn't yours, he'd be under a sod by now."

"Cuckoo!" exclaimed Aunt Lizard. "Poaching pheasants? Oh, *no*. . . ."

Mr. Hassall bent to pick up another feather. He said, still kindly:

"I found him out there myself, not an hour ago, after the birds. I thought I'd give him a fright this time, and I lifted my gun, and the blighter—do you know, he turned round and *snarled* at me? I had to laugh." Cuckoo lowered his eyes and bit a grass seed from his fur.

"Cuckoo!" said Aunt Lizard again.

"So, if you'd keep him at home, would you, for a week or two? I wouldn't like you to lose your cat, Miss Izard. . . ."

It was easy to pamper Cuckoo with meals of boiled rabbit. It was not so easy to keep him from hunting for sport. Ralph abandoned his summerhouse on the roof, left Santa with Fergus or Aunt Lizard, and spent his evenings patrolling the fringe of the bird-field. The cock chicks now had brief tail feathers, which would grow long and dark. Close to the keeper's lodge there were two coops which he often visited. One held fluffy partridge chicks, coloured brown and primrose; the other a brood of young golden pheasants, to strut under the Spanish chestnuts in the mossy ride known as the Ladies' Mile.

Already there were one or two "paradise birds" in the woods, the keepers told Ralph. The owner liked to see a silver or a golden pheasant, just as he would have a row or two of scarlet oaks, and Canadian maples, and Japanese crabs, among the sapling oaks and beeches in the forest nursery. In the same way, a former owner had planted Californian redwoods in the Groves and the pleasure ground; and another had built the orange-house and the tropical house in the garden, to shelter exotic trees. It seemed to Ralph a pity that only one orange tree should remain, while date palms and pineapples had gone to make room for peach and plum trees. But fashions changed, Uncle Laurie told him; and now the foreign fruits came in by air, and were no longer rare and curious.

One hot night, Ralph waited to see the paradise chicks leave the grass and nestle under their mother hen. He was a stray chick himself; at any moment he might hear Aunt Lizard's whistle summoning him to bed. He sauntered along, skirting the field where the hens were calling their young. All at once, he noticed that they had changed their note: they were shrieking "danger". Suddenly he saw, a few yards away, what seemed like a reddish brown snake rippling along the edge of the wood. He stood still, holding his breath; then, with a gasp, he saw that it was not a snake but a weasel, weaving rapidly to and fro, nearer and nearer to the coops. In another second it would have reached the nearest chick. Ralph, with a shout, raced towards it, waving his arms and crying, "Go away!"

The weasel turned, reared up and stared at him. He ran closer, not slackening his pace, expecting it to run like a rabbit. The weasel flew at him, snarling like a tiny savage tiger; it was Ralph who turned and ran. His shouts had alerted the keepers, and the weasel fled back into the wood.

Telling Aunt Lizard and Fergus of his escape, Ralph said, "It would have jumped at my throat, you could see, and sucked my blood. And you should have heard it chatter!" Feeling his throat, he shivered. "He *was* a fierce little bitch!"

There was a pause. Ralph looked up, and saw that he had blundered somewhere. Over his head, Aunt Lizard murmured to Fergus, as if in excuse: "He hears new words at school. Everyone does."

"Fitch, if you like," Fergus said to Ralph, smiling. "Though that's really a pole-cat. Not bitch, except for Dittany."

At fifteen, he found the eight-year-old amusing, where a younger Fergus might have been censorious.

"It only means someone cross," Ralph argued; adding rashly, "Nat says Governess is one."

"Oh dear," said Aunt Lizard. "Well, I promise you, she's not."

He sighed. His story had fallen flat. Perhaps he had not really been in danger? And he resented this grown-up alliance of Aunt Lizard and Fergus, leaving him odd-man-out: a child, liable to absurdity. He said, getting up from the floor in a huff, "Oh, well. I think I'll go to bed." ·

"*I* think," said Aunt Lizard, "that you should have a camera."

PART THREE

11

Beau Temps

small box camera cost twelve and six. How was Ralph
ever to find such a sum? His pocket money was twopence a week. But a camera he felt he must have; as soon
as Aunt Lizard spoke, he knew exactly what she meant. If only
he could have taken a picture of the weasel, or of the owls, or
of Vole . . . if he could have gone out that night, instead of
going to bed, and chosen his camera, and brought it home, it
would not have been soon enough: he would still have had to
wait until morning to begin using it. He lay in bed, looking
out at the late sunlight in the elm grove, and brooding on
ways and means.

His birthday was not until January; no help there. He
thought of Fergus and the daffodils; but of course daffodils
were over long ago. Aunt Lizard found him awake at eleven
o'clock, waiting to ask:

"Do you think you could pay me a penny when I shell the
peas?"

"Perhaps. And now I'll pay you a penny to go to sleep."

The next evening she produced a basket with six pounds
of green gooseberries. "I'll pay you sixpence to top-and-tail
these—and I'll help, so you won't be too late to bed."

"It's too hot to go to bed at all," Ralph protested.

It was certainly too hot to stay indoors. They sat on

cushions in the shrubbery, under a tall cedar, and worked at the gooseberries. Top-and-tailing was duller even than shelling peas; but the thought of the camera kept him at it.

The evening light streamed through the young trees. A sweet acrid scent came from the dying Spanish chestnut blossom. Santa lay panting on the turf, then began to tease Cuckoo, who could not bear him too near. When the hare had twice jumped over him, Cuckoo retreated into the long grass, where he flushed and stalked the old tame pheasant until it bridled like a turkey cock. Then he found a grass-snake and tortured it, ripping the writhing body with his claws.

Fergus came out to join them, and lay wearily on the grass, looking up into the cedar. His School Certificate examinations would begin in a few days' time, and his evenings were spent at work. Squinting up at the top of the tree, he said with a yawn:

"Look at those two pies up there."

"Magpies? Oh, where?" Ralph tried to see.

"Wood pigeons." Fergus rolled over, laughing. "Would-be pies, good for supper, with mashed potentials and young green might-have-beans."

"And moonshine," added his father, joining them with a glass in one hand and a deck chair in the other.

But the pigeons, fattened on garden peas, were safe. The gun stayed on its rack over the kitchen cupboard; they preened their feathers undisturbed. Fergus chewed a grass stalk and sighed over his book.

Exams were in the air, Ralph thought. A large sealed box had arrived the week before, with papers written by students for a gardening diploma. Uncle Laurie had spent all Sunday marking them, and two evenings since. He had just finished. Suddenly he said, "How lazy I was, when *I* was twenty!"

At that age, he told them, he had been a decorator in a famous country house, choosing and arranging flowers, decorating dinner tables, making bouquets and buttonholes. Work began at six in the morning and went on until six in the evening, often later; and there was no Saturday half-holiday. But the owner of the house was a devoted cricketer. The young men on the estate, Uncle Laurie among them, passed many summer days in the cricket-field. In winter, too, when the lakes froze, work would take second place to skating and ice hockey.

The sun went down behind the forest. A breeze cooled the air. Indoors they ate green artichokes, thin bread and butter and strawberries, while the gardener told them of days gone by. ("Days gone by," repeated Ralph, listening: the words filled him with a kind of happy melancholy.)

One spring day he had never forgotten, Uncle Laurie said. The woods were full of wild daffodils, and he had gone out to look at them, thinking he would use them to decorate a dinner table.

"I remember lying out there in the woods all the morning, listening to the birds. What an idler I was! I should have been reading for exams, I suppose." He shook his head over his sloth; but Ralph felt that he did not really regret that far-off April morning.

It was hard to picture Uncle Laurie as an idle youth. Now he had silver hair, like Grandfather; and like Grandfather, like the gamekeepers, he seemed to work at all hours quite happily. But to Ralph, child of a newspaperman, this did not seem unusual.

In the late summer dusk, Ralph would hear the gardener go out and walk through the glass ranges—vineries, peach houses, and the warm cell where melons hung ripening in nets—to read thermometers, check rat traps set by the duty-man, and adjust a glass light or a ventilator. A rat in the melon house, he told Ralph, might ruin a whole crop in an hour, treating the melons as otters sometimes treated salmon: one bite, and on to the next. Or a stray bee in the orchid house, when the orchids were flowering, could be just as mischievous.

Soon after six in the morning he would be going downstairs, and Ralph would hear his tap on the barometer by the front door. At breakfast one morning he remarked that he had just picked two hundred nectarines for market, and seventy Duchess of Cornwall peaches.

The summer holidays began, and for days the barometer needle stayed at Beau Temps. In the apple fences, little Irish Peaches ripened, and tart red-speckled Beauties of Bath. Green fruits swelled on the outdoor peach trees, fanned across the garden walls. Each fruit was mounted on a slip of wood, like a jewel on a velvet pad. On the indoor trees, peaches and nectarines were already crimson and yellow. For the journey to Covent Garden market, they were swathed in ruffs of cotton wool and laid in padded boxes. From July to September, packing would go on, in the long, cool fruit room: cherries and apricots, peaches and nectarines, plums and figs. Ralph learned a string of new names: Early Rivers, May Duke, Moor Park, Peregrine, Reine Claude, Brown Turkey; and now, watching the packers, he could tell a chip from a punnet, or a trug from a strike. After the blazing sunshine, the room was shaded and chill as a cave underground, and with its fruit smells and glowing colours Ralph thought it as dazzling as the antirrhinum beds outside in the Dutch garden. When the melons were cut, the fruit room scent became rich and lush. Then Ralph was joined by Cuckoo, who stole in whenever the door was opened, spurred on by a violent fancy for melon. Someone had let him taste a spoonful; now he would prowl to and fro, mewing and gazing at the high shelf where the melons rested before they were packed into nests of woodwool and sent to London.

The garden office close by was interesting too, with a good smell of ink and paper, new shiny catalogues and wooden walls. The walls were covered with white cards, lettered in gold, red or blue: "Gold Cup", "Silver Medal", "First Prize", "Second" or "Third". When Ralph first saw the cards, he remembered others like them in Grandfather's office at Nine Wells, and cried in surprise: "But where are your horses?" He knew now that apples and dahlias could win show prizes, like Grandfather's hacks and hunters.

It was in the garden office, turning over a seed catalogue, that he had an idea. Some time before, he had spent an evening hour on the duckboards behind the lupin bed, popping the black seed pods, and scattering the little grey beans inside. He had forgotten this game until, passing the same way, he had noticed a bed of bright green lupin seedlings. He had sown them himself! Now, in the catalogue, he read: "Lupins. Apricot Queen. Sunset. Pink Sugar . . . sow in boxes or open ground, July to September." He looked up at the pigeon-holes over the table. They held seed packets, and he took one down. "Sweet Pea. Blue Butterfly", he read on the packet. He shook it, and heard a husky rattle as of dried peas. He went back to the catalogue. There it was: "Blue Butterfly. Magnificent . . . highly recommended . . . 2s. a packet."

He went for a walk in the garden; not along the main paths, but on the straw between the peach wall and a faded June flower bed. Here and there he poked a withered stem; seeds poured like brown pepper from a foxglove, black shiny commas from a larkspur, brown full-stops from a polyanthus. He studied the patch of lupins he had sown. "Oliver's Tested Seeds," he muttered, and ran indoors to the Sky.

He was out again in a few minutes, carrying something Aunt Lizard had given him; a packet of little envelopes, part of a sample sent by a stationer's shop. His camera fund had stuck at two shillings and elevenpence. He would go into the seed business at once, not even waiting for dinner. "Put mine in the oven," he begged Aunt Lizard, and was gone. He rifled the early flower beds, shaking seeds into a dozen envelopes: soon he had collected one packet each of Oriental and Iceland poppies, foxglove, sweet william, delphinium, larkspur, columbine, polyanthus, forget-me-not, rock rose, violet and lupin. He found he knew most of the names, and wrote them lightly, in pencil, on the envelopes. Uncle Laurie would tell him the rest; but not now. He had a busy afternoon in the Sky, painting the seed packets with flowers in brilliant shades from Aunt Lizard's water colours. By the time he had finished six, the first was dry. On the front he printed: "Oliver's Tested Seeds"; on the back he let himself go in lyrical praise copied from the catalogues: "Glorious . . . vigorous habit . . . free-flowering . . . gold cup winner." He helped himself to a sample packet of postcards, and printed on each: "Oliver's Summer Bargains", with a tempting list, "only a penny a packet". He used up a bottle of ink and emptied the stamp box. The lists were addressed to China, to Nine Wells, to Aunt Emmy in London, to Mrs. Duffel, and to Nat, who was staying in Dorset. He saw them off by the afternoon postman, and went back to his seed packets. By tea time they were sealed and ready. Exhausted and very pleased with himself, he enjoyed his baked marrow and cold peach pie at leisure.

It was not until next day that he noticed the flaw in his plan: the seeds were not his in the first place, and would have to be paid for. But Uncle Laurie, amused, made him an offer: Oliver's Seeds Ltd. might have its stock for nothing, if Ralph

in return would spend part of his holidays gathering bluebell
seeds and sowing them under the beeches just where the home
drive entered the forest. Coming back in May, he said, when
the beeches were in bud, he had thought how well this would
look with a carpet of bluebells. Glad to agree, Ralph only
wished the bluebells might come up overnight, like the
Dragon's Teeth. "But they won't flower till May, will they?"

"Oh, they'll flower in about five years."

"Five *years*!" But his dismay was lost on the gardener, who
had spent his life waiting for seeds to come up.

"What a time everything takes," he groaned to Aunt
Lizard. "It'll be weeks before I sell any seeds . . . I'll *never* get
my camera." His optimism of yesterday was gone. Even the
gooseberries were over: top-and-tailing was finished. "How
soon do you think I'll get some orders?"

"Why not ask Uncle Laurie for a job?" Aunt Lizard
countered.

"A job? In the *garden*?"

Yes, said Uncle Laurie at once, he might have a job. He
could keep the herbaceous borders clear of dead flowers.
"And I'll pay you half a crown a week."

"Like a ratcatcher," said Fergus.

Ralph felt that all his troubles were over. In four weeks he
would have his camera. The money from Oliver's Seeds
would pay for films. It was arranged that he should begin
next day; and before the seven o'clock bell rang, he was
down in the kitchen, drinking tea with Uncle Laurie. The
flower beds were still drenched with dew. Blue and purple
morning-glories opened across the eastern wall of the Dutch
garden. He began there, with the antirrhinum beds, armed
with a trug and the kitchen scissors. By eight o'clock, when
the garden bell rang for breakfast, he was covered with yellow
pollen like a bee. Aunt Lizard had his breakfast ready. He

swallowed it, and was ready before the half-hour bell. Santa followed him, and for the rest of the week they were lost together among towering dahlias, heleniums, phlox, lilies, hollyhocks, asters and Michaelmas daisies. The borders in the upper garden were banks of red, pink, mauve, purple and blue; in the lower garden they were orange, tawny, flame, yellow and brown. Lush-smelling African marigolds scented his fingers. Butterflies floated like airborne flowers in front of his eyes. The garden was filled with the sound of bees humming, pigeons cooing, and with the tuneful whistling of the young "journeymen" gardeners who lived in the bothy by the bell yard: enviable young men, who, their day's work over, would dash away for the evening on splendid motor cycles.

When Ralph tired of snipping dead flowers, he and Santa played at hide-and-seek. Ralph would remove himself to the other end of the garden, count to a hundred, and then creep back through the jungle to look for Santa. He thought the hare understood the game thoroughly; often he would lie hidden among low thickets of zinnias, salvias, helichrysums or calendulas, so that Ralph had to hunt in earnest. When it was Ralph's turn to hide, he tiptoed away into the densest part of the jungle, and crouched there until he heard the soft scrape of hare's feet on the dry soil as Santa came to find him.

Hearing his elders talking of war in Spain, Ralph thought that, if an army ever invaded England, they could all hide in the herbaceous borders. Who would find them in that jungle? They could live on plums and peaches from the wall trees, and shelter from bombs or shell-fire in the pit by the fig house, protected by its iron lid. Sometimes, for practice, he let the lid close down over his head, and sat there in the dark on the waterpipe. He had a bad fright one day when the garden boy left a wheelbarrow on the lid while he and Santa were practising inside. He banged frantically and shrieked until he was released; he had been shut in only for a minute, but it had seemed a long time. "Crikey!" said the astonished youth, "I thought it must be a pixie," and Ralph's sobs changed to giggles as he blinked at the sunlight.

It was delightful to be able to run home for a drink whenever he was thirsty, or to put his hot face and hands under one of the garden taps. He also had the freedom of an Alpine strawberry bed. The little fruits were not sent to market—there were not enough for this—and once or twice a day he would gather a handful of the crimson berries and run out to the elm grove to rest and eat them, lying full length in Fergus's tent.

The tent had come by post on the first day of the holidays. Pitched in the west park, clear of the elms, it was all that the boys had hoped; canvas spruce as a new leaf, spotless guy ropes pegged down with hazel forks, ground sheet and sleeping bag spread inside, and camp fire correctly laid near the camp, waiting for evening. Fergus slept there every night with Santa. Soon he and Peter would set off on their walking tour. By day, Ralph wriggled through the flap and lay sniffing the blend of hot new canvas and crushed grass.

One night, waking in the dark, he heard Aunt Lizard groping for her slippers. She whispered, "I'm going out— I've forgotten to shut the ducks again." Instantly he was out of bed: "Oh, I'm coming too."

The ducks' coop was in the elm grove. The night was warm and still, filled with the sweetness of buddleia. The harvest moon was high. Ralph and Aunt Lizard crept past the sleeping bothy, and climbed the fence into the west park. They stole past the tent, footfalls hushed in the grass. Suddenly they were brought up short by a trip wire. It caught Ralph round the shoulders. At the same moment there was a great clatter.

They had blundered into some kind of booby trap. Fergus rushed out of the tent waving a stick. "Don't shoot!" Aunt Lizard begged in a loud whisper.

Fergus shone his torch and showed them what had happened. Three farm horses had been turned out to graze in the park, and, fearing an iron-shod hoof through his tent, he had rigged up a fence with sticks and wire before he went to bed, and had hung it with old tins from the garbage pit. "A scarehorse," whispered Ralph, and squeaked with laughter. Then he squeaked again as he tripped over something else in the grass.

"Mind out," Fergus warned. "It's my tame hedgehog. Look, I'll make some tea, shall I? It's too late to go back to bed."

No one else had been roused; the bothy windows remained dark. Aunt Lizard found the ducks safe in their coop. Fergus blew his camp fire embers into a blaze, and hung his billycan over it. They sat on a rug, drinking the smoky tea out of thick white jars which had once held marmalade. Ralph said musingly, "Gipsies eat hedgehogs, don't they?"

Fergus laughed. "As a matter of fact," he admitted, "I thought of that when I found it. I was going to knock it on the head, and plaster it with mud, and bake it in the ashes. And then I gave it some milk. And then . . . well . . . *you* know. . . ."

"*I* know," said Aunt Lizard. "'Fergus—Hedgehog: Hedgehog—Fergus.' You just can't eat a *friend*." She added after a minute, "Who is to wring those poor ducks' necks I cannot think. I'd as soon wring yours, Ralph."

"Just keep forgetting to shut them up," said Fergus, "and a fox will save you the trouble."

Ralph finished his sleep in the tent. When he crawled in, the moon was sinking in the west, and the sun coming up behind the pleasure ground. Over his head there were three lights: moonlight, starlight and daylight.

That evening, Fergus called him out at dusk to see a glow-worm under the elms. Wandering to and fro, they found several more, and Ralph put them together under the cedar in the shrubbery. By day, they were little brown grubs; at night they shone with green fire, a necklace of emeralds. More than ever, he longed for his camera. He imagined a picture of them, shining in the dark: "A shine of glow-worms," he would call it.

Glow-worms, like stars, shone every night; one need wait only a few hours to see them again. "Everything else takes so long!" he repeated, when he found a large green caterpillar under a privet bush. The caterpillar was honey green, marked in rose-pink and white. It would hatch into a beautiful moth, Uncle Laurie said: a privet hawk moth: but not until next summer. Given a pot of earth, it buried itself out of sight.

Uncle Laurie brought a glass-topped case of butterflies and moths from a cupboard, and showed Ralph a moth with wings four inches across, rose-pink and brown: "That's what it will be."

"And it'll come up next summer?"

"Perhaps. Sometimes they hibernate two years, like a Christmas pudding."

Ralph hung over the collection. He liked the pink hawk moths, the primrose-coloured brimstone butterfly, and the little blue butterflies, like the ones he had seen on Hurst Castle downs. His favourites were a green-and-red spotted tiger moth, which had flown through the window of a train in Kilkenny one June day, Uncle Laurie said; and the peach-blossom moth, fawn-coloured and pink, like the March buds in the orchard house.

A day or two later, going into the spinney below the

keeper's house to see if the bluebell seeds were ripe, Ralph found a dead butterfly under a fern. It was apricot-coloured, its wings veined in black like a salpiglossis bell. Underneath, it was palest green and silver. A silver-washed fritillary, said Uncle Laurie; and Ralph had carried it home so carefully that it was still perfect.

"But what did it die of?"

"Not old age, anyway. It's newly hatched."

Uncle Laurie showed Ralph how to set his butterfly. He produced a box labelled "Watkins & Doncaster, Strand, London", with pins, little cork boards grooved down the middle, a drop bottle still smelling faintly of chloroform, and a green butterfly net, on a folding ring, made to fit into a walking stick. The dead fritillary was stiff, and had to be relaxed in a tobacco tin lined with damp sand and blotting paper; then it was placed on a setting board, its body in the centre groove, its head secured by a pin. With a needle, Uncle Laurie coaxed the wings to spread, and made them fast with slivers cut from a postcard. In a few days, the butterfly would be ready to go into Ralph's glass case: a cigar box with the lid removed, covered with a pane of glass from the carpenter's shed.

Now, as he worked in the flower beds, he looked eagerly at the butterflies, willing them to drop dead. Again he wished impatiently for his camera, seeing his pictures in colour: a Red Admiral on a purple Michaelmas daisy, or a sulphur butterfly on a tiger lily.

12

Dragon's Teeth

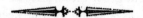

The first seed order came from Aunt Emmy, who did her gardening in three tubs on a Chelsea balcony. She asked for pansies, forget-me-nots, and a dozen lemon pips, to grow lemon bushes. Aunt Lizard made an extra jug of lemonade, and the order was sent off, with a sticky free sample of peach stones.

It was time for Ralph to carry out his side of the agreement. Bluebell stalks in the spinney below the lodge were covered with yellow pods. Ralph filled a sack with them, and shook the seeds—glossy and black, like a mouse's eyes—into a shoe box. On a hot afternoon he trudged across the north park to the beech wood bordering the drive.

The park was no longer a bird-field. The coops were gone, and the young pheasants were living in the coverts. Morning and evening, Ralph heard the keepers whistling them to be fed in the rides. Ralph slithered over the dry grass, with Santa wriggling under one arm, and the box tucked under the other. He was glad to rest for a minute when he reached the shady wood, before starting work. He had not brought a rake, but he found a beech bough that would do instead, and raked aside the leaf soil to scatter the mouse-eyes. He remembered the Dragon's Teeth, and wished the seeds might sprout into something more interesting than bluebells; an army of mice, perhaps, like the frog army he and Nat had seen.

It was a mistake to have brought Santa. The hare was growing wilder. He kept skipping beyond the beeches into the park, and Ralph had to leave his job to bring him back. In the distance, he saw Mr. Hassall working with Dittany's son, Dirk; the keeper was hiding or throwing a dummy pheasant—a stuffed birdskin—with the order "Fetch", or "Seek". Dirk would grow into a serious, clever gundog; but just now, excited as a child by the keeper's attention, he sometimes galloped in a wide circle with the birdskin, before taking it to his master's hand. Ralph was afraid for Santa. If Dirk frightened him, he might bolt into the woods and lose himself. After fetching him back three times, Ralph shovelled the rest of the seed underground and sat down against a fallen beech, holding his pet in his arms. He began to realize that the bluebell sowing would be a lengthy business. Next time, he would leave Santa at home.

The beech, uprooted in a winter gale, was held in the arms of a neighbouring tree; it sloped at a steep angle, like a palm tree in a prevailing wind. Looking up at the tilted bole, Ralph saw that it had once been struck by lightning; a deep groove ran down its length, and he imagined how rain would stream down this gutter in wet weather. Presently, he thought, he would try climbing up the gutter. But he felt too lazy to move. Santa lay across his chest. Ralph's head drooped, and he closed his eyes.

He was aroused by Santa's shriek, which he had not heard since the fracas in the woodshed, long ago. With a sharp yelp, Dirk brushed past Ralph's feet and stood with his front paws on the beech trunk, whining and frisking his tail. The hare had dashed up the gutter in the blasted trunk. "Blast *you*!" Ralph cried to Dirk, and started up the tree after Santa.

Far up among the branches, he saw the tips of Santa's ears. The smooth trunk on either side of the groove was slippery. He must catch the hare before he reached the top of the groove; if Santa tried to run on the smooth bark, he might slip and fall. Ralph could hear the scutter of his claws. Looking up, he saw that Santa had stopped, and was huddled in a niche between the "gutter" and the lowest bough. A ray of sunlight caught his pricked ears. Calling softly, "Santa! Good boy—wait for me!" Ralph climbed on. He did not dare to look down. It was easier than walking up a chestnut branch . . . he was nearly there. Leaning from the groove, he reached out his right hand to grasp the scruff of Santa's neck. He could not quite reach. He chirruped to the hare, drew himself out of the gutter and planted first one sandalled foot, then the other, on the smooth trunk. He put up his hand again.

In the same instant, Dirk yelped again. Santa made another dash upward. Ralph grabbed at the empty air, lost his balance, and fell head first out of the patch of sunlight into deep shade below.

A bright light was shining in his eyes. Fingers pressed his head, and his head hurt. He opened his eyes and tried to say so. He looked into the face of a stranger, who said quietly, "I'm the doctor," and went on pressing finger tips over Ralph's skull.

"Doctor! From *Dublin*?" Ralph asked, and the stranger smiled.

It was all very well to smile. Ralph remembered quite well how Grandmother had said, "Not the doctor. Only for broken bones or double pneumonia." That was when he fell off the donkey and sprained his wrist. He tried to explain. Then he found that Aunt Lizard was sitting by his pillow. She said, "Don't talk, Ralph. Keep still."

He shut his eyes; but he was puzzled. He had seen his lion picture, hanging on the wall, where the round looking glass should be: the one that made rainbows in the morning sun. And his bed was the wrong way round, somehow. Was he not at Nine Wells, then? And was it night or day? Something else was troubling him, but he could not quite remember what it was. He winced under the probing finger, opened his eyes and said clearly, "Santa?"

Before anyone could answer, he was sliding into a dream. He fancied a voice—Aunt Lizard?—said from a long way off, "Don't worry. We'll find Santa." But already he had found his pet for himself. They ran together through the beeches, over a field of bluebells, in and out of shadows. The dream was Ralph's last game with Santa. He was never seen again.

13

Harvest

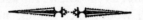

Agarden spider had spun her web across the corner of the bedroom window, anchored to a trail of creeper. In the early morning, the gossamer threads hung down in loops, heavy with dewdrops like silver pinheads. The web blew gently in the breeze, and then sparkled and dried in the first sunlight. "Guy ropes," Ralph thought. The spider— fat, pale brown, with white markings on her back—waited in the top corner, scampering out when she felt a tug at the web. Sometimes it would be a fly, to be taken to her larder at the back of her web; sometimes she was tricked by a drifting thistle seed or a flake of cedar cone.

Ralph lay in bed for a month watching her. After a few days his head was better; the queer bruised feeling died away, and he was as hungry as the spider. The doctor said he must stay there for a while, and, to his own surprise, he did not mind. He did not even want to read, but only to watch the spider, or talk to Cuckoo, who lay purring at the foot of the bed.

Cuckoo knew that Santa would not come back. He walked about the house with a flouncing air, jumping gaily in and out of windows, or rattling imperiously at door handles. He too was intrigued by the spider. When a large bluebottle buzzed in the web, he sprang to the window sill and watched wide-eyed, like the staring wooden cats in Aunt Lizard's inkstand;

but he never put a paw to the web. Downstairs, Aunt Lizard said, he had again taken possession of his wicker basket by the range, deserted when Santa came.

Ralph was sure he would find Santa again, when he should be well enough to search the wood. It was not until the third day after his mishap that he remembered what had happened. Aunt Lizard told him all she knew: the keeper had found him lying in the beech wood, unconscious, and had carried him home. "You didn't wake up for hours, Ralph. And when you did—"Aunt Lizard hesitated—"you said 'Santa'."

Ralph looked at her, and round the room. He asked: "Where *is* Santa?"

"We can't find him," she admitted. "Did you take him out with you? Can you remember? Mr. Hassall thinks you were up a tree, and you slipped off."

Then it all came back to him. He remembered losing his balance, and diving off the high tree; but he could not remember hitting the ground. He grew excited, and was given warm milk and left to sleep, while Aunt Lizard walked across to the beeches to look for Santa. Later she told Ralph:

"He isn't up in the tree now, that's certain. I think he came down that night, when it was all quiet again, and he's living wild. He'd be quite happy, you know. And think how fast he is—he could outrun any fox."

Ralph said slowly, "He *was* going wild, I know." He lay still, thinking of beautiful mad Santa frisking through the bracken, among the young pheasants; stealing the grain that the keepers scattered, and nibbling short woodland grass and woodruff. Perhaps he would find a hollow tree for a refuge, like his chimney in the woodshed.

Watching him, Aunt Lizard said, "He'll be all right."

Ralph nodded. It was no use worrying; nothing more could be done until he was up. If Fergus had been at home, he would have begged him to search; but Fergus and Peter were gone, with tent and rucksacks, on their long-planned journey west. Ralph lay quietly, looking at a picture of Stonehenge on a postcard they had sent; watching his spider, and listening to the sounds inside the house and out. Downstairs, he could follow Aunt Lizard's movements, hearing the clattering lids of the kitchen range, the whirr of the coffee-mill, the grating door of the stone-flagged cellar where she kept her butter cool. Sounds from the garden came through his open window. He remembered that first morning, when they had seemed mysterious. Now he understood them all: the creak of the greenhouse lights, the sliding of glass lids from the frame yard, the tap of a cane on pots that were being watered, the flap of step ladders by the peach walls, the soft rumble of a rubber-tyred cart leaving with a load of peach boxes for Hurst Castle station. After tea came the squeak of the hose reel as it was wheeled up and down beside the flower beds. He could even make out the squirming noise of the great hose, like a snake on the path; and then the swish of water from its nozzle.

He wondered who would cut off the dead flowers now; and whether someone had picked his secret yellow plum on the top of the wall by the orchid house; and if anyone else cared to gather the Alpine strawberries; and how the mice were faring in the harness-room; and whether the dead rat in the orchard had changed to a skeleton yet. But none of this troubled him. Concussion had left him calm and patient: everything could wait for another day, another week, even another year. The bluebell seed, for instance: "I'll finish it next year," he told himself languidly.

Aunt Lizard was clever at finding small amusements to match his mood. First she brought a basket of Spanish chestnut leaves from the shrubbery, and he lay for an hour or two, tearing them into "fishbones". Another time she brought in an armful of rushes. He plaited them in threes, sixes and nines, knotting the green braids at either end. When I have time, he thought, I'll sew them into a mat: like Meg Merrilies. The third week, Aunt Lizard brought a box of small green acorns and new conkers, with pins and reels of silk. She showed him how to make acorn men, and little chairs from flat conkers, with silken chairbacks woven with thread on four pins, like the spider's web. She would come upstairs every hour or so to chat to him, to bring him a drink or a peeled grape, or to read aloud long letters from Grandmother and Father. She moved her work table and her little wireless set from the Sky, so that he could watch her sketching clustered-bellflower and lady's-tresses, and share her evening concert. The set was always turned low, and beyond the music he could hear a robin singing on the garden wall; beyond that, the *Krrrk, Krrrrk* of cock pheasants in the forest. When the light was out, she would recite *Meg Merrilies*, or remember old riddles and verses: "I gave my love a thimble", and—

> *"In marble walls as white as milk,*
> *Lined with a skin as soft as silk,*
> *Within a fountain crystal clear*
> *A golden apple doth appear . . ."*

and another about the new moon—

> *"In Mornigan's park there walks a deer . . ."*

which he would say to himself over and over as he went to sleep.

One afternoon, Aunt Lizard came upstairs with a book from Fergus's shelf, and began to read aloud. It was called

Children of the New Forest. He listened politely at first to the story: how Jacob, an old verderer, saved four Royalist children when the Parliamentary troopers burned their father's house. The orphans settled down to live in Jacob's cottage; then Jacob and the eldest boy, Edward, set out to hunt deer in the forest. At this point there came a knock at the front door, and Aunt Lizard had to break off. Returning, she found Ralph engrossed, and went away quietly. At tea time he was still reading. When dusk fell, Aunt Lizard brought his soup and sandwich; he put the book down and asked urgently, "Why can't I get up?"

His languor was gone. The New Forest story overwhelmed him. He thought of the mossy rides, the high bracken, the wild apple tree, the great beeches, the deer, the deer. . . . He must see them again as fast as possible. He would build a cottage like Jacob's—he knew exactly where; close to the spot where he had sown the dragon's teeth and climbed the sloping tree. He would stalk deer in the fern, and bring down a hart royal, and skin it with his knife, and return to the cottage laden with deer meat. He would trail wild cattle in the park, and set springes for hares and rabbits. *Yes*; but for Santa he would set a special trap, to catch him alive, as Humphrey caught the goldfinches. . . . The cottage would be under siege from robbers, and he would fight them off. He looked at Aunt Lizard, ready for combat, repeating, "*When* can I get up?"

She answered calmly, "You're getting up tomorrow, as it happens. You're going to hospital—for an 'X-ray'."

"To hospital! Where Fergus went?"

Fergus had told him of the day when his tonsils were taken out; how he had driven with his mother, in the pony trap, in the rain, three miles to the cottage hospital, then three miles home again, dreamy and sick from chloroform. But

Ralph was to go to another hospital, twelve miles away in a town. Uncle Laurie drove him there, in the old car that Aunt Lizard called the barouche-landau. The day was cool and cloudy. He was not allowed to sit in the dicky seat, where one could enjoy the breeze and see the countryside; but he noticed how yellow the bracken had turned since he last saw the forest.

The hospital had an odd, sharp smell—from ether, Aunt Lizard said. The thought of the X-ray camera prompted a hundred questions; he was given no chance to ask them. A nurse told him to sit with his forehead pressed to a table, and his head was clamped firmly between two boards while the photographs were taken. The doctor brought them to show Aunt Lizard three days later. They were not shown to Ralph, but he was told that he might get up for a few hours next morning.

"And on Monday? And Tuesday?"

"Yes, and Wednesday," the doctor agreed. "And on Thursday you may take a little walk." He murmured to Aunt Lizard, and Ralph heard, "Four, five weeks at least . . . on the safe side . . . amuse himself quietly out of doors?"

"Yes," said Aunt Lizard thoughtfully.

Next day was Harvest Sunday. The chapel beside the garden house was decorated with little sheaves of corn, pyramids of glossy apples, and vases of red dahlias with dark leaves: Bishop of Llandaff, they were called. A bunch of purple grapes hung on the lectern eagle, vegetable marrows were heaped around the pulpit, and a giant cottage loaf rested on a garland of vegetables and flowers by the chancel rails. The senior choirboys, Fergus and Peter, carried a basket of apples and pears to the altar. The basket was Cuckoo's, borrowed at the last minute, hastily brushed clean of mouse-tails and grey fur.

Looking out at a clump of beeches, Ralph thought he saw Cuckoo; then, with excitement, he saw that it was a grey squirrel, quite a rare animal: he had seen only one before. Was it burying a nut? Before he could be sure, he had to sit down for the first lesson. Gazing into the yellowing treetops, he wondered whether Cuckoo's father might have been a grey squirrel? He was so like one . . . then his straying attention was caught by the Vicar's reading: "And in process of time it came to pass, that Cain brought of the fruit of the ground an offering unto the Lord. . . ." Overtaken already by his winter cough, he thundered with fearful effect: "And the Lord said unto Cain, *h-r-r-r-mm!* Where is Abel thy brother? . . . the voice of thy brother's blood, *h-r-r-r-r-ugh,* crieth unto me from the ground. . . ."

In the fruit room, as in the chapel, it was harvest festival, Ralph thought; all was safely gathered in. The shelves along one side, from floor to ceiling, were packed with apples of all sizes, from little sweet Golden Knobs to giant cooking-apples. The apple smell here was very different from that of the basement at Nine Wells; it was faint and delicate, because bruised fruits were quickly banished before they could rot. Uncle Laurie was packing apples and pears to compete in a fruit show in London. Watching as the beautiful fruits were swathed in tissue paper, Ralph thought they were even finer than the ones in the chapel. He said so, and Uncle Laurie said musingly:

"H'm. I wonder why Cain's offering wasn't accepted?"

"Cain's . . . ?"

"Yes. D'you think he'd kept back the best for an autumn show?"

"One of Father's gentle jokes," Fergus told Ralph kindly. He was helping with the packing, lining boxes with wood-wool and white paper. Ralph wandered up and down, eyes and nose taking in the scene. There were trays of filberts in catkin-coloured husks, brown and golden pears, sugary split figs, one box of Sea Eagle peaches, one of late plums, crimson and yellow, and a punnet of raspberries. Bunches of blue grapes hung from a rack, each with its stem in water in the neck of a tilted wine bottle. There was also a basket of little dark grapes from a vine on the wall of the Dutch garden; these Aunt Lizard was planning to make into wine.

But—taking a deep breath—Ralph thought the room smelled of sad autumn now: once it had been like the breath of summer. The air seemed bleak, as though a chill rose from the brick floor. He wanted to escape to the sunshine outside. He went back to bed rather gloomily, after choosing himself an apple—a golden apple, tasting of honey: a St. Edmund's russet—but quickly forgot his gloom in reading *Children of the New Forest*.

On Thursday, setting out alone for his promised walk, he remembered this autumn mood. He was like a sleeper awake. That hot late August day in the beech wood seemed long ago, and he had awakened in a cool bright autumn world. The herbaceous borders were still full of flowers, but with more greenery than he remembered. There were still scarlet flowers, too, on the lush vines of the runner beans, overrunning their township of wigwams in the lower garden. But the onion bed was empty now, the beautiful onions gone; like rows of burnished apples, they had looked, their tops turned over all one way to make a trim pattern. The lawns, unmown for the past week, were vivid green, dotted with pink and silver, with daisies and small cold mushrooms. He could not find his glow-worms under the cedar; instead, he found little mauve flowers, like rabbits' ears laid back. An oak tree on the south lawn was ringed with autumn crocuses. The ground there was dotted with ripe acorns. Two birds were cropping new grass by the yew hedge. They did not hear Ralph's step, and he came close and stood watching them, admiring their smooth neat feathers, coloured buff and French grey. The blue spruce tree behind them repeated their silvery tints. At first, he thought they must be tame bantams. Then he remembered the partridge chicks in the field. Mr. Hassall had said they would have fawn and grey feathers. Could these be two of the fluffy twittering mites he had helped to feed? Suddenly the birds caught sight of him. Instead of flying, they seemed to panic, and began to run in flurried circles, making small sounds of distress, and limping as though paralysed. He put out a hand to catch one. Then, shaking off panic, they rose in whirring flight, skimmed the yew hedge and landed far out in the east park. Yes, they were partridges, he was sure. "*When* I have my camera . . ." he thought.

The seed business, of course, had lapsed while he was in bed. Now, looking at the fat yellow acorns on the lawn, and then at the slim tan-coloured ones under a Turkey oak, he planned an autumn list: "oak seed, Forest Giant Minimus. Grow in pots. Only a penny a dozen." He could have beech seed, too, and conkers, and Spanish chestnuts. He crossed the drive to a sweet chestnut tree, growing behind a grassy hillock which, Fergus said, had been an ice house in Victorian days. He looked again at the barred wooden door in the mound, picturing great chunks of ice being hacked from tanks and stored there; icebergs that would have stayed solid, perhaps, even in the summer? The Spanish chestnuts were not ripe; the boughs were still covered with green burrs. He looked across the north park to the beeches, thought of the cottage he would build there, and ran home over the cricket lawn at Aunt Lizard's whistle.

Uncle Laurie was still in London, and Fergus was back at school, but there was a third at the table. The author had come to collect the last of Aunt Lizard's flower drawings, and he stayed to eat baked venison and red-currant jelly, followed by stewed pears. Aunt Lizard had found, by accident, a good way to cook the stony-hearted pears from an old tree in the orchard. She would slice them into a brown stew pot, with sugar, a clove or two and a drop of lemon juice, put them in a warm nook under the oven, and "forget" them for three days. They came out pale pink, sweet and tender.

The author, who told Ralph to call him David, thought it was romantic to eat venison from the forest; as did Ralph himself. He asked about the forest, and about the ruined tower beyond the east park. Ralph told him of the smugglers, and then of Queen Elizabeth and King Charles.

"No more legends?" he smiled.

"Yes, I have one of a sort," said Aunt Lizard. "Uncle Laurie actually bought his car from a descendant of Jane Austen."

"Surely not?" said David, after a moment's thought.

"No, no, what am I saying?—from a *relation* of Miss Austen. Steventon isn't far, you know—and Selborne."

"And the New Forest," said Ralph to himself.

He told David about the cottage he meant to build in the wood, from beech branches thatched with bracken; and David told him about bears in Russia, where he had been the year before. When the bears were ready to hibernate, he said, they built themselves dens of pine boughs, and then snow fell and made the dens into igloos; and hunters could trace the sleeping bears by the "chimneys" of melted snow in the igloo roofs, where their warm breath came up from below.

He went on to tell other travellers' tales, and Ralph was sorry to see him go.

It was two mornings later that he found a typed letter by his plate at breakfast, addressed to Ralph Oliver, Esq.; he thought the letter must be to Father, but Aunt Lizard thought not. Opening it, he took out a sheet with a printed heading: Baillie & Scott, Publishers. He read:

Dear Sir,

Flowers of the Forest

Enclosed please find our cheque in payment for your services, for which we thank you.

Yours faithfully,

M. GRANT,

Secretary.

Mystified, he looked at the green paper pinned to the letter. "Pay Ralph Oliver—ten shillings." He glanced across the table. Aunt Lizard also had a typed letter and a green slip of paper.

"What's the matter, Ralph?"

He handed her the letter. She nodded and said:

"*Now* you can buy your camera!"

Astounded, he asked, "But what does it mean?"

"Mean? Why, that they thank you for your services, and enclose ten shillings. Five for Nat, I think; and five for you."

Smiling at his dazed expression, she added, "You remember the pansy, don't you? And the orchids?"

"They've *paid* me—for those flowers we picked?"

"Yes, and me too. You for finding them, and me for drawing them. It was David's idea. He hopes you'll tell him if you ever find—oh, a wild tulip, or a scarlet pheasant's-eye."

"I will anyway, if I do." Ralph's porridge cooled as he struggled with a sum in his head. "The gooseberries—and my weekly twopences—and two weeks in the garden—and the lemon pips—and five makes—Aunt Lizard!"

There was a long pause.

"Doesn't it come to enough?" Aunt Lizard asked.

"It comes to *more*. It comes to—d'you think I could buy a rabbit for a shilling?"

14

Brownie

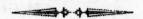

S ally, the garden pony, was cheated of her Saturday afternoon in the paddock. Aunt Lizard harnessed her and drove the trap to Hurst Castle, where the innkeeper tied her in a stall.

She settled down to retaliate by kicking through the nearest plank in the wall. Aunt Lizard and Ralph could hear her from the station platform as they waited for their train. This was the first time Ralph had seen the station in daylight. He wandered up and down, remembering the lamps, the high footbridge and the clatter of the signal bell. He was surprised to find a slot machine that sold a bottle of scent for a penny—"Attar of Roses"—and would gladly have bought one for Aunt Lizard, but she demurred: "Keep it. We'll need all our spare pennies to pay for that stable wall."

Fergus met them in the market town. They bought the camera. Ralph carried it, clasped by its loop, sniffing the curious pungent smell of its shiny black covering. Attar of Roses would not have smelt sweeter.

They went on to a livestock show in the town hall. The high roof echoed with the trilling of canaries, squeals of guinea pigs and the thudding feet of rabbits thumping unfamiliar hutches. Ralph had not known that there were so many different breeds of rabbit. He was spellbound in front of a proud beauty, a snow-white Angora with pink eyes, whose owner set it on a bench and combed its fur to a froth of airy whiteness. It was bigger than a Polar bear cub. The card on the hutch said: Best in Show.

He loved the little dapper black and tan rabbits, the silver rabbits, the Flemish giant, the Chinchillas, the Belgian hares, and the Abyssinian guinea pigs with clean pink skin showing under thick rosettes of fur. He peered hopefully into a cage labelled Fancy Mice, but could see nothing.

"Oh, you know what those are," Fergus told him. "Haven't you ever lain awake at night and *fancied* you heard a sort of scampering and scrabbling in the walls? They're not real mice at all, though. Just fancy mice."

Ralph gave him a distracted look. He had grown wary of Fergus. The morning before, he had heard him say to Aunt Lizard:

"Thousands of crabs on the lawn in the rose garden."

"Oh," said Aunt Lizard, "little green ones?"

"No, big shiny red ones, but they make good jelly. Shall I get a basketful tonight?—if they're not all swept up by then."

"The green ones have more bite to them."

"I'll go and get them!" Ralph had cried. "Crabs!—where have they come from?"

"Siberia, I suppose," said Fergus absently, strapping his satchel.

Ralph could not wait to see this invasion of crabs. He remembered the horde of frogs he had seen in the summer. Taking a chip basket, he ran through the orange house and across the pleasure ground to the rose garden. He reached the rosebeds and walked to and fro; at first cautiously, then with growing disappointment. He could not see a single pair of claws. At last he looked with sudden doubt at a scattering of small red apples under a tree. The tree label dispelled his doubt. It said: Siberian Scarlet.

Now, as he thought of this, he found Aunt Lizard at his elbow. "Ralph. There's a man here selling baby rabbits."

It was growing dark as they came out of the hall. Ralph was still carrying his camera in one hand. The other was tucked round a yellow cardboard box which had once held the camera. Now it held—not a Chinchilla, or a Belgian hare, or an Angora, but a little plain brown doe, shifting uneasily from one side to another, so that he was in danger of dropping the carton; but he would not part with either of his purchases. He thought the little rabbit should be labelled: Best in Show. She was so soft, so bright-eyed and intelligent. He had nothing left to wish for.

The innkeeper at Hurst Castle greeted them with relief. The stable plank had held, after all. He had bribed Sally with oats, apples and carrots; she was skittish as ever. In the lantern light, the innkeeper looked exhausted. Holding her head while they got into the trap, he began to tell Aunt Lizard: "I was in the Cavalry, ma'am, and never have I met with such a divil——" the rest was lost as Sally took the bit viciously between her teeth. Fergus dropped his bicycle and ran to grab her: too late. The trap lurched out of the inn yard, and the pony, mounting the pavement on the far side of the road, plunged between a lamp post and the stone wall of the park. Ralph shut his eyes. The gap was far too narrow. He was going to be killed. It seemed a pity, after such a happy day.

But, as in a nightmare, the crash did not come. Ralph opened his eyes. Tilting on two wheels, somehow the trap had shaved through. They were inside the park, and Sally was careering homeward. The long hill up to the edge of the forest sobered her. She slowed to a crawl. At the top of the hill she began to trot daintily, like a show pony in the ring.

Ralph sat with the camera and the box on his knees. By the flicker of the carriage lamps, he could read, in black print on the yellow carton, the name Brownie. That's right, he thought; that's what I'll call her. The trap rolled on through the forest, and he sat contentedly, watching Fergus's bicycle light bobbing after them in the dark.

Dormouse

15

Dormouse

T he swallows were long gone from the brewhouse, and the turtle doves from the cedar tree. Winter was coming. A square bulge in the inner wall of Ralph's bedroom, enclosing the chimney, grew warm from the wood fire below, lit once again in time for breakfast. Lying awake in the quiet autumn nights, Ralph sniffed the scorched smell of hot soot from the chimney, and listened to scampering sounds inside the thick outer walls. They were not made by "fancy mice": Cuckoo heard them too, and pricked his ears. Aunt Lizard said the intruders must be fieldmice, settling indoors for the winter. They were welcome, she added, so long as they brought their own stores, and stayed inside the walls.

Ralph remembered the dormouse that he and Fergus had set free in the copse by the old garden. He wondered if he could find it again, and bring it back to be photographed in its winter sleep? Everything, now, must be photographed.

A misfortune had befallen the first film. On the morning after the rabbit show, Ralph had taken all the photographs, by himself, before anyone else could interfere. It was a beautiful morning. He wandered from the garden house to the stables, through the pleasure ground and the shrubbery, taking pictures in a trance of happiness. He photographed

Cuckoo, Brownie, the two ponies, Biddy and Sally, looking out from their stable doors; then the autumn cyclamen under the cedar tree; and at last, after a long, patient wait, sitting under a red-berried berberis clump—the tame cock pheasant. Then he wound off the film, past the succession of black hands, domino dots and black numbers, until the window showed only a dark blank. Fergus took the film with him to school next day, promising to have it developed and printed as fast as possible. Aunt Lizard promised him a new film as soon as they should have seen the prints of the first. Ralph waited in a fever of impatience.

But there were no prints. Reluctantly, Fergus broke the news to him. He had made a mistake. In the shop, when the camera was bought, a man had explained to him how to use it; but he had been too wrought up to take it all in at once. He had not understood that the film did not move forward of its own accord: that it must be wound on every time the shutter was pressed. He had taken all the pictures on one space. The film was a failure.

A new one was put in, and he set out again, on a sunny morning. At first he felt downcast. He had taken such fine pictures that first morning. Could he ever repeat them? He photographed Brownie at the window of her hutch—windows neatly replaced by Fergus after the owl had wrecked the others; then Cuckoo, sunning himself on the rainwater tank; then a great blue morning-glory on the garden wall. His excitement returned, and he ran to the stables, but the ponies were out. He ran through the wild orchard and across to the paddock to the old garden, and photographed a toad in a rhubarb bed. Then he climbed the fence into the copse, and began his search for the dormouse.

The oaks in the copse were covered with yellow leaves and little green acorns. Below were thickets of hazels, green and gold, their nuts already stripped by the red squirrels. Under the hazels were briars, with green and scarlet hips. Ralph found a spray of white rosebuds, half open, filled with cold dew. There were a few dog-violets, too, in the moss under the bushes, and primrose buds, and clusters of pale gold flowers in the ivy twined round the oak trees.

His camera, slung by a lanyard across one shoulder, bumped his knees as he wriggled among the briars. He saw two nests, round as cricket balls, and studied them hopefully. They were rather like a long-tailed tit's nest, but woven from grasses instead of lichen, and not bottle-shaped, like a tit's nest. Were they dormouse nests—summer nests, deserted now in October, as he had deserted his own summer-house on the roof? A brown wren ticked at him from the fence. Were they old wren's nests? But they were smaller and neater than the wren's nest in the churchyard fence; and that was made of dead leaves, not grass. He remembered a linnet's nest which Nat had shown him—a little cup of grass wisps; but *that* had no roof. Anyway, the nests were empty: his probing fingers found no mouse inside.

He pressed on through the hazels, jumped a ditch, and came out into the Groves: a double row of pines, firs and redwood trees, bordering the "church path". The only churchgoer who used it now was the old sexton, who came that way every Sunday from a neighbouring village; but Ralph and Aunt Lizard loved this grove, with its carpet of thick springy moss, and its June garden of wild roses, honey-suckle and ragged-robins. Ralph skipped over the moss, keenly scanning the briars on the high bank beside the ditch. He came to a clearing where he and Nat had feasted on wild strawberries, on Saturday mornings in July. Now there were only red leaves on the strawberry runners. He sat on the moss, picking up thick yellow catkins that had fallen from among

134

the green needles overhead. They puffed out yellow dust as he played with them. Looking up, he saw something in a high briar that stretched from the bank to the lower boughs. Another nest. . . . He stood on tiptoe and gently poked at it with a stick. A small head, yellowish buff like the catkins, pushed through the woven grasses. He saw soft ears, black eyes, then a fuzzy tail, as the mouse dropped from the nest and ran up a briar. Ralph took one leap from the moss to the top of the bank, trying to steady his camera for a picture. His hands were shaking with excitement. Peering into the viewfinder, he saw only briars and shadowy pine boughs. The dormouse was gone, springing away into the sheltering hazels. Ralph did not click the shutter. Now he had found the nest, he could come back and wait for his picture. He would come in the afternoon, when the sun would shine through the clearing, straight on to the nest. He would save the rest of his film for the dormouse. Now he would go away, and leave it in peace.

Luck was with him this time. In the clear sunlight of midafternoon, he ran down the church path, climbed on to the bank, held his camera level with the nest, and gently shook the briar with his left hand. He heard a rustle before the head pushed through the grass wall. His left hand came back to steady the camera. The soft nose probed into view; and still he waited. Then the mouse was there, sitting on a twig beside the nest. He pressed the shutter, and quickly, quickly, wound the film on, ready to snatch another shot before the mouse could disappear into the branches. His eye was on the viewfinder. Seeing no movement, he looked up; he was just in time to see the tips of ears and nose as the dormouse retreated into the nest. Was it going to bolt from the other side? He moved round the bush and waited. From the nest came a faint scuffle; then silence. He stood until he was cramped. Then he looked up at the homing rooks and said aloud in his amazement:

"It's gone back to sleep!"

The sunlight moved from the briar to the wild strawberry bed, and away into a redwood tree beyond. Somewhere a woodpecker was tapping. Still he stood there quietly. The nest was in shadow when at last he dared to shake the briar again, so gently that he might have been a breath of wind or a hopping linnet. Nothing happened. The mouse stayed inside.

"Asleep . . ." he whispered aloud. Surely, if the dormouse were really asleep, he might take it home now for the winter?

Putting his camera safely on the moss, he pulled out his pocket knife and began to cut the briars that held the nest. The stems were surprisingly tough. He was hacking at green skin, like thin leather, and hard white pith that frayed under his knife, but did not break. He heard a rustle from the nest, and stopped in panic. He must not disturb the sleeper. He stood for a moment, thinking; then sprang off the bank, took his camera and raced for home.

Aunt Lizard was buttering toast at the kitchen table. Cuckoo stood beside her on his hind feet, one paw laid on her wrist, waiting for a crust. Ralph whirled past them into the breakfast room, put the camera away, and tried to pull the scissors from the work basket without a sound. He had a feeling that the scissors might cry, "Master, master!" or rather "Mistress!" like the bags of gold in *Jack and the Beanstalk*. Sure enough, the blade clicked against the pin box and betrayed him. Aunt Lizard called alertly:

"What are you going to do with my scissors?"

"Oh, *please*—I *have* to cut something—quickly——"

"Not paper? It blunts them."

"No, no, not paper, I promise——" He was gone, by the

front door, scissors in one hand, and in the other the yellow carton in which Brownie had come home. Suddenly a warning voice came to him from his earliest years: *Never run with scissors*. It was his mother's voice. He stopped short. The evening sky was clotted with gold-edged clouds. It was as though she had leaned out of a cloud to warn him. He put the scissors into the carton, took it in both hands and ran back to the Groves.

It was twilight there; but he could see well enough for his purpose. Scrambling on to the bank, he snipped the twigs about the nest with infinite care, so as not to jerk the mouse inside. The nest, enclosed in briars, went into the carton. He closed the flaps, wrapped the scissors in a sheet of moss and laid them on the box. He ran past Frank, the horseman, in the west park, and did not see him. Frank stopped and stared after him. The box was clasped against his jersey, and as he ran, he whispered, "Oh, mouse, mouse, mouse," in a chant of rapture.

The carton was hidden under his bed. No sound came from inside. When he went to bed, all was still; he put the box in his cupboard, to be safe from Cuckoo, wedging the door with a slipper, so that the mouse might have air. Did it *need* air? He could not be sure. He had no book about dormice; but there was the Dormouse in *Alice*: "I breathe when I sleep . . . I sleep when I breathe." Yes, he had better leave the door ajar. He lay in bed listening for the snore which Fergus had told him to expect. Once or twice, he thought he heard a rustle; not the galloping sound of the mice in the wainscot, but a slight whisper like a mouse turning on a bed of grass.

At daybreak he was on his knees beside the box, unravelling the grasses to inspect the sleeper.

She was not asleep, and not alone. With her in the nest were four babies, new-born, naked, greyish pink, each the size of a thimble. He put out a finger to stroke one; and then the temper of the mother dormouse reached snapping point. He withdrew his finger with the mouse swinging from it, her front teeth fixed in a ferocious bite. Then she dropped back into the box beside her young.

His first feeling, when he saw the babies, had been one of sheer delight. It was followed by a pang of fear. Peter Hassall had had a white mouse, and it had a family, and when Peter moved them into a better cage, it had eaten every one. He knew this grisly tale was true; Mrs. Hassall had told him so. Peter should have left them alone, she said, for three or four days, and then the mother wouldn't have taken fright.

He saw what he must do. Back in her own wood, under her own bush, the mother dormouse might let bygones be bygones. He wrapped a handkerchief round his dripping finger, and tied it with one end held in his teeth. He did not mean to tell anyone what he had done. It seemed so cruel, although he had meant no harm: how could he have known she would have babies? Setting off for the wood, he tried to make it up to her, putting a handful of hay into the box as he passed the loft, and hazel nuts, blackberries, acorns, hips and haws to make a store for her. He left the box under the bush, and went away.

He had told himself that he would not go near the nest for three days; but by evening his resolve had already weakened. Next day, he could hardly keep himself from going. Then the weather kept his promise for him. In the night a high wind rose. He woke to the dull roaring of the elms and the drumming of rain. The day was dark and wild. The distant silver streak of the sea was blotted out. The chimneys smoked. Yellow wistaria leaves shivered on the front wall, and beech leaves drifted thickly into the Dutch garden, where yesterday the snapdragons were still in flower. The vegetable man appeared in gleaming oilskins and fisherman's helmet; rain ran like quicksilver from his cauliflowers. Ralph visited the barometer by the front door several times, hoping to see the needle drop down past Pluie to the dramatic Tempête. Uncle Laurie, who kept weather records "to send to Kew", told them in the evening that over an inch of rain had fallen. Ralph privately thought the rain gauge unreliable: there was a puddle quite four inches deep by the brewhouse.

Aunt Lizard had never before kept him indoors because of bad weather; but now she said, "You'd better not catch a chill." For three days he did not go outdoors, but played up and down the greenhouses in the upper range. He walked for hours round and round the orange-house, up and down between rows of budding chrysanthemums, higher than his head. He popped the fuchsia buds and swarmed up the slim trunk of the single orange tree. Among the green leaves at the top, he found two or three green oranges, and a pale yellow one.

"Would you call them English oranges?" he asked Uncle Laurie.

"Well, yes . . . if you talk of English pheasants?"

"Or peaches," said Fergus.

"Or crabs," thought Ralph.

In the central house, between the early peachery and the muscat house, grew a tree with shiny leaves and little dark red fruits; guavas, Uncle Laurie told him, and gave him one to try. It was soft pink inside, like strawberry ice, and tasted of strawberries. He shared it with Brownie, who ate her half with relish.

In the muscat house it seemed warm as summer. The sloping glass roof held four spreading vines, and golden bunches were still hanging among the leaves, the grapes round and smooth as glass. Once, Uncle Laurie gave him a sprig of little shrivelled grapes, pale brown in colour. He bit cautiously, thinking they looked rotten, and was amazed at their delicious taste, sweeter than sultanas. He spent half a day in the tropical house, watching the goldfish in the tank; and another half day in the potting shed next door, where a garden boy was scrubbing pots. But this last afternoon went slowly. The little dormice would be growing up, he thought. He had left the carton on its side; he hoped it would have sheltered them from the rain. If only he might go and see!

He woke to a sunny morning. Not waiting for breakfast, he crossed the park. The rain had not doused the maple trees; they flamed like torches. He ran through a squelching thicket at the top of the church path, through a swinging gate, and down the Groves. Ducking under the briar, he looked into the sodden yellow box and saw—nothing.

Nothing. The floor was bare. Not a shred of the nest remained, not a wisp of hay, not a crumb of the nuts or berries; not a trace of the mother dormouse and her babies.

So this was what came of setting things free! he thought bitterly. If he had risked keeping them, they wouldn't have been eaten by some rat or weasel. He stood upright.

He found himself looking at a new dormouse nest in the briars. It was woven, not of the coarse sedge grasses of the wood, but of fine meadow hay. He gently shook the bush, and a yellow nose poked out.

Watching the nest day after day, he saw four young mice running in and out. The mother dormouse had carried the old nest and the hay, wisp by wisp, from the box to build her new cradle. She must have carried her young ones up, one by one, as Ralph had seen old Soldier at Nine Wells carrying her kittens. The family flourished in the warm sunshine of

St. Luke's summer. Ralph named the four young mice Edward, Humphrey, Alice and Edith, after the Children of the New Forest. Their mother, because she was fierce and brave, he christened Boadicea.

16

"In Mornigan's Park . . ."

Before he could begin his cottage, Ralph had work to do. The fieldmice in the wainscot were not the only creatures to need winter stores; Brownie would still expect two meals a day when there were no more "bolted" lettuces in the kitchen garden, or feathery carrot leaves, or dark bitter-smelling leaves from the parsnip bed. Ralph laboured for two mornings, picking up the handsome brown acorns from under the Turkey oak, and yellow ones from the English oaks, and tipping them into a barrel in the brewhouse. Later, he would add sweet chestnuts. Secretly, he meant to gather enough for two; he still hoped to find Santa. The finest acorns he saved for his seed packets. Photography was startlingly expensive; but for a thoughtful present from Father, he would have had to wait for his third film until after Christmas.

The prints of the second film taught him a lot. The portrait of Brownie was a maze of wire netting and two ears; that of Cuckoo showed mainly a tilting dark cliff of tank; the toad and the morning-glory looked fuzzy, and oddly alike; but when he saw his two last pictures, he was too pleased to speak. The first was so clearly and unmistakably the mother dormouse and her nest; the second was a little blurred—"out of focus", he had learned to call it—but this was his favourite.

He had taken it after a long wait, and there was the new nest, and one of the babies, and the tail of another, curled round from behind the nest. The weeks of looking forward to his camera, the toil of top-and-tailing gooseberries, the hours in the flower beds, going without sweets...all had been worth-while. Aunt Lizard thought so too; she made him write down the dormouse story, just as it had happened.

One morning he crossed the park to the beech wood where he had had his fall. Nearly two months had gone by. The beeches were no longer green, but bronze and brown above, and bright yellow below. He wandered about for a time, calling, "Santa!" He saw only a red squirrel, which whisked up a beech trunk and sat jerking its tail and scolding him: a noise which he could imitate, he found, by clicking the front of his tongue on the roof of his mouth. They gibbered at each other for some time. Looking about him, he found the place he had had in mind for his cottage; a pair of oak saplings grew side by side, with low horizontal boughs that would do for the framework. He began to collect dead branches to make the walls. The woodmen had been busy all the summer in another part of the forest, and the flotsam of last winter's gales still lay there, waiting to be gathered. He dragged branches from the undergrowth, and planted them deeply in the leaf mould beside the saplings. He ran back over the park to the carpenter's shed by the stables, and found enough scraps of wire to rivet the branches to the growing crossbars. The roof would be of leafy boughs torn down by the latest storm; these, too, he would wire to the oak beams. The four walls standing, he set about gathering bracken to thatch them. His pocket knife was not sharp enough; trying to break the stems, he gashed his finger badly—the same finger on which the dormouse had left her mark—and had to stop work to suck at it. The one o'clock bell from the garden took him by surprise. It was tedious to have to trudge away to dinner, and then to rest on his bed; the afternoon would be half gone by the time he returned. He appealed to Aunt Lizard: "Can't I take dinner out? And I can rest just as well in my own house. I could make a lovely dry bed of leaves and things. Governess told us," he suddenly remembered, "people used to stuff their mattresses with beech leaves, in the olden days."

"You must come back to dinner," Aunt Lizard said, "then I know you haven't had another disaster . . . and you must have your rest, the doctor said so." Then she made a compromise; he might take his pudding out, while the fine weather lasted, and he must rest for half an hour. He returned to the wood in triumph, carrying two apple dumplings in a napkin, Uncle Alfred's army cape, the kitchen egg timer, and an old pair of leather pruning gloves, one of several pairs in a kitchen drawer: his hands were lost inside them, but he would suffer no more cuts.

He piled a bed of dry bracken and beech leaves inside his house, and spread the waterproof cape over it. The dumplings finished, he lay down, staring up at the brown beech leaves and the chinks of sunlit sky. The egg timer hung from a twig by his head. He watched the sand slip busily through, and turned and re-turned it: "as long as it take to boil ten eggs," Aunt Lizard had said. It occurred to Ralph that ten eggs might very well go into one pan, but he did not cheat. It was delightful to lie there, sorting out his plans. Tomorrow he would have a roof over his head. This, he was determined, was going to be a real cottage, very different from the flimsy shelter which had contented him last winter. And when it was built, he would have a gun and go in search of deer.

The cottage was finished on a still golden morning, so quiet in the wood that Ralph could hear the tapping of beech nuts falling one by one from the trees. He set out in the afternoon, equipped for stalking: beech stick gun under his arm, skinning knife in his belt, and the camera slung over his shoulder. Sometimes the gun was modern, a ·410 like the one at the garden house; sometimes it was a forest ranger's gun with a long barrel, as used in the New Forest. Mr. Hassall had said that there were deer in the woods that lay to the north-west, bordering the High Forest road. He ran out of the beeches into a green avenue that cut through the forest. A faint breeze blew down the ride, touching his left cheek. He knew that he must stalk his quarry upwind.

He went along the Ladies' Mile, a mossy path under Spanish chestnut trees. A good word, "Spanish", he thought: there were Spanish irises too, and Spanish gold, and the Spanish Main. Old silver beech trunks, long felled, lay in the sunlight on a high slope above the path. Dogwood leaves glowed crimson; spindleberry thickets were massed with berries, shell-pink, green and lemon-coloured, like the "satin cushion" sweets in the village shop. He found a sloe tree with powdery blue fruits, wrinkling in the sun. He turned and plunged into the forest, making his way upwind, alert for the first sight of a deer.

This part of the forest was wilder and deeper than any he had seen before. Ancient oaks were thickly coated with moss. Dead leaves from past years lay in drifts, knee-deep, among bracken clumps and brambles. He found strange things; dark purple toadstools, and clusters of little brown slimy caps, and beautiful wicked-looking ones, cream-coloured, stippled in brown, like thimbles for a giant's daughter. Under the oaks he saw masses of fungus like tiny pale green cups—"ant's-egg cups", he thought; and patches of dark moss, shaggy with soft red hairs like butterflies' antennae.

A rustling and thrashing noise caught his ear. In the distance, he saw what looked like a fox cub jumping a fern leaf.

He dashed through the undergrowth. It was not a fox, but a red squirrel struggling in a trap. It was caught by one paw. The squirrel jumped to and fro, squealing with pain and fear, then lay panting on the moss. Crouching beside it, Ralph saw that the mangled paw was held only by one sliver of skin; the squirrel had almost torn itself free. With his knife he cut the skin. At the same moment, the squirrel flew at him and bit his hand, then flashed on three paws up the nearest tree. It stopped in the first fork to chitter angrily at Ralph.

Sitting back on the moss, he frowned at this ingratitude, and sucked his own wound, spitting on the moss as with rattlesnake poison: it was best to be on the safe side. Blood ran freely, and he watched it for a moment with interest. "Things always go in threes," Katy Wood had told him. Now he had three scars: from the dormouse, the bracken and the squirrel. He prised the trap open and took out the tuft of red fur and nails that had been a front paw. Slipping it into his pocket, he found a forgotten apple there and began to eat it.

Across a wilderness of fern, he noticed a dead branch sticking up. He fancied it moved. He began to watch it: why should it have moved? There was no wind blowing here. Then he paused, with his mouth full of apple. The branch had moved again. It dipped out of sight, then reared and bobbed up and down.

His apple lay forgotten on the ground. He crouched, and began to crawl through the standing bracken, high thistles and ragwort. Now he was in an open stretch of turf, ringed with grey thorn trees, old and gnarled. He made no sound on the grass. He found a fallen oak, embedded in fern, and began to crawl along it, inch by inch. Leafless boughs grew from the trunk; antlered boughs, like the one he had seen. At the end, a curtain of bracken fronds arched over the trunk. He found a gap in the curtain and peered through it. He came almost face to face with a fallow deer, lying under a rowan tree.

He and the deer took one another by surprise, the boy with a mouthful of apple, the deer with a mouthful of grass. Stockstill, they eyed one another. The deer's head was tilted, its nostril flared, its eye, black and shiny as a rowan berry, stared at the face in the bracken. Ralph swallowed his gasp and held his breath, waiting for the fairy-like creature to vanish. Then his heart seemed to turn over; for the deer sank back on its fragile knees, flicked its ears and *began to chew*. It was not afraid of him!

Ralph went on gazing. The deer had come out from between the blue and gold covers of the New Forest book, into the autumn afternoon. Its antlers bobbed, fawn and silver coloured, above the old fawn and silvery bracken. Its hide, whitish fawn as the autumn grass, rippled over a fading dapple of white spots, then twitched as a fly, peacock-blue in the sun, came down from the rowan berries. The deer shook it off. The bright eyes had never left Ralph's face. Ralph swallowed his mouthful of apple unchewed. It scraped his throat like a mouthful of conker shells, but he did not choke.

The fly alighted on Ralph's forehead, and he did not stir. It crawled down his face. He was in torment. He put out his lower lip and blew upward at it, a tiny puff of breath that could hardly have moved a piece of thistledown; but the deer heard it, and sprang up. Bracken swayed, thorns crackled, and then there was silence. Ralph stayed where he was, staring at the faintly hollowed grass under the rowan.

A long time passed, and he found that the sunlight was gone. His right leg was cramped, his hands and feet prickled with pins and needles, and he noticed that both knees were deeply furrowed from the oak tree bark. He dropped to the grass, and noticed his gun and his camera. Strange; he had forgotten that he was carrying them. What a picture he might have taken! But he did not care. The picture was in his head.

He limped back through the wood, and came up out of the Ladies' Mile into the rabbit warren. The sun had gone down behind the beeches. The far-off park lay like a quiet sandy shore under the dark cliff of the forest. A new moon hung in the sky, thin and white, a squirrel's finger nail.

Ralph began to run like a mad child down the warren, dodging rabbit holes. A rhyme came into his head, and he stopped and said it half aloud:

> *"In Mornigan's park there walks a deer,*
> *Silver horns and a golden ear.*
> *Neither fish, flesh, feather nor bone,*
> *In Mornigan's park he walks alone."*

The white gate clinked in the distance as the garden men went home. Lights shone from the bothy and the garden house, but Ralph could not bear to go indoors yet. He was not cold, but he found that he was shivering. He groped through the beeches to his cottage, and lit two candles he had hidden there, and warmed his hands over them. Far away, he heard the shrilling of a whistle, without realizing that it was for him. Fergus, cycling home, saw the glimmer of candle-light from the drive, and went to investigate. He found Ralph crouched on his beech leaf mattress, looking dazzled, as though he had just woken from a long dream.

PART FOUR

17

Treason and Plot

"The breaking waves dashed high
On that stern and rockbound coast,
And the woods against a stormy sky
Their giant branches tossed."

Standard Four bellowed in chorus against the roar of the north-west wind. Already at three o'clock the school-room was nearly dark. An Arctic gale rocked the forest, hurling wet leaves and beech nuts against the windows. The Virginia creeper leaves were gone from the schoolhouse wall; their naked white stalks remained, and made a hissing noise when a blast of wind caught them. It was the fifth of November, and Ralph's first day back at school.

Uncle Laurie, before leaving to visit the estate in Ireland, had arranged for the lily pool in the Dutch garden to be drained and cleaned. First, the goldfish must be caught and transferred to the tank in the tropical house. Yesterday, the garden boy, Billy, had been given this job, and Ralph had gone to help him. They caught the fish in nets of butter-muslin tied to canes, and put them into a bucket of water. When a dozen or so had been caught, the bucket was carried to the tank, and they began again. For an hour they worked steadily, under the eye of an old gardener who was planting polyanthus in the flower beds. By that time most of the fish were caught, leaving only a few agile brown ones which eluded the nets, hiding under the lily baskets, or lying low in the clouded water. One by one they were netted; but the fishermen had grown dangerously reckless. At last only one was left. It dashed from side to side. They tore round and round the brink, laughing and dodging each other, lunged together at the fish, tripped over the bucket, and fell together into the pool. Ralph had the worst of it; he was underneath, lying full length in thick water, mud and slime, gasping like the stranded fish that were spilled over the flagstones. Billy picked up the fish, and the old gardener picked up Ralph, muttering, "Knew how it would be. Two boys is no boy at all." Ralph was plastered with evil-smelling mud; his coat would never be the same again. Peeling off his clothes in the scullery, Aunt Lizard snapped, "Tomorrow, my lad, you'll go to school!"

Aunt Lizard did not often snap; but for the past week she had been on edge, listening for a telegraph boy, getting up early to take in the letters, walking two miles to Hurst Castle in the evenings in case another letter might have come: Aunt Emmy was expecting a baby any day, she told Ralph, and as soon as it arrived, she was going to London to see it. Ralph was to stay with Mrs. Hassall. He had greatly looked forward to this; at the keeper's lodge there were glass-fronted cases of shining guns, ferrets in the woodshed, antlers in the hall, a stuffed fox in the attic, and queer bedroom windows level with the floor, so that you had to kneel down to look out at the kennels in the back yard. He might help Mr. Hassall to clean a gun or a trap, or exercise the dogs. School would be a poor exchange. Coming down from his bath, he asked sulkily:

"Are you going to London yet?"

"Not yet. The message hasn't come."

"What does Aunt Emmy want a baby for?"

"Oh . . . most people do, some time or other."

"What's the use?—it'll only grow up."

"And a good thing too," she retorted tartly, buttoning the ruined coat on to a hanger.

The summons came next morning at breakfast: a telephone message, brought by the caretaker from the great house. Aunt Emmy had a daughter, born that morning; and Aunt Lizard set off at once, lit with excitement, in the station taxi, dropping Ralph by the keeper's lodge among the other children. Ralph had got over his chagrin at going back to school. At least he and Fergus would sleep at the lodge to-night, and tomorrow would be Saturday, and a holiday. Peter and Fergus had built a bonfire in the paddock by the empty pheasantry, and they would let off the box of fireworks that had come for Ralph from Father—not from China, but from a shop in London.

Ralph jumped from the taxi into a crowd gathered outside the lodge, waiting for the guns to arrive for a pheasant shoot. All the dogs were there; the retrievers, Rain and Ring, Deuce and Dittany, Niger, Jet, Trace and Turk, and the spaniels, Maggie and Tulip; and all the keepers, and a throng of beaters from the estate and from neighbouring villages: among them Fergus and Peter, who had a half-term holiday, and were equipped like men with sticks, sandwiches, matches and cigarettes. The schoolchildren lingered in a bunch by the looking glass, staring enviously at elder brothers and sisters, ranged in a line along the grass avenue beside the forest. They were "stops", Nat said. They had lit grass fires to keep warm, and were ready with their sticks to wave back the poor fugitives when the drive should begin.

"My skull's been fractured," Ralph told Nat.

"Coo," said Nat politely. "*We* heard you were dead."
Did he sound disappointed? But he was friendly as ever, and
Ralph perched on his bicycle step as he raced, "no hands",
down the drive. In the woods they filled their pockets with
sweet chestnuts, Nat climbing the trees while Ralph scuffed
among the fallen leaves for nuts. Nat eyed him from above
and remarked:

"Gov'ness *said* it would teach you to go climbing."

"Oh!" Ralph stared. "Oh . . . did she?" He began to
swarm up a sapling. It was no harder than climbing the
English orange tree. Soon his fall was forgotten, and he
climbed as daringly as Nat.

The schoolroom felt draughty after the sheltered forest.
The two stoves smoked, the wind moaned, the children
shivered. Only the infants were lucky. They had an open coal
fire; their room was like a nursery, with pictures, rocking
horse, dolls' house and giant teddy-bear: gifts from some
country house, carefully treasured. Passing the door, Ralph
had a glimpse of five tots pressed against a high fire-guard,
their faces pink in the firelight, under a snug picture of a
squirrel. Miss Hazel, their teacher, let them stand there in
relays all the morning, Nat said enviously; and Mrs. Duffel
used to let her children do the same, but Governess had
stopped it, saying it gave them chilblains: "and we *got*
chilblains, anyway."

They arrived warm from their journey, but the glow soon
faded, and they sat numb, hands too cold to write, feet growing chill in stiff winter boots.

It was not only the icy air that made Ralph shiver. All day,
the sound of the guns was blown from the forest as the
pheasants died. It was like listening to a battle. At break, the
little boys dashed about yelling, "Ma-a-a-ark over!" and
"Woodcock over the left! *Bang!*" It was all very well for

them, Ralph thought. They had not seen the little pheasants growing up almost from the eggs, changing from chicks to fledgelings, only to be slaughtered in their home rides where the keepers had treacherously fed them. And he had had a fellow-feeling for them, ever since he had heard that they came from China. Then he thought of the deer in the wood by the Ladies' Mile. Would it be shot like the pheasants? Would it run for its life? It would be *terrified*.

He had told no one about the deer. Now, racked with anxiety, seeing its dark eyes wild with panic, he felt he must tell someone. After break, for their composition lesson, Mrs. Duffel told the children to write a letter. Ralph asked how to spell "rowan", and began, "Dear Aunt Lizard, I saw a Deer. Under a Rowan tree." He stopped then, listening. There had been a lull, but now the distant gun-fire began again. Would the deer find somewhere to hide? He read what he had written, and saw that it was like a poem. More lines came into his head, and he wrote them down: "Its horns were silver like a fern. It flicked its ears at me, And ran away into the Forest." After a while he added, "When I came home the wood was dark. And I saw a new Moon over the park. Love from Ralph." After this he wrote, "I hope Aunt Emmy likes that baby." His fingers were cold again. He could not write any more. He knew it was not the kind of letter Mrs. Duffel expected, and was quite unprepared for the fuss she made about it; not a scolding fuss, however, but a flurry of pleased surprise. She read the lines aloud, and then went into the little room to read them to Miss Hazel. When she came back, she asked, "What baby?" Ralph explained, and then Mrs. Duffel took the page out of his exercise book and put it in an envelope with a stamp, to be posted to Aunt Lizard. Ralph wrote down the address in Chelsea. He was glad Aunt Lizard would have the letter, but it did not help his disquiet over the deer. He longed for the day to end; tomorrow he would go and search for it. In the afternoon, the guns were banging away in the very wood where he had seen the deer. It was a relief when the reciting began, and he had something else to think about. The poems were new to him, though not to the performers, who were already sick of "that stern and rockbound coast". This came from a poem about the landing of the Pilgrim Fathers, and before long Ralph, too, had it by heart: Governess wanted them word-perfect for a concert at Christmas.

Half past three drew near, and the children looked out at the swaying forest. Grey clouds were scudding before the wind, and drops of cold rain spattered the windows. It must not rain on Guy Fawkes' Night! Most of them had a bonfire and a handful of fireworks ready at home.

> *"Remember, remember, the fifth of November,*
> *With gunpowder, treason and plot . . ."*

It was cheeky Randy who piped up with this, when Mrs. Duffel said:

"Five minutes to go! Now, who'll give us something new? A solo? Francie? Jack? Roy? Anything you like!"

Governess heard the laughter, and pounced, asking the cause. Then she kept them an extra five minutes, wiping the grins from their faces with a sombre account of Guy Fawkes' fate. She described the difference in his signatures, before and after torture; the first elegantly flourished, the second a pathetic scrawl. The children waited glumly for release; but, once outside, with their faces turned towards home, they forgot to feel guilty, and again looked forward to their bonfires. The wind behind them, they galloped down the hill like ponies. Ralph left Nat at the top of the bank, and ran through the dark wood towards the Ladies' Mile. The rides were quiet now; but no bird chirped and no rabbit hopped in the fern; those that had survived the day of terror were huddled under cover, or straying in another part of the forest. Ralph sniffed curiously at the gunpowder tang that lingered under the trees. In clearings here and there he found empty cartridge cases, scarlet and yellow, with shining brass heads. He gathered a double handful, and wandered on, looking among hazels and dogwood thickets for his deer. A branch, blown from a high tree, landed near by and startled him. Then he heard a far-off cry; it was only a lowing cow, perhaps, or a motor horn, but he could not help remembering the phantom chairmender. He cut across the forest, back to the road, and on to the keeper's lodge.

Mrs. Hassall was looking out for him. He crossed the cobbled floor under the stone pillars of the lodge, and went in. They shared tea and buttered toast while Ralph admired the hunting prints, *The Meet*, *A Check* and *Full Cry*, with their gay scarlet, greens and russets, in the lamplit sitting-room. The men would be in presently, Mrs. Hassall said; if he liked, he might go and see the ferrets—"Only mind your fingers." First he took a candle and tiptoed upstairs to visit the snarling fox in its glass case. Then he went into the kennel yard. The weary retrievers were gulping supper; all but Dirk, who was too young to go out with the guns, and had spent a wretched day alone. He jumped against his barred gate, greeting Ralph with a plaintive whine. Ralph looked in the end kennel for his favourite, gentle Dittany, but could not see her; perhaps she had already gone to bed in the inner kennel. He wandered to the upper yard, where the day's bag in the game cart was being checked; brace upon brace of dead pheasants hung there, that would never cry at dusk, or strut under the oaks again, looking for acorns. Ralph went back to the house. Mr. Hassall followed him, but did not speak.

Fergus and Peter were standing by the back door, with an under-keeper and two men from the estate. The head keeper went past them into the house. The men looked at each other, and Ralph heard:

"A silver high-bird. Seen it get up myself."

"Captain Brock's bird, wasn't it?"

"Ah. But old Bert—'Never had no silver in me cart all day,' he says. 'Never clapped eyes on one.'"

"Plenty more missing." The men grunted. Peter said:

"Old Dittany——" Ralph did not catch the rest.

"Your dad sent her after the silver high-bird. 'High lost,' he says. But he never seen. . . ." More whispering.

"Beaters . . .?"

"Your dad knew something was up. He was waiting——"

"Them foreigners?"

"—had his eye on them."

The muttering broke off as the head keeper came out of the back door with two torches and two stable lanterns. He spoke sharply.

"Now then. Come on. You take the spinney, Fred. Peter, cut off down to Withy Piece, you and Fergus. Double whistle if you find her. Dick, we'll make for the Larches and work over." His glance fell on Ralph. "Well, my boy, you must wait a bit for your bonfire, but we'll have it later, never fear." They were gone. Ralph ran into the kitchen, bursting with questions. Mrs. Hassall stood by the window, an absent look on her face. The kettle steamed; the big teapot stood waiting. Ralph cried, "What's the matter? Who's lost?"

She picked up the empty teapot and put it down again before answering. "It's Dittany."

"Dittany lost? How could she? Oh . . . will they find her? Poor Dittany——" He was shocked.

"Don't worry." Her thoughts seemed a long way off. Ralph asked, "Mrs. Hassall—what's a silver high-bird?" She gave him a startled look.

"Hybrid . . . a silver hybrid—pheasant. There are one or two in the forest. . . ." He waited. The clock ticked loudly on the shelf. Someone called to Mrs. Hassall from the yard. She went out, and Ralph was alone in the shadowy kitchen. His mind was made up. He darted along the passage, grabbed his macintosh from the peg and slipped out of the front door. A torch was jigging far down the drive. "The Larches," Mr. Hassall had said: this was the quickest way, Ralph knew— down the drive a bit, and then up the straight ride through the chestnut copse. He raced after the torch, and saw it swerve into the ride. He ran as fast as he could. The light stood still, and he heard both keepers give the long shrill whistle they used for the dogs—like Grandfather calling his sheep dogs. "Dittany!" That was Mr. Hassall. "Here, girl, Dittany, here, here, then!" They moved away up the ride, calling and whistling. Ralph padded after them. He thought he had made no sound, but Mr. Hassall shouted, "Who's there?" and the torch beam blinded him. He feared that they would send him back, but they accepted him, as though he were a tiresome puppy that had followed and must be allowed to tag along. Perhaps the macintosh helped; he was glad he had thought of it, for the rain was streaming down now, and his jersey would have been soaked. No grown-up, Ralph knew, was too busy to order you home for your own good. But the keepers strode on, glancing back now and then to see him running at their heels. They stopped every dozen yards to whistle and listen; but the only sounds were the roar of the wind, the beat of the rain and the distant rumble of a train.

They turned down a cross-ride, then another and another,

until Ralph felt utterly lost. The keepers flashed their torches under trees and bushes, and he realized that Dittany might be lying somewhere, hurt . . . or *dead*? He had no breath for questions, and knew better, anyway, than to open his mouth. Suddenly he ran full tilt into something that rapped his face sharply, making him yelp. The torch flashed, and he saw that he had knocked down a hazel stick: a split wand, with a white card stuck in it. He remembered seeing sticks like this in the morning, as he and Nat crossed the Broad Ride; they were marks, Nat had said, for the Larch Wood drive. They must be near the Larches now.

Then, above the gale, came a sound that made Ralph clutch at Mr. Hassall's coat. It came again, and all three listened: once more they heard it—the faint yelping of a dog. But was it in the forest? Or blown on the wind from the kennel yard?

"There! That's her! Dittany!" Ralph heard the joyful note in Mr. Hassall's voice, and knew he had dreaded what they might find. Mr. Hassall turned abruptly towards the sound, Dick and Ralph following. He whistled, and the yelp came again. It had an odd, almost muffled note, Ralph thought; the way his own voice might sound from the pit by the fig house. But why? He remembered the pitfall that Humphrey dug in the New Forest book, to catch wild cattle. Could there be something of the kind here, and could Dittany be trapped? He could tell by their muttered exchanges that the keepers too were puzzled. The dog's bark came distinctly now, but still with that trace of—was it an *echo*? Perhaps she's in a hollow tree, he thought, struggling after them through switching hazels, his hands over his eyes. He stumbled on a stone, and then stopped.

"Mr. Hassall! Mr. Hassall! I know where she is!"

They looked back at him. He gasped:

"The old well! She's fallen down it!" He kicked at the stone. "Look . . . it's a flint. The old cottage. . . ."

With a curt exclamation, Mr. Hassall slewed round and went straight from the spot to the clearing where the broken walls stood. Stumbling after the men, Ralph forgot his aching legs and the stitch in his side. Here was the well! Two torches shone down into it, and Dittany gave a low excited whine. Ralph could see her dark head and waving tail. She leaped, and dropped back; she was too far down to clear the coping. Before either of the keepers could speak, Ralph was over the side; he landed beside her with a soft flump, and cried out in new amazement:

"Feathers! I say! Mr. Hassall! There's *hundreds of* dead birds down here!"

From above him in the darkness came a murmured parley. The torches had been switched off. Then Mr. Hassell spoke in an urgent whisper.

"Ralph?"

"Yes?"

"Listen. Pipe down. Keep still. Not a sound. *Someone coming*. . . ."

Silence. The dark shapes of the two men were gone. He could see only a circle of murky sky, a little lighter than the darkness in which he stood. He crouched down on the slack bodies of the dead birds, his arms round Dittany. She had heard the keeper's order from his tone; she made no sound, but licked his hands and moved from one foot to another, shivering with excitement. What did the keeper mean? "Someone coming?"

Then he recalled the muttered conversation at the back door. Something about missing pheasants. A silver hybrid. Someone had shot it, and it wasn't in the game cart. Bert was the man in charge of the game cart, and he hadn't seen it. Now there were all these birds, a great mound of them, hidden down here in the well. And here was Dittany—what was *she* doing here? What was happening?

Straining his ears, Ralph heard a faint click from above, like a twig snapping, or a foot touching a flint. Then the wind howled again, and he heard a tree creak; the old apple tree, perhaps. Was that really a footstep? He clung to Dittany. He had begun to tremble from head to foot. He did not quite know what he was afraid of, or who the prowler could be, but he had begun to guess. In another minute, someone would reach the well, and shine a torch down, and find . . . what he knew was there. Stolen pheasants. But also he would find what he didn't expect: a boy and a dog. Oh, where were the keepers gone?

He opened his mouth to shout: he could not help it. But his call was lost in sudden uproar. First there was a sharp cry, as though in warning; then Mr. Hassall's voice—"Got him! Grab hold of t'other one!" Then shouts, curses, whistles, and then the crash of bushes, the sound of running feet, more shouts, a volley of shots; and then nothing. The shouts, the crashing footsteps were gone into the distance. They were alone again, he and Dittany, with rescue no nearer. Supposing the keepers were outnumbered and overpowered? Supposing *they*—the enemy—came back to the well?

Ralph sat down. His aching legs had given way under him. He propped himself against the brick wall. Dittany whined and leaped, and he put his arm round her neck, whispering, "Up, Dittany, sit up, shut up, don't make a noise!" She sat for a moment, padded in a circle, came back to nudge him. They sat listening together. The wind made a queer whining sound in the well, and Dittany whined again. Then all was quiet, except for the wind in the trees. They leaned against one another. The feather bed was warm. Dittany was warm. A long time passed, and they dozed.

Ralph woke with a jump, wondering what had disturbed him. He caught a small scratching sound from above, like a finger nail on the brickwork; then a rustle, like a stealthy footstep. His teeth were chattering. Someone was up there. Not a friend, a keeper, or it would have called out to him. *It.* Why had he used that word? Was it a keeper, after all—the ghost of the dead keeper who had lived there long ago? No, no, he musn't, he must *not* think of Nat's tales now, not the dead keeper, not the chairmender, please God, *no.* Something shone for a second in the darkness, above the brickwork: two green eyes. He felt a prickle at the back of his scalp.

Only last night, Fergus had told him a story, a joke, and he had laughed at it. How did it go? A sixpence lost down a drain, that was it, and a Thing that chanted, *I am the ghost with two green eyes.* And the chant came several times, to an Englishman, an Irishman . . . and then it ended with a Scotsman: *Ye'll be the ghost wi' twa black eyes if ye dinna gie me back me saxpence.* Ralph shuddered. Last night, it had seemed funny, but it was horrible, horrible. Was that a dark shape peering over the well-head? Then Dittany leaped, with a shrill bark. The green eyes gleamed again, and disappeared with a scuffle, a spitting and a long mournful miaow. Ralph began to laugh. Mr. Hassall found him a few minutes later, propped on the mound of pheasants, laughing as though he would never stop, while Dittany wriggled and licked his face in sympathy.

Another mewing, spitting howl came from the thicket as the keeper handed Ralph up to another man above. This time it was Mr. Hassall who laughed. "Wild cats," he said, and bent down to lift Dittany.

They had the bonfire after all. It was very late when the

hot whisky and water, tea and bacon and eggs had been finished in Mrs. Hassall's warm kitchen, and they had heard the story of the chase: how the returning poachers had shone a torch on to Mr. Hassall and Dick, who had grabbed them; and how two more had joined in, and they got away, and the keepers had given chase; and the gang (not knowing the forest really well, it seemed) had run out on to the drive, "right slap bang" into the arms of the police and another search party, warned by Mr. Hassall's shots; to be marched off to the police house in the village.

Dittany, of course, was the heroine. She had been told, "Fetch", and she had fetched; or tried to. The three boys could not make enough fuss of her, but she paid little attention to their flattery; sitting with dignity beside Mr. Hassall, and only stirring her tail slightly at the sound of her name. There was the famous silver hybrid, lying on a bench in the lobby, having been brought out of the well with the rest of the pheasants. "And it was young Ralph thought of the well," Mr. Hassall remembered. "And how did it feel, young man, trapped down there all alone? Wished you'd stayed at home, didn't you?" All eyes on him, Ralph admitted, "It was spooky." With Fergus and Peter listening, he tried to sound offhand, amused.

Mr. Hassall took Dittany to her kennel, and came back saying, "The rain's over. It's a clear night now. How about that bonfire?"

Drenched in paraffin, the fire blazed up in the paddock, against a file of black fir trees. Rockets soared, and little fireworks whizzed, flashed and spat gold sparks. Ralph watched calmly, smiling. "He's asleep on his feet," teased Mr. Hassall. "Ah well—Saturday tomorrow."

It was Saturday today when Ralph curled down in bed, in the room with the low window. He had not been asleep on his feet, but quiet with amazement, reliving the events of the night. He had been in a real ding-dong grown-up fight; or as good as in one. He had seen a ghost—or as *bad* as seen one; he had seen a "wild" cat; he had tasted whisky. A night to remember. "Remember, remember, the fifth of November. . . ." What a long time ago it seemed, that schoolroom hour. Burrowing deeper, falling into sleep, he heard a sound like breaking waves. "The woods against a stormy sky . . ." before he could trace that echo, sleep closed over him.

18

Day-boy Prefect

The north wind had raked the brown leaves from the beeches and whitened the grass in the east park. Buff-coloured leaves still clung to the oaks, and at sunset the withered bracken was tinged with pinkish gold, like a frosted rose. A full moon swam up from behind the bracken fields; white and gold, barn owls swooped to and fro, calling loudly. In the pleasure ground, where the lawns had been in shadow all day, the soaking grass was frosty blue as the spruce trees; but it was still autumn, Ralph thought, not winter yet. The tulip tree rustled with bright leaves, and there were a few buds in the rose garden.

Ralph had been down to the Groves to see his dormouse family; but they were gone. The nest in the briars was empty. The mother must have moved them all to a winter nest somewhere. He hoped it would be cosier than High Forest schoolroom. Still, he was warm again now, after running home from the crossroads, after toasting hands and feet at a log fire, eating hotpot and buttery seakale, and dashing down to visit the dormice. He dawdled in the bright twilight, behind the laurel hedge that sheltered the rose garden, and listened to the owls in the east park. Nat said he knew where a barn owl had its daytime roost. He had promised to show

Ralph. But Ralph at this moment was thinking, not of owls, but of red squirrels.

For—it had struck him, as he came home from the Groves, under the sighing trees—might it not be better to find a squirrel for a winter pet? Dormice went so thoroughly to sleep, as he had seen for himself in March. Really, they might as well be dead, and then you could stuff them, like the fox in its glass case at the lodge. But a squirrel would only doze, and then wake, and frisk about a bit, and eat nuts; it would be a real pet, like Brownie. He did not say to himself: like Santa; but this thought was never far away. Often he would stop and think in panic—Where's Santa? before he remembered. Santa had been his companion for so long. Docile Brownie could not quite take his place. But a squirrel too would be beautiful and playful. He remembered the one he had released from the trap, its soft fur, the colour of redwood bark, its fringed ears, big eyes and feathery tail. It had not been in the least afraid of him. They might have made friends, if he had kept it . . . but how did one set about keeping such a wild bold little thing, with such sharp teeth? A hutch was out of the question; and indoors it would be worse than Santa: it could climb better. He laughed at the thought of a squirrel romping up the curtains and along the picture rails; but Aunt Lizard, he feared, would not laugh. Certainly, Uncle Laurie would not.

Not indoors, then, at least until it was tame. Somewhere outside, where it could have space and freedom until it fell asleep. He thought of his cottage in the beech wood. On the afternoon of that languid Saturday after Guy Fawkes' Day, he had gone to rebuild the bracken walls, where the wind had loosened them. Sitting inside, close to the window, he had watched a red squirrel come nearer and nearer, until he could have touched it easily. Supposing he set some kind of trap, baited with nuts? There were the fishing nets in the potting shed; not the little muslin ones that he and Billy had used, but two large nets, wide-meshed, on long poles, for clearing twigs and scum from the lily pool. Supposing he were to borrow them, and make a springe, that would bring the net down over the squirrel without hurting it? He could set one by the cottage in the wood, and another in the pleasure ground, under the three redwood trees, where the mowing machine stood all the summer, so that a pleasant smell of oil still lingered there; squirrels lived high in their boughs, he knew, tearing out the soft red bark to make their nests. Then, when he had caught a squirrel, what next? He frowned, and had a lightning inspiration. Here, here, behind the laurels, under his very nose, was the thing he needed: a big outdoor cage, about eight feet square and five feet high, made of wire netting and wooden stakes.

For weeks, earlier in the autumn, the dewy grass inside the cage had been set with rows of apples, turning scarlet and russet in the crisp air. Orchard boxes had been stacked there, full of apples—left "to sweat", Uncle Laurie had said, before being stored. At night they had been covered with a tarpaulin. Sometimes a few bruised ones had rotted, and then Ralph fancied the place smelt like a kitchen when a batch of bread was rising. But now the cage was empty; apples and tarpaulin were gone. There it stood, doing nothing. Supposing he "planted" branches inside—beech branches, and hazel, and fir—and made a drey out of redwood bark and twigs?

No one would come here now, until next September. He could keep the squirrel there, a secret, and surprise them all later on with a tame pet, trained to sit on his shoulder. In snowy weather, he could carry the drey up to the woodshed ... he ran back through the dusk to the house.

In the kitchen, Aunt Lizard was peeling boiled chestnuts for soup. "Oh, do let me help," cried Ralph. "You'll burn your fingers!"

"And you'll burn your tongue."

"I'd only eat every other one."

From the inner room, Uncle Laurie said:

"Once, when I first went to Ireland, there was a hedge of young trees I wanted thinned, and I said to old Paddy Grace, 'Leave the one at the end, and take out every other one.' So he did. I've never used that expression since."

Uncle Laurie and Fergus were sitting writing at opposite sides of the long breakfast table. Ralph, going to the wooden chest where he kept his toy soldiers, read from Uncle Laurie's top page: "Dessert For The Christmas Dinner." Uncle Laurie wrote two weekly articles for different gardening papers. He looked up again to ask Fergus:

"How would you describe the taste of a medlar?"

"Ugh," said Fergus.

"You wouldn't say, 'clean and delicate, like a water ice?' No?"

"No," said Fergus. "Musty, or rusty, or fusty, or . . . sawdusty."

His father wrote peacefully, and after a while Fergus asked which he had put.

"I've put: 'the medlar, with its refreshing tang, may be used to clear the jaded palate, cloyed with a surfeit of sweets'. How would the Head like that, d'you think?"

"Well . . ." said Fergus, "I'm afraid he'd say something like . . . *Perhaps rather mannered in style.*"

His father smiled and wrote on. For twenty minutes there were no sounds but the scratch of Uncle Laurie's J nib and Fergus's fountain pen, the flicker of the fire on its bed of white ash, the soft grind of Aunt Lizard's wooden spoon on the wire sieve, and the tap of cartridge cases on the floor, as Ralph set out his coloured regiments, gathered from the forest rides. These he preferred to shop soldiers, because they smelled of gunpowder.

Uncle Laurie finished his ten sheets of copy, blotted the last and reached for an envelope. Fergus sat back and began to read aloud:

" 'Thin ice crackled under my bicycle tyres as I rode over puddles in the dark. Hoarfrost glittered everywhere in the light of the setting moon. I was on my way to school. It was 5.30 a.m.' "

"Is it a story you're writing?" Ralph asked.

"No, it's my essay. It's called, 'The Trials of a Day-boy Prefect'."

The school in the market town, where Fergus and Peter Hassall were day-boys, had been endowed in the eighteenth century "to instruct twelve boys in the Mathematicks" with a view to sending them to sea. The school had prospered, and now had two hundred boys, many of them boarders. The present Headmaster cared less for "the Mathematicks" than for English and its grammar. This term, as a Sixth Form boy, Fergus had to write a weekly essay for the Head, on a subject of his own choice. The Head's criticisms were courteous but incisive. Fergus, however, had some criticisms of his own in mind. For the past year, he had been one of two day-boy prefects, and he thought this promotion brought too many unnecessary "trials". It seemed to him, in fact, that the school no longer really welcomed local boys: that the boarders had the best of it, and day-boys, even prefects, were never Optimates. His essay, on the surface, was an ingenuous account of a school day, but the Head would recognize it as a blast of the trumpet against this system.

Ralph had known no school but High Forest. Most of the

trials so obliquely described were lost on him. He understood, however, that Fergus, Peter and their fellow-travellers were excused morning prayers at school, as their train arrived too late for them to attend. After prayers, the Head would read out various items of school news and outline future plans; but it was no one's business to pass on these items to the late-comers. "The youngest First Former", wrote Fergus, "knows more about school affairs than the absent prefect."

Nowadays, however, Fergus was not always absent. Sixth Form prefects took turns, week and week about, to read the lesson at prayers, and this was not excused. Twice a term, Fergus would have to get up at five and catch a workmen's train, reaching the town with two hours in hand before prayers.

One paragraph in the essay described the discomforts of the dinner hour on a wet day, with day-boys milling about the gymnasium and passages, eating their sandwiches in snatches. As the other prefect went home to dinner, Fergus was left alone to keep order, and was blamed for any trouble that arose. "Some schools", this piece discreetly ended, "provide a second dining room, where day-boys can sit down and eat in comfort at table."

Ralph thought of dinner time at High Forest—the sheltered copses, the fireplace which the big boys had made from an old bucket, the fires of sticks and cones, the toasting of sandwiches and cheese, the baked potatoes and chestnuts and sizzling wild crabs. He would not change it, he thought, for table cloths and forks; but he did not say so.

A week later, Fergus showed them his essay book again. At the bottom of the page, in red ink, the Headmaster had written: *Matter interesting*. On each page of the essay, in tiny lucid handwriting, appeared marginal comments in red ink; beginning, "Surely—" or "Is it not the case—?" or "would it not be better—?" Fergus headed a new page, "The Trials of a Day-boy Prefect: II", and went on to explain where the Head's suggestions were at fault.

The book came back, and Fergus found only a row of red-ink ticks. At tea-time he had news. That morning, he said, a copy of the Head's daily announcements had been pinned to the school notice board under a new heading: "Day-boys: Information".

"There's a letter for you," said Aunt Lizard.

Fergus slit open the cream-coloured envelope, read the letter and handed it to her. Under the school crest was written: "The Headmaster requests the pleasure of F. Metherell's company as his guest at the Schoolhouse for the week beginning Sunday, December 12th."

"It's my week for reading lessons again," said Fergus. He looked taken aback; almost shocked. There was a minute's silence.

"That's very kind of the Headmaster," Aunt Lizard said crisply.

"I don't think he means to be kind," said Fergus slowly. "I think he means to *learn* me." Then he laughed, and began to eat his dinner. He seemed suddenly in high good humour. Ralph asked:

"But what will you write about, this week?"

"No more Trials," said Fergus. "I think I'll have a shot at something quite new. A modern poem, say."

The cold spell had given way to a span of mild, misty days, with thrushes singing and violas budding in the rose garden, under the bushes. Aunt Lizard had arranged a bowl of late rosebuds on the table. Fergus nodded at them and said blithely:

"I'll call it 'Roses in December'."

Despite this romantic title, the poem he produced was resolutely "modern". The book was returned, and in the familiar hand appeared a polite remark: *This may be better than I think.*

Was Fergus dismayed at the honour he had brought on himself? Ralph could not tell. As it happened, that was the last term in which boys travelling by train would need to miss school prayers. Perhaps the Headmaster and the school governors had something to do with this; but after Christmas a new train appeared in the timetable, reaching the town just before nine. Fergus would neither have to get up and leave "in the light of the setting moon" to read the lesson, nor again face six evenings *tête-à-tête* with the bachelor Headmaster. But he told Ralph regretfully:

"To tell you the truth, I liked the workmen's train. We used to stop outside a signalman's cottage, out in the middle of the downs, and fill up a special water tank, because they hadn't any well. And I used to get coffee and sausages at a lorry drivers' stall, and on market days I used to walk round the pens and talk to the drovers. It's a bit feeble, just getting to school on time."

But the bad old days would not be over until Christmas. On Sunday, December 12th, in the freezing darkness after tea, Fergus set off with a small suitcase to become the guest of the Head. Behind his bicycle, the others heard the door of the Dutch garden clap to. The frosty wind moaned round the chapel with an eerie sound. Uncle Laurie murmured, "A youth who bore, 'mid snow and ice, a banner with a strange device——"

"Fair play for day-boys," finished Aunt Lizard.

Ralph, sitting on the sofa between Cuckoo and Brownie, looked bleakly at the grown-ups. It was all very well for them to laugh; but he had a secret worry which was growing every day more urgent. Fergus had gone away just as Ralph had decided to beg for his help.

19

A Squirrel by Christmas

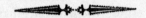

It had all begun so quickly. Even now, looking back, Ralph could not see how he had gone wrong.

Since the evening by the apple cage, he had been making ready for his squirrel. His pattern was Humphrey, in the New Forest book, who made hay and gathered fodder and built a cowhouse before his wild cow was captured. Ralph had his squirrel cage ready made, and on the next Saturday he worked hard to make it into a homely place for a squirrel. Two days of high winds helped him, and he dragged fallen branches of hazel, oak and lime, and wove them into the netting. He uprooted bracken and thatched the walls to the north and east. The drey he left until later. The squirrel might like to amuse itself by making that, he thought. In one of the sheds by the stables he found a box, and lined it with hay and fern. Set on its side, it would do at once as a shelter—if he brought the squirrel home today.

It was too late to think of storing hazel nuts. The squirrels had long ago stripped the copses, and the orchard filberts and Kentish cobs were stored in barrels in the fruit room, between layers of salt, waiting for the Christmas market. Even acorns were not so plentiful. Hares, rabbits, deer and pheasants had been after them, Fergus said. In October, as he bicycled down the drive, he could feel acorns squashing under his tyres, and brittle beechmast splitting; but now the road felt clear again.

Turning over the leaves in the beech wood, and under the chestnuts of the Ladies' Mile, Ralph found that there were nuts still to be had, if one took a little trouble. Beech nuts did not make much of a showing in his sack; after an hour's work, he seemed to have only a handful. Chestnuts were better. He gathered nearly two pounds of them, wet, red and shining, the kernels crisper and sweeter from their weeks of burial. A squirrel scolded him from an oak tree, and he stood still to admire it. Tomorrow he would set his springes.

It took him the whole of Sunday afternoon to get them right. The one in the beechwood was the more hopeful, he thought. The pole of the net was poised on a bracken stalk, so that the squirrel would knock it down when he went for the bait—chestnuts, and two hazel nuts from a chocolate bar. He used Brownie to test the trap, coaxing the rabbit to brush against the bracken stalk. The net fell neatly over her. Before starting, he had rubbed his own hands and Brownie's paws in the leaf soil, as Mr. Hassall would have done, so that the squirrel should not smell them. But was Brownie grown too plump and heavy to test a trap for an agile, frisking squirrel? Well, he would soon find out. Perhaps tomorrow morning. . . . The second trap was set under the redwoods in the pleasure ground. The oil smell here was a good thing: the squirrels must be used to it, and it would hide the smells of boy and rabbit. The net was balanced on a crag of redwood bark. Ralph did not take so long over the testing here. It was pitch dark by now, and since his fright in the well, the thought of ghosts came more readily to mind.

Before eight o'clock next morning, Aunt Lizard found him in coat, scarf and gumboots, waiting for his sandwiches. He told her, "I want to start for squirrel early."

"For where?"

"Oh!—I mean, for school."

"Child, have you had any breakfast?"

Yes, he had helped himself from the porridge pot and milk can. No, he didn't want any bacon, honestly. *Yes*, he had fed Brownie. Cuckoo, cheated of bacon rinds, went back to the fire. Ralph took his sandwich packet and apple, and fled, forgetting his thermos of cocoa.

The trap under the redwood clump was exactly as he had left it; but in the beech wood the trap had been sprung. True, there was nothing caught; but on one of the chestnuts he found what could only be a squirrel's tooth mark. Another had been dragged away from the pile, and a hazel nut was missing. He reset the trap; better go away at once—a squirrel might be watching. Deep in thought, absently finishing the sandwiches, he crossed the beeches and a copse behind the pheasantry, and dropped from the bank into the High Forest road.

Despite his hunger, he went straight to his traps on the way home. Again the one in the beeches was sprung, and empty, and the bait was scattered. He reset it, brooding over it. Tomorrow, he was certain, he would be lucky.

The trap under the redwoods was a failure, the chestnut bait untouched. The squirrels in the pleasure ground were spoilt, he decided, and used to the best of everything—crabs and mulberries, cherries from the garden wall, plums, Alpine strawberries, walnuts, redskinned filberts. But the trap in the beechwood must do its work. It was only a matter of time.

And every morning, inspecting both traps, he repeated: only a matter of time. Once, the net had been knocked down and the meshes were tangled; the squirrel must have struggled free, lifting it to escape. Then he weighted it with apples, tied round the wire ring and padded with sacking and woodwool. Stones would be heavier, but he must not stun his squirrel. Next day, the net had fallen, but this time it had caught on a dead foxglove near by. He rooted up the foxglove. Soon, now . . .

Then came the day of his blunder.

All at once, with the darkening days, a change had come over the big schoolroom. Only two weeks to the concert! Lessons took second place. Instead of Scripture reading, they practised carols. Sums and compositions were set for the younger children, but never finished. Instead, they watched the big boys making steeple hats and hempen beards for the Pilgrim Fathers, and the girls sewing at sacking cloaks, or pasting crêpe paper screens for the play. The play would be the event of the evening. Recitations, country dances, Tim Lamb's solo, Katy and Dora's Shakespeare scene, with Randy groaning in at Enter Touchstone . . . even the final tableau of the stable at Bethlehem, all were nothing to the delights and hazards of *The Night Before Christmas*: a Children's Play with Music, as Mrs. Duffel's copy announced. Scene One: Christmas Eve: a family of children discovered hanging up their stockings and bickering over their letters to Santa Claus; all but one good little miss, who would ask only for a doll. Scene Two: Midnight: enter Santa Claus, to read the letters and fill the stockings. Scene Three: enter the Wicked Imp, to steal everything but the doll, overlooked in his glee. Scene Four: Dawn: the greedy children disconsolate, until, flash! Enter the Good Fairy to put things right, and point a moral.

Ralph, as the Imp, in black jersey and tights, would appear under a green limelight: Mrs. Duffel's bicycle lamp, masked in green tissue paper. Pecky Sylvester, a sharp-featured, clever boy, took charge of lighting and effects. The big boys, as a rule such a trial to Governess, were now her right-hand men. Hoppy borrowed his father's tools and made a manger for the tableau. Kinger produced a silver star and a wand for the good fairy, and a wicked mask for Ralph, to make the watching mothers squeak.

Outside, mists hung over the forest, and rain dripped from the black trees. Inside, the gala atmosphere mounted. Governess was wreathed in smiles, excited as the children. The air was heady with the smell of gum, crêpe paper, and paraffin from the hanging lamps which burned all day. The sulky stoves seemed to glow with the warmth and gaiety of Yule logs. Desks were piled with costumes and borrowed "props". Uncle Laurie lent two pairs of woollen stockings. Six stockings, threaded with red and green tapes, were to be hung by the family in the play: Ralph must remember to steal only five. The climax of the plot was in his hands. Rehearsals filled the afternoons; then, as time grew short, they began in the morning, directly after prayers. The desks were pushed back to leave a stage, and Mrs. Duffel, in bright green knitted dress and Russian boots, strode to and fro, listening, drilling, deciding, encouraging. *Lochinvar* and *The Pilgrim Fathers* rang out at all hours; or Vincent, who owned a sailor suit, would be set to declaim at concert pitch: "*The Sea!* BY BARRY CORNWALL!" Tim Lamb was the other junior soloist, with a plaintive little song about a squirrel in winter, hunting in vain for a lost nut. Tim was the youngest performer, and by far the best. Governess and all the girls listened, with needles poised, when Tim sang. Mrs. Duffel gave him star billing, just before the play. The neatest writers were busy copying out a hundred programmes.

Because of the early darkness, school ended half an hour earlier this month. Some of the children came four or five miles, from outlying farms and woodmen's cottages. Freedom at three o'clock gave the crowning touch of frivolity to the day.

This evening, Ralph told himself, there would be a squirrel in his trap.

Nat had taken it into his head to cycle home by a new route, through the shorn oak forest on the left-hand side of the hill. They passed foresters at work, planting young oak trees four feet high, and fencing them in with wire. Farther on, a chestnut copse was being felled. They overtook Tim, setting off to find his father, who worked in the woods and would take him home after dark. Nat clicked his broken bicycle bell and swerved past, with Ralph astride the carrier, his feet trailing through dead leaves. Nat glanced back, braked, skidded and stopped, waiting for the child to catch them up. He muttered in Ralph's ear, "Funny. He's *howling.*"

"Howling" did not mean bawling aloud. Tim made no sound, but tears were pouring down his face. He rubbed his puckered face on his sleeve. He would have run past, but Nat stopped him.

"What's up, then? Hurt yourself?"

Tim shook his head.

"Go on, tell us. Someone give you a clout?"

They waited. Tim sniffed, gasped, shuddered and brought out at last: "I-I-I-I don't want to sing in no concert!"

"What?" Nat and Ralph were astounded. "But you like singing, Tim! You're always singing in break!"

More sobs. "Like it . . . out here . . . by myself. Don't like it . . . in school . . . people looking at me. . . ."

This made sense. Neither Nat nor Ralph would ever be called on to sing alone in public, but they knew that they would not enjoy it. They tried to think of something to say. Nat pointed out:

"We're all doing things, see? You won't mind, on the night." *On the night* was a phrase on everyone's lips. Governess and Mrs. Duffel used it every five minutes. Tim gulped and cried:

"But . . . not even dressing up . . . like all the others!"

So that was it. Again, the two listeners took the point. Nat, as a Pilgrim Grandchild, would have a sacking tunic, a staff and a lantern. In the Nativity tableau he would wear a Vicarage dressing gown, and a striped turban, and carry a shepherd's crook lent by Hoppy's father; if Hoppy could get hold of a lambskin, from a stillborn lamb, he might even carry a stuffed lamb under his arm. Ralph, as the Imp, had the mask to wear, fiendish with luminous paint. But, only this afternoon, Mrs. Duffel had praised Tim's scarlet jersey and said:

"Be sure you wear that jersey *on the night.*"

It was one thing to dress up as a shepherd, or "the fiery heart of youth", or a wicked imp. It was quite another thing to be Tim Lamb, in your everyday jersey, having to sing by yourself in front of everyone. Tears poured down Tim's face again. Ralph thought of a play Aunt Emmy had taken him to, with children dressed up as squirrels and fox cubs, all in red fur . . . better not mention that. He said:

"Look, Tim. Don't cry. Look . . . supposing I lend you my tame squirrel? If I get him in time, I mean. . . . He could sit on your shoulder while you're singing. Would that do instead of dressing up?"

Tim looked at him. His face suddenly cleared. He blinked, and his eyes took on their usual dreaming look. He saw himself singing, but not alone; he felt the squirrel perched on his shoulder, brushing his ear. He beamed.

"Oh Ralph! A tame squirrel! Oh, yes!"

"Well, if I get him by Christmas . . ." Tim was not listening. With a spark of returning common sense, Ralph added:

"Mind, it's to be a secret. You mustn't tell anyone, not till the night, or Gov'ness would most likely stop it."

Tim gave them a brilliant smile and darted away. Ralph looked after him thoughtfully. He had better hurry up and get to the springe. The squirrel mustn't get away now.

Nat said coldly, "You got a tame squill, then?"

"N-not yet. Not exactly. But I shall have."

"Where fwom?"

"Well . . . from a trap."

"You mean a *wild* one?" Ralph did not answer. Nat repeated slowly, "You're going to catch a wild squoggy, and tame it—by Chwistmas? In time for the concert?"

"I shall," Ralph said angrily. Nat snorted.

"Tim thinks you've pwomised. Say you don't get one? What's he going to be like, on the night? He'll cweate. What'll Govvy say? 'Delibewate lying and deceit. . . .' "

"You see if I don't." But his heart sank.

Tim was out of sight. Sick of such folly, Nat jumped on his bicycle and rode away. Ralph jogged home alone. By the time he reached the beeches, he was not really surprised to find the trap empty, the net still poised. Still, there was plenty of time. Two weeks, nearly. Santa had been tame in half that time.

Yet it was strange how much less sure he felt, now that he *must* have the squirrel by Christmas. It was almost as though his anxiety frightened off the squirrels. The bait was no longer touched. He began to suspect that rats or mice might have made the teeth marks he had seen before; and the net might have blown down, or just fallen. He went on setting the traps. He varied the bait, bringing all his share from the basket on the kitchen table; pippins, richly coloured, a pear, a guava. If he were not greedy, like the children in the play, perhaps fate would be kind. Fate, strict as that Good Fairy, liked to point a moral.

Then—there might be other ways of getting a squirrel. He might trace one to its winter lair and take it, nest and all, as it slept. On Saturday, he studied the trees in the Groves and the pleasure ground. He saw several dreys, but all were swung out of reach, at the end of slender, drooping boughs that would bear only a squirrel's weight. He grumbled to Fergus:

"If I were a squirrel, I'd live in a hollow tree, like squirrels in books, not stuck right out in the middle of nowhere!"

"If you were a squirrel, you'd have more sense."

He went to the lodge and asked Mrs. Hassall:

"Do you—did you ever know anyone with a squirrel? A tame one?"

"A tame squirrel!" Mrs. Hassall laughed. "Why, yes—my mother. Her cat, rather. Her kittens died, and she cried most pitifully, and then she went off to the woods and came back with a little squirrel, new-born. We thought the nest might have blown down, and the cat found this little thing inside. Anyway, she brought it up, and we named it Pussy, and it was tame as your Santa."

"I knew it would be!" Ralph cried. "Oh, *couldn't* your mother lend it to me? Just for one night?"

"Why, it's been dead, twenty years or more."

Of course he had guessed as much. And now he lost heart. Too late, when Fergus had gone to stay at the Schoolhouse, he thought Fergus might know a boy with a pet squirrel. Tim sparkled at the thought of their secret; darting meaning looks at Ralph when he had to sing his song. He sang without having to be coaxed, his face bright, his notes clear. Ralph felt sick.

At night, Ralph looked out at the flashing December star-light and prayed for a live, tame squirrel: "If *only* You'll help me, just this *once*, I'll never promise anybody anything, ever again. . . ." But the Almighty shunned him. So did Nat; adopting the lofty, *don't-drag-me-into-it* tone so familiar to the unfortunate. It was new to Ralph, and wounding. And every morning the traps were empty.

A Squirrel by Christmas

The only time when Ralph still felt happy was at rehearsal, as the Wicked Imp. Mrs. Duffel had chosen better than she knew, he thought darkly. What a row there was going to be, on the night! Perhaps he should break the news to Tim now, at once, and get it over? Yet he waited. God might relent, after all.

But the last Saturday came, and he did not even visit the traps, but spent the day helping Aunt Lizard in the kitchen, plastering a Christmas cake with almond paste. Fergus was going to decorate the cake on Christmas Eve. Then there were the first mince pies to be crimped, and cherries and almonds to blanch for a second-best cake. It was dusk, and he thought, Too late now to look at the traps. Anyway, what was the use?

On Sunday afternoon, Fergus and Peter invited him to come rabbiting. They had spent the last few Sundays chasing through the elm groves, the shrubberies and pleasure ground, with a spaniel, Maggie, and a ferocious old Sealyham called Pip. But Ralph shook his head. He was taking Brownie for a run in the orange house, among the chrysanthemum pots. Tomorrow the great curled beauties, bronze, yellow, wine-coloured, would be cut for market. Tomorrow, he would face the music. Tomorrow night was *the night*.

It was comforting to come in to Sunday tea by the sitting-room fire, with scones and celery, and the dark bramble jam which the boys called bumble bee jam, full of whole berries, black and "furry". Fergus and Peter arrived, laughing at some nonsense of their own. Uncle Laurie asked:

"How many rabbits?"

"Well, none," Fergus admitted, while Peter added:

"*We* can't catch 'em with our bare hands, like some people." Ralph would not live this down in a hurry. "Oh, sir," Peter went on, "I'll have to borrow that wheelbarrow

183

again, old Pip's fagged out." Pip, the Sealyham, had a "tired heart", which failed him after three hours' yapping and digging.

"Have your tea first, boy," said Aunt Lizard.

Peter slid into a chair and shook his red head at Ralph. "All the same . . . when you *do* set traps, you've got to look at them every day, always. That's a rule. You ask dad."

Ralph dropped a scone.

"Otherwise it's cruel," Peter finished airily.

"Traps?" Aunt Lizard glanced at Ralph's stunned face. He swallowed a bumble bee whole.

"Yes, or snares, or——"

"Fishing lines," suggested Fergus.

"Oh, well, maybe it was Harry set it? Down under the redwoods," Peter told Uncle Laurie. "A sort of bird-net, from what I could see, only it's not a bird caught in it, it's —what did you think it was?" he asked Fergus.

"A weasel, could it be? No, too soft. More like a squirrel."

"Of course, it was dark—and carting Pip—and hanging on to Mag——"

"We'll go and look later," said Fergus.

Ralph's chair was pushed back. He was gone. He raced through the dark brewhouse, going carefully, because of the buckets of yew boughs and other "flat greens" cut for Christmas wreaths. It was lighter in the orange house. He shut the sacred glass door behind him, and then his feet were on the lawns, and he was dodging among the trees, crossing the path by the cedar, groping under the redwood branches. His hands found the net. Something was caught, yes. Something soft, with long fur, and a bushy tail. But it was stiff. It was dead. It might have been there since Friday morning.

"Oh," moaned Ralph, and dropped it again. He had caught a squirrel, and starved it to death.

A torch flashed. Fergus called, "Ralph!" Then Fergus and Peter were talking together: "Don't worry, it's all right!" —"It wasn't you caught it, it was Pip"—"He killed it weeks ago, one Sunday"—"We couldn't help it, the poor little beggar was burying a nut, under a beech, and it tried to run up the trunk and slipped off somehow"—"It didn't suffer, he killed it in a second"—"And Dad thought you'd like it stuffed, and Mr. Hassall did it for you . . ."—"We were going to give it to you at tea time, and then we found your snare, and we thought——"

"Here," said Fergus, and put the squirrel into Ralph's hands. It was as silky as Santa. Its tail felt like Grandmother's ostrich plume. And then he understood his luck.

The great burden rolled off his mind. Tim would have a squirrel on his shoulder tomorrow, after all. Alive, however tame, the squirrel couldn't really have gone to the concert. He saw that now. It was true, then, what Governess always said: God doesn't give us what we pray for, He gives us what we *need*. God had done it all right this time: a squirrel for Tim, and a tip-top sell for Nat Wood.

The stars seemed to be dancing all over the sky.

On Monday the children were sent home directly after dinner. At five o'clock, Ralph packed the squirrel into his satchel and set off for High Forest village hall. Aunt Lizard would come later. By twos and threes the performers gathered in the tiny dressing room to be robed by Governess and made up by Mrs. Duffel. Six-thirty came, and everyone was ready: all but Tim Lamb. Where was Tim? Silence fell. The teachers and the older children looked at one another, with sudden misgiving. Slowly the truth dawned on them: no one had warned dreamy Tim that tonight was the night; that he must come back, after tea, with his father and mother, to sing in the concert. Too late now: Tim, unlike the squirrel in his song, was in bed and asleep, "safe from winter cold", on the other side of the forest.

The concert was nearly over.

The tableau was ready, star and crib in place, Mary, Joseph and Guardian Angel posed, Shepherds ready to come in at the second verse, Three Kings behind the screen awaiting their cue, heavenly host packed out of sight back-stage ready to sing their loudest, led by Santa Claus—Mrs. Duffel, magnificent in red flannel, cotton wool beard and Russian boots, carrying all before her. It had been a huge success. For the first time, left alone in the dressing room, with the reek of grease paint and burnt cork, carbide and scorching paper, woollen stockings, peardrops, apples and oranges—for the first time, Governess dared to think so. The Vicar, from his seat in the stalls, had said as much already. No one had forgotten his lines, no one had been sick, *As You Like It* and *Rufty Tufty* had gone without a hitch; the play, with all its pitfalls—terrible as a full length *Hamlet*, it had seemed to her in the small hours—had run smoothly from first to last: the children had sung in tune, young Ralph Oliver had remembered to leave the doll, Pecky's flashbulb—naughty boy!— had neither set fire to the screens nor scattered what wits the Good Fairy had: a flibberty-gibbet, but how pretty she looked in that spangled net! As for Randy, he had got a laugh whenever he opened his mouth; as well he might, with four grown-up brothers watching hilariously from the back.

A pity, of course, about Tim Lamb's solo. Very disappointing. Still, one couldn't think of everything.

Now the hall was quiet again. Mrs. Duffel's voice soared out alone: *Once in Royal David's city*. . . . A shame to have missed the whole evening; but she had been so busy in the dressing room, rushed off her feet. . . . Why not slip round to the back, and just see the tableau? Nothing could go wrong now.

The door at the far end of the hall creaked faintly as Governess stole in. Randy's brothers made room for her with alacrity. Yes, the tableau was sweet, and now all the children were singing like angels. Here came the Shepherds, Ricky and Ernie Thrower, and—but what on earth was Nat Wood carrying on his shoulder? Governess craned forward, peering through her glasses. Had they got a lambskin after all, then? Her eyes were weary, she hadn't slept a wink the night before. At three in the morning she had got up and lit a candle, and come down to the cold schoolroom to put the finishing touches to the dresses. No use lying there worrying. . . . Yes, she was very, very tired. Perhaps that was why she had fancied, for one ridiculous moment, that Nat was carrying —not a stuffed lambskin, but *a red squirrel*. But now the Three Kings were coming. Nat had moved forward beside Ricky, only the top of his crook was visible. The Star glittered above. The tableau was complete. Governess let her weary eyelids droop, and the angel voices sang on.

20

Winter Holiday

The low red sun shone through the hazel copse as the trap bowled down the drive towards Hurst Castle. It was New Year's Eve, and Fergus and Ralph were taking Aunt Lizard to the London train. Tonight she was going to a fancy dress ball. It would last all night, she told them, ending with kippers and bacon and eggs in someone's studio. Ralph looked at her intently as they rode along. She was wearing a new suit of dark green corduroy, with curious buttons like silver coins. Her crisp bright hair, the colour of hazel bark, curled round her Cossack cap. Her cheeks were pink, her brown eyes shone. Ralph could see that she felt as he had done on Christmas Eve. He did not exactly want to be grown up, to be going with her; but he wished it were tomorrow, that she had come back and could tell him all about it.

When the invitation came, Fergus had told her, "You ought to go as a lizard!" And she had answered, "Shall I tell you something?—I *am* going as a lizard." They had not seen her costume—green and gold tunic, tights and snood—because she would dress at Aunt Emmy's; the things were borrowed from a theatre wardrobe. Ralph had helped her to re-gild her evening slippers, from a little pot of paint which was half clear liquid, half gold sediment, and had to be carefully shaken, every few minutes, with the cork held on.

He had used the rest of the gold paint on a Christmas present for her: a gilded cedar cone, scooped out in the middle to hold a two-and-sixpenny gold thimble. Fergus's idea; but another present had been his own idea—a bottle of scent, attar of roses, to wear at the ball. On the first day of the holidays he had gone alone to buy it from the machine at Hurst Castle station. He had twopence, and meant to buy two bottles; but when he breathed into the darkness behind the ticket window, "I want to go and buy some attar of roses," a voice had thundered from a cloud of smoke, like the Voice on Sinai, "*What* did you say you wanted?" His courage failing, he whispered, "Platform ticket, please." So there was only one bottle: a very slim phial, it proved, when he fished it out of the little iron drawer; but he had heard somewhere that it took a thousand roses to make one drop of scent. There must be ten drops at least in the phial; ten thousand roses. As he stood on the dark platform, under the wooden roof, he heard a far-off shriek among the downs. An express train. He wanted to run; but he could not. It swept round the corner and came roaring towards him, pistons working with their terrible energy, whistle screaming, wheels thundering. The monster had caught him at last. He shut his eyes and clung to the slot machine; he felt he could not bear the nearness of the hurtling train, the menace of its size and speed; his heart must fail, his ear-drums would burst; he wanted to scream against the shrill note of the whistle. He held his breath, and felt the blood running out of his ears. Then it was gone. He opened his eyes. The phial was safe in his pocket. He ran a finger over one ear; no blood, after all. The train was a mile away. The station had stopped shuddering, it stood quiet in the winter sunlight, with no sound but the chirping of sparrows on the roof.

Running back through the forest, he had come on a little

Christmas tree, three feet high, growing alone in a clearing, and spent some time decorating it with old-man's-beard and bryony berries. On Christmas Eve he had returned with his satchel full of clinking jelly jars borrowed from the kitchen cupboard, and a packet of spoilt candles, rescued from the dustbin. The visiting fieldmice had been gnawing at them; they had also left teeth marks in a box of soap, and Aunt Lizard had called Cuckoo a lazy, drowsy, good-for-nothing slug-a-bed.

Ralph remembered a party last year at Nine Wells, when he and Aunt Lizard had lined the drive on both sides with candles in jam jars, to light their guests to the front door. He put his jars in a ring round the tree, each with its candle, and tied the left-over candles to the branches. He had brought strands of flower wire from the fruit room, where Uncle Laurie had been wiring sprays of orchids and carnations for a wedding. It was dusk when he was ready, and one by one the candles twinkled out in the wintry forest. He did not know that someone had smelt the burning wicks from the road two hundred yards away; he did not hear an old forester walking quietly through the trees to see what was afire. Ralph pocketed his matches and sat down to look at the lovely tree. Then he sprang to his feet. A drop of hot wax had dripped from a high candle to a lower one; a flame sputtered, a green twig caught alight, and then the branch was flaring. Ralph dashed forward, but the old man was there first, beating out the flames with cap and stick. Ralph knew him; he was called Cap, or Cap'n Crewe; like several men on the estate, he had spent his youth at sea. He was a spry little old man, with quiet blue eyes; but now he turned on Ralph in fury.

"You young devil! Want to set the whole forest alight? Get off, before I skin you alive!"

Ralph did as he was told. It was an unexpected ending to his secret Christmas tree; but he thought that he had left enough candles behind to give all the mice in the neighbourhood a Christmas feast.

Their own feast, it seemed, was less certain. The turkey sent from Nine Wells had not yet arrived. As Ralph walked into the kitchen, Aunt Lizard was saying, "It's had time to trot here on its own two feet!" The ducks had long ago been eaten as Sunday dinners.

"Sausage and chestnuts will be fine," he assured her.

"Or roast beef," said Fergus. A sirloin, a present from Uncle Laurie's employer, was safely in the larder.

"Or a jugged hare," said Uncle Laurie absently, from behind *The Times*.

There was a moment's silence. Ralph turned cold. Then Aunt Lizard and Fergus began to talk together. Fergus should go and buy a brace of pheasants from Mr. Hassall, they decided. Ralph might go too, on his bicycle crossbar. They hurried away; but in the beeches they met Postyman, cycling to meet them with the missing turkey, just arrived by train. Postyman had been on the road since five that morning, but he had set off at once to deliver it. He hailed them gaily. They spun home, Fergus steadying Ralph, and Ralph clasping the turkey, while its head lolled over the handlebars. "I *wish* I had a bike!" Ralph said suddenly. Fergus whistled a tune.

Before dawn on Christmas morning, Ralph woke to find something propped at the foot of his bed. A bicycle. It was a complete surprise. His shout roused the house; but only for a moment. The others slept again, while he opened his stocking. The toy searchlight and anti-aircraft gun, owl whistle and torch, camera case and paint box, tangerine, chocolate frog and salted almonds, whiled away the last hour of darkness.

Then he was outside in the misty morning, cycling round and round the shrubbery path. The bicycle was a present from Fergus, an outgrown one of his own, painted red and silver, and refurbished with new bell, new tyres, front lamp and red reflector. Ralph cycled all through Christmas Day, Boxing Day and the week after.

He had ridden Nat's bicycle often enough to keep his balance, once he was started. Mounting and dismounting were his problem. At first he would push off from the park fence; then he made himself copy Nat's hop, skip and jump, with right leg thrown over the saddle. To dismount, he simply fell off; then taught himself to land safely with left foot planted on the ground.

Soon, both knees criss-crossed with sticking plaster, he began to go farther afield; up the path to the high lawns, where, in the quiet grey weather, green woodpeckers were digging for ants; and down the stony frame yard to the soft dirt-track surface of the stable yard; a wide arena now, clear of chrysanthemum pots until next summer. He could rest for a while in the harness room, or up in the hayloft, on top of the hay, under dangling strings of onions with skins as red as pomegranates. Then on through the garden door to the orchard house, to watch the peach trees being sprayed with an acrid-smelling wash against pests, Silver Leaf and Red Spider. A wrought-iron gate brought him into the rose garden, to circle round the Italian well-head; then up through the pleasure ground, tyres making a faint trail on the damp brown paths; careful not to blunder into the grass verges so beautifully kept by Harry.

Several times he left his bicycle against the fence and crossed the east park to a lime tree, hoping to see a barn owl which, Nat said, had a daytime roost there. One day he was lucky. Under mistletoe clumps and "witches' brooms" the owl sat torpid, golden wings folded, waiting for night. It eyed him steadily, six feet over his head, from round eyes opaque as mistletoe berries in a white pussy-face. Ralph backed away without disturbing it.

After tea, with the owls hooting up and down the park, he went out again, his bicycle lamp throwing a soft beam of light along the paths. The owl whistle was his favourite present after the bicycle. He blew softly into its curves; it was shaped like a chess pawn, and made a thrilling hoo-ooo-ooo like the cry of a brown owl. He turned off the lamp and sat in the dark, whistling, and thought the owls answered him; but he could not be sure. He must ask Nat. Now it was still dark when the garden bell woke him at seven in the morning. He had been surprised to find Uncle Laurie still in the kitchen at half past seven, drinking tea and reading his letters, before putting on boots and leggings polished like chestnuts, to make his first tour of the garden. Ralph asked:

"Why don't they ring the bell at half past seven . . . now it's too dark to start till then?"

"Well. If Ted rings at seven as usual, everyone's there, ready to start. Ring at half past, and no one starts till eight—and that's breakfast time, anyway." He left Ralph to puzzle over this, and took secateurs and pruning gloves from their drawer. Venturing into the walled garden later in the week, when he felt that he would not flounder into the neat box edging, Ralph found Uncle Laurie busy on his chief winter task: three months' steady pruning, up and down the apple hedges and in the old garden.

Afternoon cycling was delayed by a whim of Aunt Lizard's, that he should have a "thank you" letter ready for the three o'clock post each day. He wrote at the table in the breakfast room, looking out at a tree-creeper on the churchyard cedar, or goldcrests whispering high up. He wondered if they were the same pair that had nested there in May. He was interrupted, too, by birds coming for crumbs to the window sill, and by a cock chaffinch sparring with his own reflection in the top pane. One day Ralph heard a persistent stealthy rustling in the ivy leaves below the sill. He watched, and saw two ears, then a brown head and scrabbling paws. A churchyard mouse. It grabbed a chestnut, put there for the nuthatches, and bolted back down the ivy with the nut held in its teeth. Another day, Ralph had to chase a gang of sparrows that were tearing at the mauve and fawn-coloured winter crocuses, planted in the grass by Fergus's mother.

Still, somehow, the letters got themselves written: Monday, Tuesday, Wednesday, Thursday: Father, Grandmother, Aunt Emmy, Uncle Alfred. And now it was New Year's Eve.

Uncle Laurie too was away for the night. Peter was coming to stay; the three boys would have the house to themselves. Peter was waiting at the lodge when the trap returned from the station. As Sally trotted through the beeches, they looked at one another, aware of their freedom. Fergus decided they should have supper in his own room.

Ralph thought the south bedroom which he and Aunt Lizard shared was the best room in the house, with its private exit over the roof-tops, and its wide view to the sea. But Fergus's room downstairs was odd and snug. Fergus drew the crimson curtains, lit a fire in the grate and brought in a basket of logs and pine chips.

Aunt Lizard had left a supper of cold chicken and salad, fruit and cake. Fergus, in experimental mood, had added a German sausage and a bottle of stuffed olives from the village shop. They each chose something else from the larder: Peter a mince pie, Fergus a tin of mulligatawny soup, and Ralph a jar of pickled cherries. The feast was spread on the floor. Fergus also took down a bottle of home-made grape wine from a larder shelf, and then put it back, with a murmured word to Peter. Ralph caught the word, which was "Later". He was set to watch the fire, feeding it with cones and twigs. Cuckoo, uneasy at Aunt Lizard's absence, found his way through the stone passage and sat in the hearth, sniffing the blend of coffee and mulligatawny wafted from the kitchen. Ralph looked at the museum, to which he had added the squirrel's paw. He looked at the piles of old *Boy's Own Papers* with their wonderful serial stories: "The Cruise of the Water Bat", "The People of the White Peacock". Fergus sometimes let him borrow them; but he was not in the mood for reading now. He felt keyed up, restless and excited. He lifted the cloth to rattle the trapdoor hiding the secret passage. He longed for adventure. If we were in a *Boy's Own* story, he thought, we should be locked up by a gangster, and I'd get down the trapdoor, because I'm the smallest, and I'd run along the secret passage to the big house, and ring up the police, and they'd come and catch the gang trying to steal the silver up there; no, they'd catch them with the stuff in a sack, all tied up. . . . Ralph remembered his surprise on hearing that the Guy Fawkes' Day poachers had *not* been sent to prison, after all. In court they had said they knew nothing of stolen pheasants; they had come back to look for a lost pocket watch, dropped while they were working as beaters; and the keepers had "attacked" them, so they had fought back. The Bench had decided to dismiss the case, Mr. Hassall explained, because there was no evidence that they were making for the well. But in Ralph's adventure, the gangsters would have their paws firmly on the treasure, and Ralph's prompt action would foil them.

Intent on this story, he did not realize that the others had returned. He was caught, with the table cloth awry, staring at the trapdoor. Fergus held three soup bowls in his hands;

Peter followed with the coffee pot and hot milk. But Fergus was in a genial mood; besides, the soup was too hot for mortal lips to bear. So the bowls were set in the hearth beside Cuckoo, and with a chisel Fergus undid the screws and let Ralph peer into the darkness. By torchlight, Ralph made out a flight of steps leading downward, then the passage, then . . . nothing. A blank wall.

"If you're thinking there's a secret catch, and a door slides back, and you find a secret chamber—well, there may be," Fergus told him. "But we've looked and felt every inch—haven't we, Peter?—years ago. And there's nothing."

"But there might have been once," Peter said. "They had a real battle here in the Civil War, or a siege or something. Perhaps someone hid down there . . . perhaps his skeleton's still there?"

"Let's have supper," Fergus said quickly, closing down the trapdoor on this notion.

They finished everything, and Cuckoo feasted on chicken-bones and pickled cherries; one of his eccentric fancies. The cherries were Morellos, from a north wall. Ralph remembered lying in bed, one September day, and smelling the spiced vinegar boiling downstairs. They lingered over coffee, watching the red fir cones glowing. Fergus and Peter lit Turkish cigarettes. It was time to face the cold trek out to the woodshed for more logs.

"I know," Fergus said suddenly. "Christmas is over now —let's burn the holly."

They ran through the house, stripping holly from behind pictures and mirrors. The fire blazed and crackled; the boys warmed their hands in the white light. A few moments later they were looking at one another with mounting dismay, listening to a hollow roar in the chimney. Burning soot fell on to the hearth, and Cuckoo fled. The roar increased. They ran outside; what they saw made Ralph's heart leap with terror; flames, two feet high, were pouring from the chimney. As they stood appalled, the chimney pot cracked like a rifle-shot. Fergus cried, "Quick—fill buckets! Go on, run!" He dashed away to the bothy, where Jim, the duty-man, was sitting by his own peaceful fire, reading *The Motor Cyclist*. The other journeymen were away at a dance. Jim wasted no words; he ran for the garden hose, and climbed from the ground to the top of the water tank, from the tank to the low roof, then up a ladder held by Fergus, dragging the hose after him. The other end was screwed to the scullery tap; but before Ralph could turn it on, Fergus was calling him— "Quick, bring the salt bars—cooking salt—shelf over stove!" Ralph knew the shelf, where Aunt Lizard kept the chunks of salt used in the autumn for salting down runner beans. He scrambled on to the tank and threw the bars to Fergus, who hurried up the ladder after Jim. The flames still pierced the darkness. Ralph watched, dry-mouthed with fear. The garden house was burning down. He thought of how he had wished for something to happen. What a fool! he groaned, unable to take his eyes from the blazing chimney.

But—was he imagining it, or were the flames dying down? Jim and Fergus were throwing handfuls of salt that burned with a gritty, sputtering sound. Yes, the fire was duller now. Ralph ran back to Fergus's room. The fire was dead in the grate. The fearful roar had stopped. The hearth was strewn with soot, and there was a fine black film over the floor, the empty plates, Fergus's bed, and their four faces. But the house was saved; the chimney pot was the only casualty.

Ralph was astonished to find that it was only eight o'clock. "I thought it must be nearly midnight!" he laughed: then wished he had kept quiet.

"Bed for you," said Fergus.

"Oh no! Aunt Lizard said I could see the New Year in!"

"Yes, if you went to bed first."

"What are you going to do?" he parried. "You're not going away?"

"If you must know, we're going to mull some wine . . . when we've cleared up this mess. Now you take off."

"Don't forget to wake me, then."

The oil stove in the bathroom was unlit. The warm water steamed in the wintry air. In the hot-cupboard he found Cuckoo, curled on a pile of socks. Here was the one he had hung on Christmas Eve, a great grey stocking of Uncle Laurie's; still, the fun was not all over. He wondered if Aunt Lizard had begun to dress for the ball. He lay too long in the cooling water, then forced himself at last to jump out and get dried, teeth chattering with self-pity, as he heard music playing, and the voices of Peter, Fergus and Jim in the room below. Drinking hot wine, he thought, and playing Aunt Lizard's wireless, and forgetting to call him at midnight; he had better stay awake.

Fergus shook him out of a deep sleep. Starting up, he saw his coat and scarf held ready. Fergus himself was wound in a school scarf.

"We're not going *out*?"

"Buck up."

Peter waited by the chapel, holding the three bicycles, front lamps lighted. Now Ralph was riding between the others, up the shrubbery path, past the dark mansion, past the rabbit warren, through the beeches, then—for the first time —out on to a public road. Fergus rode on his left, holding the back of his saddle. Peter, on his right, held his front bar in the middle as they went spinning down three short hills. His feet whirled on the pedals. They passed the west lodge, the duck ponds, and then they were in unknown country.

Ralph was wide awake now. Fergus and Peter did not talk, but they seemed excited, like conspirators. Ralph too kept silent, letting the wind sting his face and ruffle his hair. They did not stop for upward hills: he was propelled between them. On a level road they let him ride alone, following Peter's red reflector. Cars surged towards them, lights dazzling in his face, and were gone. They were riding in a great starlit silence, on and on and on. The wheels hummed. Ralph felt that he could never tire. He could go on all night, as far as London . . . *could* they be going to London? To surprise Aunt Lizard at dawn, to bring her home? At this thought he pedalled faster, and ran into Peter's back wheel. The mudguards grated, but before he could lose his balance, Fergus was gripping his saddle again, holding him upright until he felt steady. Now they entered a tunnel of high trees. Peter dropped back to his right. They were on a hill. Below were the lights of a city, and a thin dark spire. Bells were pealing as they came into the streets. They followed a line of slow-moving cars with sounding horns. The cars drew in and stopped, and people began to run down the street; men in black coats and white scarves, girls in long dresses and fur wraps, talking and laughing. They leaned their cycles on the kerb and followed. They were part of a crowd surging slowly round and round a kind of tower in the middle of the street, where four roads met. A bell tolled midnight. The crowd began to cheer, and to link hands and sing: *Should old acquaintance be forgot?* Bells pealed from a high square belfry, beside a dark cathedral.

(Telling Aunt Lizard about it next day, Ralph said, "I thought of people I used to know—oh, *years* ago, in China, and Ireland . . . all of them. Did you?" And Aunt Lizard said slowly, "Yes. No—not quite all. I've known some who should be forgot . . . and *never* brought to mind." What did that mean? It sounded sad. And she had come back so happy. But of course, like himself, she was sleepy.)

The crowd did not want to break up. They went on circling, singing the songs to which they had been dancing. Peter shouted in Fergus's ear, "Get the bikes . . . thought of something. . . ." They fought their way out of the din.

What Peter had thought of was a lorry drivers' café, a mile out of the city, on the main road to the west. As Peter had hoped, it was open. They sat at bare wooden tables, in a rich smell of frying, drinking tea as dark as Nan Hanlon's brew; Ralph's mind was still running on old acquaintance. A canary dozed in a cage. At the next table a man slept, his head pillowed on his arms. Ralph suddenly cried aloud, "I say! It's 1938!" The canary woke with a shrill "Swipe!" like a greenfinch. The man behind the urn said to the bird, "Pipe down", and glared at Ralph, who had blushed at the sound of his own voice. Then plates of sausages and fried potatoes appeared from the blue haze beyond. The boys were ravenous.

They came out of the lamplit cave into the lamplit road, and headed north up a lane into darkness. Fergus and Peter towed Ralph between them, their notes echoing between high hedges, whistling the songs of the old year.

The lights were far behind when they reached a level road and turned north-west for home. The dark line of the downs loomed on their right. Far away, on the left, Ralph saw the dull glimmer of sea creeks. Sheep bleated and hustled in a fold. In Ireland, Ralph thought, stray sheep would be lying on the roadside, eyes shining in the dark, as he had often seen them when he and Grandfather and Aunt Lizard drove home at night from horse shows. The three bicycle lamps moved like glow-worms through immense silence under the blue of the night sky. A fox barked from the downs. For the first time in England, Ralph felt the night wild and desolate, almost menacing; not cosy, as it was at the garden house. The whistlers seemed to feel it too. They fell silent; then whistled a bar or two of "In the deep midwinter"; then lapsed into their favourite *Wenceslas* duet.

Sire, warbled Peter, in the delicate tremolo of the bailiff's aunt, *Sire, he lives a good league hence* . . . and Ralph could not help smiling, yet the melody caught at his heart. He knew exactly where the peasant lived: at Duck Cottage, "right against the forest fence"; the mountain sloped up beyond, dark with pointed firs; the duck pond was St. Agnes' fountain. Now Fergus was singing in the tones in which Frank *whoa-hupp'd* the ponies:

> *Bring me flesh and bring me wine,*
> *Bring me pine logs hither—*

and Ralph saw a barrow of logs bumping across the Dutch garden, on the uneven path. He wobbled, and would have fallen if Peter had not grabbed him. "Look out!" Peter said, "the kid's asleep!"

"I am *not*," he protested. Yet his legs felt curiously shaky, as after his first riding lesson; and his hands seemed frozen to the handlebars, finger by finger, like the owl's talons that night when. . . .

"Wake up!" laughed Fergus, "last lap!"

The windows of the keeper's lodge were dark. They rode by without a sound; then, a hundred yards away, Peter hooted like an owl and Fergus barked like a fox. They left Ralph behind and raced down the slope; then whirled and raced back, and swept him along with them, skidding as they crossed the gravel sweep. The stable clock struck two. Ralph did not hear it chime the next quarter.

21

Snowdrop

Ralph sat gazing glumly at a picture in a new Scripture book. The shadowy World, a yellowish globe, hung in Space. Stars were scattered across a stormy purple void. Underneath he read: "Darkness was upon the face of the deep." Darkness was in Ralph's soul; he felt wretched to the very roots of his being. It was Monday morning, and the new term had begun. Governess sat at her desk beside a new block calendar, thick with its 363 leaves. Her spectacles flashed dangerously. Already Nat Wood was in disgrace, standing behind the blackboard, and one of the big boys had been promised a caning. The Christmas truce was over.

Over, too, was all the mounting excitement of December, its carols, cards and parcels and decorated food. It would really be better, Ralph thought, not to have Christmas at all, than to come back from the holiday to the dank schoolroom, to sums and Scripture, thermos cocoa and pallid cheese sandwiches, with nothing to look forward to but the boredom of "raffia day".

Raffiawork was a favourite with Governess. On most afternoons the girls did needlework or knitting, while the boys had freehand drawing in pencil, from cardboard cones, spheres and pitchers; or made "history models"—a Roman fort, a castle, a Saxon village. On Thursdays the whole school did water colour painting: an ivy leaf, a sprig of yew, a snowdrop. Their painting books marked the seasons of the year. But Friday was a day of gloom, to be endured before the freedom of Saturday. The whole afternoon was spent in raffiawork. Ralph loathed everything about it: the great hanks of cheese-coloured raffia, the awkward, springy cane, the dullness of putting in stitch after stitch, the order, endlessly repeated: "No talking, children." Above all, he hated the length of time with no change of occupation. Even playtime was cut on Fridays, in case they came back with grubby hands. Two hours, that went like a flash in the holidays, spun out into a dreary waste of time, endlessly stitching at the hateful, bumpy little mat which would never grow large enough to "turn up", would certainly never come to look like Pecky's wonderful basket, with red heraldic lions prancing up it, which had won a prize at the handwork show. Aunt Lizard would be lucky if all Ralph's raffia days brought her a pair of table mats. And always, on Fridays, the clock hands seemed to stick at twenty past two.

This week, there was a cheering rumour that raffiawork would be shortened; a man was coming to give them a lecture. But Friday came, and hope died. The stranger arrived an hour before dinner: a solemn elderly man, with a neat grey beard and whiskers sprouting above his eyes. Ralph brightened when he unpacked a jar with an object like a green lizard swimming inside. The title of the lecture, *Alcohol and the Human Body*, had been written on the board by Governess, but Ralph had no idea what it meant. He hoped some of it would be about reptiles, and was disappointed. Afterwards he remembered only one precept; that if you foolishly drank alcohol, your inside became dingy and clouded, like the liquids which the lecturer was briskly mixing in glasses on the top table. . . . "And he never got on to the thing in the bottle at all!" Ralph cried at the tea-table that evening.

"What was it, a newt?" asked Fergus.

"I don't *know*. He didn't *tell* us!"

Perhaps the lecturer had cut his recital short, because of the long walk back to the station; or perhaps—as Randy whispered, earning a black look from Governess—he had hurried off to warm himself at the Crooked Billet.

The conjurer who came one afternoon brought no bottled creatures, but a wand, a greenish top hat, coloured balls, glass tumblers and blue and red handkerchiefs. His visit was a surprise, a treat for the children from the school managers. Christmas flowered again for a moment. The conjurer may not have been at the top of his profession, for once he showed them a green ball in his left hand, and told them to watch carefully, and they would see it "flay through the air, *so*!" —tracing an arc in front of the table—"and when I catch it in this hand, *then* see what colour it is!" He waved his handkerchief, fluttered his hands, and said hopefully, "Now! How many of you saw it flay?" The children smiled; no such thing had happened. The ball had gone up his sleeve. "Oh, then I must tray again! Now watch closely this tame . . ." and again the handkerchief was waved. "There! Who spotted it? Hands up!" The children's smiles were apologetic; they kept their hands folded, following the example of Governess, who sat at her desk tight-lipped because the sewing hour was being wasted.

The conjurer still smiled his wistful, crinkled smile.

"Once more," he pleaded. "Let's see who has the sharpest ayes. . . ." And then, on an inspiration, "Sometames I give sixpence to the one who spots it first!" The handkerchief waved, the fingers fluttered, and three hands began to waver uncertainly in the row of big boys. But Governess, with a

surge of her long grey skirts, had risen to her feet. Three slaps
rang out one after another as three ears were sharply boxed.
The hands dropped. The boys muttered, and three girls
blushed for their brothers. The little conjurer still smiled
bravely; but he looked as though his ears too had been boxed.
He murmured on a note of defiance, "Well, some of us see
more than others!" and went on to a new trick. But now the
children's smiles were wan. The treat was stone dead. Soon,
accepting defeat, he packed his box and went sadly away in
the rain. Ralph heard Governess hiss to Mrs. Duffel: "The
heighth of impudence!"

The grey month went on. After the Creation came the
Fall, and after the Fall the Flood. Singing and reciting were
out; Mrs. Duffel had "lost her voice". Ralph's raffia mat grew
one painful inch. He longed for ice and snow; Fergus had
promised to teach him to skate. He and Peter talked of a
winter ten years ago, when snow was piled in white cliffs
along the drive, and they had tobogganed on the downs above
the railway line. But the month continued mild. The ther-
mometer by the fruit room hardly fell below freezing point.
Wintersweet, with wych hazel and mauve winter irises,
flowered in the garden. There were violets in the orchard, and
already Aunt Lizard had picked a bunch of polyanthus from
the Dutch garden. Only one night was memorable, when
Uncle Laurie called them out to see a strange red glow like a
sunset in the north: the Northern Lights.

Ralph was often late home from school this month. He
and Nat had agreed to share the owl whistle. Nat could pro-
duce the owl notes so skilfully that Ralph, listening from his
cottage in the beeches, could not tell which call was Nat's and
which was an answering owl. Nat would prowl about under
the trees, calling; and often, from love, or rivalry, or curiosity,
an owl would reply, and come nearer and nearer until it

hovered overhead; but then Nat would stop whistling, for he was still scared of talons. One night the two sat together in Ralph's cottage, listening to a pair of brown owls in the dusk; one calling from the wood near the lodge, another answering—first from a distant copse, then from the park, then from the beeches close by. Suddenly there was a loud report. The owl, as well as the boys, had been deceived. The keeper's imitation—with no wooden whistle to help him—had been faultless.

When Aunt Lizard protested at his lateness, Ralph begged to be allowed to ride his bicycle to school; but she hesitated, thinking of the steep homeward run.

Ralph had another reason for being late, but this was a secret shared with Nat. In return for his share of the whistle, Nat had given him half shares in his new white mouse, Snowdrop; an elegant little creature, with spotless fur and eyes as pink as campions. Snowdrop had a cage, made by Nat's father; but he spent his days in Nat's pocket, until Governess ferreted him out. Then they had to find a crèche for him, where he would be safe during the day. They decided on the keeper's hut on the grass at the top of the warren; a pair of old railway carriages without wheels, used for shelter when this was the summer bird-field. The door could be fastened against rats and weasels; there was glass in the windows. The carriages were of the cattle truck kind, with low partitions, familiar to Ralph, but not to Nat. Finding them up there, under a ring of oak trees, had been like finding the skeleton of his dream monster. "So I was right," Ralph told himself: "the trains *do* come hunting." But, except sometimes at night, he no longer fancied this. The hut, skeleton or not, was a safe and friendly place. Snowdrop's cage rested there while the two owners were at school. During alternate weeks, when he was Ralph's, the cage

stayed there at night as well; for Ralph could not trust
Cuckoo. The grey cat might be lazy, but only when it
suited him. Ralph could not forget one day when Cuckoo
had been fast asleep in his basket, and a robin had flown into
the kitchen. Quick as a flash, the "sleeping" cat had been
after it; and the robin had only just escaped. Supposing Snowdrop managed to worry open the door of his cage? It was too
awful to risk. So the mouse was left in safety; if he escaped
from the cage, he would still be enclosed in the hut and could
come to no harm. Ralph left him reluctantly at night, and
hurried up to the warren every morning on his way to school.
On Saturday he took Brownie with him; urged to make
friends, the rabbit and mouse eyed each other doubt-
fully.

Then, on his birthday, Ralph at last got his own way.
Aunt Lizard agreed that he might bicycle to school, "just this
once, to see how you manage". He set off joyfully. It was
his week for owning Snowdrop, and he left the bicycle to
run up the warren and give him a breakfast of corn. It was
too wet and muddy for bicycling through the forest; he and
Nat escorted Mrs. Duffel on her slow ride up the hill. But, in
the evening, Aunt Lizard's fears were vindicated. Four big
boys lay in ambush for Nat and Ralph. They had hardly
mounted when they were waylaid; and, in the scrimmage,
Ralph fell off, bumping his left knee on the road. He managed
to mount and escape, flying down the hill after Nat, and
braking safely before he reached the crossroads; but at home
he could not hide his limp. The birthday cake, with its nine
candles, waited on the table while he was bandaged and
reproved: unfairly, as he pointed out. Aunt Lizard did not
actually say, "I knew how it would be"; but she looked
worried.

Next morning, the knee was swollen and puffy. Ralph

could not walk. It was "water on the knee", Aunt Lizard said. She made him lie on the sofa, and doctored the knee with hot poultices, "as hot as you can bear it". He and Aunt Lizard rarely agreed as to how hot he could bear it; but, apart from the hourly poultice, he enjoyed his holiday. Fergus brought the whole pile of *Boy's Own Papers* and dumped it beside him; a hundred and twenty of them, he counted; some, passed on to Fergus, dated from the year before he himself was born! He was surprised to find them less old-fashioned than he expected. He read them through, stories, stamp pages, tales of birds and animals by a naturalist called "Hedgerow". At the end there was always a page of jokes called "Under the Spreading Chestnut Tree". He read these aloud to Aunt Lizard, who bore it more calmly than he bore his poultices. He missed Snowdrop, but knew that Nat would take care of him.

In the evenings, Uncle Laurie taught him draughts, playing with nine men against Ralph's twelve; showing him how to wait and plot for the final glory of "giving" one king and then sweeping all Ralph's kings from the board. To even things out, Ralph played with Aunt Lizard, who rarely won. When Ralph hopped up to bed, he left Uncle Laurie and Fergus settling to their long evening game of chess by the sitting room fire; picnic supper beside them, soup and celery and the Stilton cheese begun at Christmas, to be eaten casually, eyes on the board.

Ralph did not mind going upstairs alone here. The house was so small and compact, the staircase short, and there was only one empty bedroom, not the deserted wing beyond the landing which had daunted him at Nine Wells. The garden house, enclosed in the forest and gardens, felt like part of a little hidden town, where people had lived in safety for a thousand years. If there were ghosts, they were gentle and aloof as fieldmice. "If ever I'm a ghost," Ralph thought, "I'll come back here and walk in the orchard."

One evening he was allowed to stay up late. From his sofa he watched Uncle Laurie and Aunt Lizard feeding Seville oranges from a crate into a little slicing machine borrowed from the grocer. The juicy slices in the cauldron looked tempting; slipping one into his mouth, he was astonished at its bitterness. Aunt Lizard, glancing up, stared at his puckered face and watering eyes. Then he swallowed, and she laughed, enlightened. "You'll like it tomorrow." Next day the house was filled with the smell of simmering oranges, and for tea there was new marmalade, dark gold jelly striped with thin peel.

In the second week his knee was back to its normal shape, but it felt bruised, and Aunt Lizard would not let him walk. For his birthday, Uncle Alfred had sent *The Jungle Book*. Under its spell, he lay for hours staring out at the cedars, making up a story about an English boy, lost in the forest as a baby and brought up by foxes. Some day, he thought, I might write it down: *Merlin of the Wilds* would be a good title.

The week had been sunny; but on Sunday he woke to see the peaks of the pleasure ground trees whitened by a snowstorm. Surely he could go out, he cried after breakfast. But Aunt Lizard was firm. He might slip down, and start the trouble all over again. "I don't want you blaming me some day, because you can't play football!" He looked at her in surprise. Why should he want to play football? Uncle Laurie came in and asked, "Who's coming to church?"

"I will," said Ralph.

"Well, I think not," said Aunt Lizard.

"Too much prep," said Fergus lazily.

Uncle Laurie shook his head at him. "You should have

lived at my old home. No excuses. And no prep on Sundays. If one of my sisters ironed a chiffon scarf, even, it was like Sodom and Gomorrah."

Half an hour later, Uncle Laurie returned to find them still hugging the fire. Others had had the same idea, he said; even the old sexton had rheumatism and for once had not arrived.

But the Vicar had slid down the hill from High Forest on his motor bicycle, and he and Uncle Laurie had shared Morning Prayer; Uncle Laurie making the responses, while they read the Psalms verse and verse about, and took a lesson each. Hymns and sermon had been abandoned. Now they heard the motor bicycle chugging away up the shrubbery path.

"If you were the only one——" said Fergus dreamily, "The padre shouldn't have started, 'Dearly beloved brethren'."

"No, no, he started, 'Dearly beloved Metherell'." Uncle Laurie took his walking stick, and ten minutes later Ralph saw him in the pleasure ground with the duty man, shaking snow from the fragile spruce boughs so that they should not break. Was that work? Ralph wondered. And there was Aunt Lizard in the kitchen, roasting the joint and making one of her Yorkshire puddings, crisp and brown, like a ripe puffball: wasn't cooking *work*? He looked across at Fergus, whose prep seemed to consist in sorting fishing tackle. At least that wasn't work; yet he could not feel that Uncle Laurie's parents would have approved.

On Tuesday the snow was still falling and melting and falling again, in twirling blizzards that made his head spin a little if he stood at the window too long. Uncle Laurie went to a flower show in London, and Aunt Lizard went with him. Mrs. Tann came to keep Ralph company. He was fond of Mrs. Tann, who usually spent Thursdays helping Aunt Lizard, and who never threw away anything she swept up—

even a scribbled piece of paper or a cigarette card—but kept all rubbish in a neat pile, to be claimed by the owners. Beside this endearing habit, which had often saved a child distress, Mrs. Tann was charming to look at, with kind blue eyes and coiled flaxen plaits. Aunt Doll, the forest children called her; although she was really aunt only to two of them, Katy and Nat Wood.

At dinner he told her about his fall from the bicycle, enjoying her sympathy. Nat, she said, had come home with his jacket half torn off; and his mother had been so annoyed that she had taken him with her the next day, when she went to nurse their Grannie in Dorset for a while: "he'll go to school down there," she explained, "and his mother can keep an eye on him, instead of fretting about what he might be up to at home."

After dinner, while Mrs. Tann finished her work in the sitting room, he helped her by rubbing pink plate-powder, mixed to a thin paste with water, on to all the cutlery. He sat perched on his sofa with a tray on his lap, holding files of spoons and forks, little silver butter knives, teaspoons with rose handles, and the sugar spoon shaped like a violet leaf. He invented a kind of chess to play with them as he worked. If only, he thought, you could make up a game to help with raffiawork! He had tried pretending to be the young tailor, in a fairy tale read to them once by Mrs. Duffel, who was under a spell, and had to mend countless tattered coats, and had his head cuffed if he spoke: a hazard not unknown, of course, to Governess's pupils. The story was called *Silence!* Another time, Ralph had made himself stitch right round his mat before looking at the clock. But the breakfast room clock, with its merry tick, seemed to go twice as fast as the one in the schoolroom. By the time they had polished the silver, it was time for Mrs. Tann to cycle home and get her husband's tea. Fergus would soon be home, he knew; and before that he could talk to Billy, who would come in to refill the coal scuttle and the log bin. He hopped about the room, trying out his knee, and sniffed appreciatively at the flowers on the table: frail white irises, big snowdrops, white hyacinths, wintersweet, mimosa and pearl catkins, in a honey-coloured bowl. It was snowing lightly again. He wondered what Billy had been doing all day; sweeping paths, perhaps, or oiling the mowing machine, or "crocking" pots in the potting shed. A snowflake drifted in the open window, and Ralph caught it on the back of his hand. It was "white as snow"; as white as Snowdrop; now it was melting.

Snowdrop!

The thought went through him like an icicle. Who was feeding Snowdrop?

What had Mrs. Tann said?—"Nat came home with his jacket half torn off . . . his mother took him with her *next day*. . . ." Could it be that Nat had gone to Dorset, not knowing that he, Ralph, was a prisoner? He wrung his hands, and then began counting on his fingers. He faced a cruel sum: Snowdrop had been shut up there, at the top of the warren, without food or water, for fifteen nights and days.

And it had been cold. It had been snowing. Ralph groaned again at another grim thought. Snowdrop had not even had his usual bed of sawdust and dry bracken to keep him warm. On the Sunday, Ralph had scrubbed out the cage with a toothbrush, and put in a pile of newspapers to soak up any damp. He had meant to take a bag of hay in the morning; then, in the excitement of cycling to school, he had forgotten. Snowdrop had had no covering but his own fur; and only newspapers, cold as linoleum, to sit on.

Struggling into his gumboots, Ralph gasped to himself, "How *could* I? How *could* I?" He dragged his coat from its hook. Aunt Lizard's orders were forgotten. This was a matter of life and death. No—with his hand on the latch, he thought, "It's a matter of death." He had murdered Snowdrop. How could the poor mouse have survived? Yet he must go and see, in case . . . in case . . . he did not dare to finish. It was dusk outside. A thin wind made him shiver on the wide cricket lawn. He swished through a layer of soft snow, like white sugar. The forest looked sad and wintry. The grass in the park fence was biscuit-coloured, as it had been that summer day when he lost Santa. This ill omen took him by surprise. He began to cry, and to run. His knee did not seem to hurt, and he ran faster, over the drive, over the fence, up the warren, slipping on the snowy turf. He came to the oak trees, and looked back at the desolate landscape. There was no comfort anywhere. Snow had gathered in little drifts among the oak roots, and muffled the windows of the hut. He opened the door and went in, and crouched on the floor by the cage. Peering through the wire, he called, "Snowdrop!" There was no answer, no whiskers and nose at the window, no eager rustle of paws. Well, he had known there would not be. He must get the worst part over. He unlatched the door of the cage.

What he saw staggered him. Surely he hadn't left anything there but newspaper? Yet the cage was furnished, from floor to ceiling, with a maze of white tunnels, nests, little caverns and grottoes, stretching back from the doorway. He touched the stuff. Then he began to understand. It was paper, or papier mâché. Snowdrop, like a little white mole, had set to work and had tunnelled and built up the newspapers, page by page, layer by layer, into this honeycombed cliff. He must have bullied the paper, and trampled it, and danced on it, and chewed it into shape. *Perhaps he had been able to eat it?* With frantic hope, Ralph began to pull the cliff to bits. Now he was calling, like a rescuer digging for a trapped miner—"I'm coming, Snowdrop, I'm here, wait for me, I'm . . . oh, Snowdrop," he said, as his fingers touched something crouched in the farthest corner. He picked it up and went to the glimmer of light by the window.

Snowdrop was a sorry-looking mouse; eyes half shut, coat dull and grubby, tail drooping; but he was not a corpse. Ralph held him for half a minute, afraid to believe this, before he realized what the prisoner had lacked: water. He ran out to scoop up a snowball, and held the mouse's nose to it. Snowdrop's lips sucked feebly, his tongue flickered. Was it too cold? But the taste seemed to rouse him. He sucked again, blinked and shook himself. His ears pricked. Ralph remembered the dormouse in April. He thought: Snowdrop's been hibernating. That's what he's done. And he's still alive, but he looks so poorly. What should *I* want, first, if I were *him*? Not an ice . . . feeling ready to sing for joy, he saved his breath and raced for home with the mouse clasped in both hands.

"Do you think hot toast is the best thing?" Fergus asked.

They were sitting in front of the fire. Snowdrop, almost himself again, had drunk two saucers of warm milk. Now he nibbled at the rich brown toast, which Ralph had cut into fingers, as Aunt Lizard prepared his toast when he was ill. So grateful to Snowdrop for being alive, Ralph could not do enough for him. The mouse sat on a velvet cushion; butter dripped gently on to it from above as Snowdrop ate from Ralph's hands. Cuckoo, banished for the night, was sulking on the warm pipes in the vinery. Ralph explained:

"I thought—if I'd been shut up somewhere for two weeks, in the snow, with nothing to eat but newspaper—I think hot toast is what I'd like to start with."

22

The First of March

Back at school, Ralph found himself without friends. Governess had kept in the boys who had attacked himself and Nat; they had had no playtime for a week. Nat was still away, so Ralph must take the blame. When he protested, he was shouted down: he shouldn't have gone falling off and hurting himself. "Shows you're daft," summed up Hoppy. Ralph told himself that he didn't care. He would be Merlin of the Wilds. At playtime and at midday he wandered off into the woods, or along the downs, in the dazzling white sunshine of February, out of earshot of the clicking marbles in the boys' playground, and the swish of the girls' skipping ropes. Mr. Hassall had told him that, last year, there had been a litter of fox cubs near the Larches, in a den under a fallen tree. He searched for the den, and then for the wild cats near the ruined cottage. There were sheets of snowdrops under the apple tree. He sniffed their cold green smell, and the bitter tang of elder buds. Birdsong rang through the forest. Crisp moss, pushed upward by frost, crunched underfoot. Hazel copses were yellow with catkins; there were buds like silver scuts on the pussy-willow trees, tinged with pink under the silver. He solved, at last, the puzzle of Katy's "palm tree", when she picked a handful of the willow twigs for their painting lesson.

The First of March

The month had turned mild again after the snow. Holly trees in the forest were still covered with scarlet berries. Ralph found little piles of cone scales in a pine grove where the squirrels had feasted. Running down the hill alone one evening, leaving the rest behind, he thought he saw a squirrel crossing the road. It stopped, and he saw that it was a beautiful stoat. The red-brown snaky body, the creamy bib were bright on the slate-blue road, between the purple birches. Ralph was so near that he could see the satiny shine on its back. He thought the eyes were *blue*. As he gazed, the stoat glided into the bushes.

Ralph went down a green forest ride which would bring him out by Snowdrop's hut at the top of the warren. He came to a clearing where Cap'n Crewe was burning brushwood. The flames were pure crocus-gold in the frosty air. He paused to look with envy at the shelter that the old forester had made for himself from close-pleached hazels. Here he could keep dry in heavy rain. Pointing south, it caught the rays of the low winter sun, and at dinner time Cap'n would sit there sunning himself like an old fox. He nodded to Ralph, then broke off a twig and came over to give it to the boy. "You wear that tomorrow."

"Why, Mr. Crewe?"

" 'Tis Ash Wednesday. They'll tread on yer toes else."

Ralph looked at the twig, with its pointed black buds.

"What is it?" he asked.

"Ash stick. You pin it on yer coat."

"But—why would they tread on my toes?"

" 'Tis Ash Wednesday," said Cap'n, closing the conversation.

The sun was dipping behind the Hurst Castle woods. The forest here was already in deep shadow. Frost tinged the brown oak and chestnut leaves along the rides; but the green leaves and white candles of a laurel thicket made him think of spring. Then he found a primrose bud. Climbing up into the warren, he suddenly felt stifled in his tweed hat and knitted scarf. He tore them off, and let the cool sea wind blow on his face and neck. Spring was coming.

At home, he found Aunt Lizard cooking pancakes. Of course, it was Shrove Tuesday; he remembered the Scripture lesson, about Lent, which he had heard ages ago: this morning. He ate his dinner, and still it was light outside. He could take Brownie for a run in the pleasure ground. Aunt Lizard gave him a hot pancake, folded over a layer of lemon juice and sugar. He held this in one hand, and tucked Brownie under his other arm. The latch of the orange house door could be managed with his elbow.

Brownie, like himself, felt a surge of springtime gaiety. She sprang about the lawns, kicking up her heels. Closing the glass door, Ralph followed her, and stood down by the angle of the garden wall, nibbling his pancake, and fingering the strings of pearl catkins on a tree. Some memory was teasing him. Once before, he thought, he had touched those catkins . . . and eaten pancakes. He could not remember when. The five o'clock bell rang out; and then all at once he remembered. His first morning here. And—he thought of Governess's calendar—today was the first of March. It was March when he came to England. He had been a whole year at the garden house.

The thought intrigued him. He remembered so vividly the strangeness of all the things he had seen. Now they would not seem strange at all. The glass mountain, the house with poison gas, the house with the peach blossom and the rabbit's tail wand—now they were familiar, the orange house, the carnation house, the orchard house. He had seen Ted using the rabbit's tail to take pollen from one tree to another; you got more peaches that way, Ted had explained. Standing there, keeping frisky Brownie under his eye—for there might be stoats here, as well as in the forest—he could picture to himself exactly what was growing now in all the glass-houses; white-flowering early strawberries in pots, bright green mustard-and-cress, scented lilies of the valley, the first lettuces. He realized that he even knew the name of the tree with the pearl catkins, *Garrya elliptica*: he had read the name hundreds of times from the metal label, as he skipped to and fro with Brownie. And the other trees . . . at some point in the long year, he had learned to tell them apart; he did not know when. The knowledge had grown on him, like lichen on a tree.

Lugging Brownie under one arm, he ran to tell Aunt Lizard that they had been there a year. He thought of the garden now as home, or "our place", as the forest children said.

Tea was ready indoors. Fergus was back, and the three were at table. Ralph slid into his chair, and was about to burst out with his discovery, when something stopped him. An odd silence seemed to have fallen. The copper kettle bubbled softly on its stand. Why were they all looking at him? He turned to Aunt Lizard. It must be all right. She was smiling.

Fergus handed a magazine across the table to Ralph. It was the new March number of *Field and Forest*. He looked, as it seemed he was meant to do, at the open page, and his own name caught his eye. Then, with unspeakable surprise, he saw something equally familiar: his own picture of the mother dormouse at her nest. He could not mistake that; he had looked at it thousands of times; he had carried a crumpled print in his pocket for weeks. He gasped, "They've printed it! In a paper! My dormouse!"

It was several minutes before he could grasp how it came there. Then he took in the heading: "Photographic competition: prize-winners." There was a list of names, and underneath: "A special prize is also awarded to the youngest competitor, for a good effort with a box camera, and an interesting story." Aunt Lizard was explaining that Fergus had sent in a print of the dormouse picture, and the account she had made him write out. "That's printed too, Ralph, look." He nodded, and went on staring at the page; but not at the picture or the printed story. His attention was held by the sight of his name and address. The type seemed to underline his thoughts in the pleasure ground. There it was, in black and white: Ralph Oliver, of The Garden House, Hurst Castle, Sussex.

PART FIVE

PART FIVE

23

Water-hide

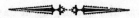

Bicycling up the lane beside the east park, Ralph spotted two blackbirds' nests without dismounting. This was the beginning of a new game: bicycle bird-nesting.

Spring-like February had given way to summery March. The lane was already dappled with shade from horse chestnuts in leaf. Someone said it had been "the warmest March for 150 years". Coming home from school one afternoon in the middle of the month, Ralph found tea laid in the little garden as though it were midsummer. The light of the western sun shone through the chapel windows on to clumps of daffodils and aubretia. A vivid scent came over the wall from the massed polyanthus—bronze, tortoiseshell, apricot, butter-yellow and white—in the Dutch garden.

Uncle Laurie liked to have tea in the garden, Aunt Lizard said, because it had been a family custom of his youth. His father had often begun it in March, and they had continued until the darkness and mists of autumn drove them indoors. Once, visiting them in January, she and her sisters had found themselves drinking tea outside in the afternoon sunlight, wrapped in rugs, with snow on the ground. To the three girls from Ireland this had seemed extraordinary; only the madcap English, they felt, would enjoy such antics. And in fact old Mrs. Metherell did not enjoy them at all: she would

223

have agreed that "it is never safe to sit out of doors". But she loyally made no protest, beyond providing rugs for the faint-hearted, and hassocks for each of her ten children, even on the hottest day, to keep their feet from the damp grass.

This March, however, the turf was already dry enough to have satisfied anyone but Mrs. Metherell. The summer weather, the light evenings, the park with its new green grass gave Ralph a sense of wonderful freedom. To have such weather so early was like getting up at dawn with an endless day ahead: eight months of summer, perhaps. In the evenings he hardly knew where to go first, there were so many nests to visit and so many new ideas to try. One idea had already proved a success: home-made crystallized violets. The wild orchard had been planted, years ago, with violets from the garden frames, single and double, purple, pink, ruby, yellow and blue. Ralph had picked a handful of the large purple ones, soaked them for three days in thick sugared water, and spread them to dry in the sun, on clean paper, on his bedroom window sill. Unfortunately the first batch had been eaten by Cuckoo; but a second batch, dried in the oven, had survived to decorate Aunt Lizard's birthday cake.

Then he had decided to hold a Boat Race on a little green pond in the derelict rock garden. This wilderness, between the orchard and the wych elm grove, had become his favourite retreat, as the harness room had once been. It lay in deep shade, with rocky pinnacles and caves, winding paths, ferneries and dark yew trees. Most of the plants were swallowed up in bishop-weed; but there were some dark red polyanthus, which Nat called spring-flowers, and white forget-me-nots, and a tangled rose bush which, in June, would have a few exquisite roses; single, deep pinkish gold in colour, and nearly as big as saucers. Last year he had picked one for Aunt Lizard, and then Uncle Laurie had taken cuttings for the rose garden, and Ralph had felt like an explorer who had found a forgotten treasure. But it was the wildness and secrecy of the place that he valued, and the knowledge that no one else would want to come there.

On Boat Race Day, however, he brought Nat. They skimmed the weed from the pond, and made toy canoes by splitting the hollow brown stems of a bamboo-like plant that grew there. Nat had brought a cocoa tin full of tiny frogs to show Ralph. They tried using the frogs as crews, but found them too unruly, and searched instead for ladybirds in the forget-me-nots. But, whereas the frog crew had jumped overboard, the ladybirds took wing. The boys leaped to and fro over the pond, using hollow stems as pipes to blow their boats along. Ralph's new sandals squelched with green weed. Tiring of make-believe, Nat had suggested that they should go down to the duck ponds and take out the punt. No one would know, if they kept quiet and didn't frighten the ducks.

They went up the wych elm grove, among daffodil fields and clumps of grape hyacinths, through the oak woods, and over a water meadow where Nat had collected his frogs. A pair of peewits wheeled and cried over their heads, dipping and circling, their wings making an odd hoarse sound, like swans in flight.

"Nest somewhere near," said Nat.

"What does a peewit's nest look like?"

"Why . . . like that," said Nat, pointing, "there's one." And indeed at their feet there were four brown eggs, spattered as though with ink, in a shallow earthen cup. The parent birds were abruptly silent. The boys looked down at the nest, and then, with awe, at one another. Nat said slowly, "You'll never find another one, just like that."

Ralph was never to find another there at all; search as he

might, all through the spring, up and down the meadows, with peewits wailing in his ears.

The duck ponds, like the pheasant coverts, were out of bounds at nesting time; but no one saw Nat and Ralph as they slipped down the steep mossy slopes of a beech hanger, passed Duck Cottage and came to a strip of turf, a bridge between two ponds. Celandines, spread wide to the sun, blazed on the short grass under an oak tree. The little timber boat house stood close to the bank; inside, the punt floated on a shallow dark pool. They climbed in; Nat took the pole, unhitched the rope and drove the punt out over the dazzling water. Dark cliffs of fir trees loomed above them. Across the pond, one duck gave a long shrill quack, and they waited, holding their breath, for the clamour and mass flight which would mean disaster. It did not come. Nat steered away from the reed clumps, away from the little islands in the middle of the ponds, into a wide lagoon. The heat was like August. They stripped off their clothes, dabbled their feet, and spoke of bathing; but the water was deep and neither could swim. They lay in the bottom of the punt, talking in whispers: forlorn and shipwrecked brothers. An aeroplane buzzed overhead, and they waved to it soundlessly, laughing and grimacing. Ralph thought he had never been so happy. A boat was far the best thing to have: better than a horse or a bicycle, better than an aeroplane, even. He wished he had found the punt long ago. He must bring his camera; he would make another "hide", in the reeds, and wait for the otter which Mr. Hassall had seen there.

They were both astonished to see that the sun was setting. They tied up the punt, and went home to be scolded. Everyone had been looking for them. Ralph found he was burnt deep red by the sun; he had had no idea that the sun had been so fierce on that windless stretch of water. That night he could not sleep; dazed with light and air, he thought only of getting back to the punt next day. But, as he climbed the stile at the top of the hanger, Mr. Hassall stopped him.

"Don't go near the ponds again, Ralph. Not while the ducks are sitting."

The boy's face was a picture of guilty surprise. The keeper laughed. Ralph said lamely, "We didn't know anyone saw us."

"You left enough footprints. New sandals, too, weren't they?"

The new sandals were drying at home. Ralph looked more mystified than ever. The keeper explained:

"Everyone's footprints are different. Easy to tell where *you*'ve been." Then, nodding to a meadow at the edge of a distant copse, he murmured, "Just look at that, will you?"

Inside a gate, close to a gorse patch, three young school-girls lay basking in the sun. Their bicycles, leaning against the hedge, were hung with bunches of primroses. Mr. Hassall and Ralph exchanged a grin. The gorse roots were the home of many grass snakes, which often slid out to bask on that very stretch of turf. The children might waken to find they were not alone. Ralph whispered:

"Shall we tell them?"

Mr. Hassall shook his head. He was always reluctant to disturb quiet picnics. Rowdy boys or egg collectors would be another matter. But Ralph hoped the long-tailed tit, sitting on her eggs in the gorse, would not be disturbed by shrieks.

It was a pity, he thought, that his water-hide must wait. He might have been able to watch sedge-warblers and willow-tits.

The prize from *Field and Forest* had changed his life. It was a book by a naturalist called Richard Kearton, and was about photographing wild birds and animals. As he read, Ralph seemed to be learning a new language; or to be saying to himself, over and over—"Yes, yes. That's what I meant . . . That's what I want . . . That's what I shall do. Of course. . . ." Now the cottage in the beeches was not a cottage in a game; it was a hide, for watching squirrels; although the wood was too shady for photographs now that the trees were coming into leaf. His camera, too, had new meaning. Now he did not wander about looking for things to "snap". His dormouse pictures, which Fergus said were beginner's luck, had shown him what he wanted to do. Richard Kearton's book told him he was right, and explained how he should go about it. He must build hides; and he must have a jacket, like the Kearton brothers'—green on one side, brown on the other—for lying in green fields or dead leaves. His outgrown winter coat was brown, but the inside was of red tartan. Finding a tin of green paint in the carpenter's shed, he tried to paint the lining. This was not a happy idea; the paint rolled itself into drips and gobbets, and then refused to be scrubbed off. It was far too hot for a coat, anyway. Lying in the east park, looking for hares, it was too hot even for a shirt. Soon he was sunburnt to the colour of dry bracken, and that contented him until his new hide was ready.

Slung between three hawthorn bushes, with walls of brushwood and old bracken, this was designed for watching baby hares; but soon he found that a pair of goldfinches had begun to build in one of the bushes, using red and white cow-hairs plucked from a barbed wire fence. By tiptoeing quietly across from the far side, he could use the hide to watch them, as well as the long-legged hares which he would never see without thinking of Santa. Aunt Lizard had lent him an old pair of opera glasses; with these and his camera, he felt like a veteran

naturalist. Also, he was keeping a written record. He had
remembered the fine leather-bound diary which had been his
mother's, and which he had brought from China. Some time
in April, the pages were blank: she had tired of writing in it.
His own entries went back to early March, when he had first
seen a thrush building in the plantation. At the end of the
book, however, he found ten pages headed: Addresses:
Memoranda: Books to Read. Rose Izard had entered no
address or memorandum, and whatever books she meant to
read, they were not recorded. Keeping his style terse, he had
spun out the pages until today. On this date, his mother had
put her last brief note.

Bicycling up the lane, he thought: today I can start a
proper diary. He must start with a flourish. Blackbirds' nests
were no good. Even the goldfinch's nest was stale news. He
would go on to Brookside and look for the kingfisher that
nested there in a lime tree. He had told Aunt Lizard he might
go as far as the ruined tower; the brook was only a little
farther. Even if the kingfisher failed him, he would see minnows and wagtails. The stream there was marked on his own
map of the district; since the day when he and Nat had been
missing for nine hours, Aunt Lizard would make him point
out on the map which way he meant to go.

The idea of a map had come from Governess. In the last
week of the term, she had set a piece of homework: each
child was to draw, first, a plan of its own home; and then a
map of the district. It sounded easy. Before he had fairly
begun, Ralph found it was not. By the time he had finished
his two plans—upstairs and down—he realized that he knew
far more now about the garden house than ever before. The
map of the estate was far harder. He had thought he knew it
so well. He discovered that he was not even sure exactly
which way the drive to Hurst Castle ran, or whether High

Forest lay north or east of the great house. Aunt Lizard, Uncle Laurie and Fergus were all pressed into helping him and contradicting each other. "What you need," Fergus said, "is an aeroplane." But the map was done at last, and drawn out in indian ink. So now, as he cycled along the lane, Ralph knew that he was heading due east.

This was the lane haunted, according to Nat, by a headless lady; but in the sunlight it seemed tame and reassuring, bordered by copses full of periwinkles, primroses and anemones. There were striped stars-of-Bethlehem too, and the yellow deadnettle which Nat called weasel-snout. He passed the tower, already explored with Nat: there was nothing to see inside, only an empty dark chamber where jackdaws nested, and blank windows open to the weather. He reached Brookside, and went to look again at the cottage where King Charles had slept.

Circling in the narrow road, he heard the sound of trotting horses in the distance. Now he was not a naturalist, a bicycle bird-nester, but the Royal fugitive, fleeing with a troop of horse at his heels. He sped along the road, came to a hump-backed bridge over the stream, flung his bicycle through a gateway—it was his horse, and he had turned it loose—then ducked down and crawled into the darkness of the bridge. The brick arch was low, but so was the water. He was able to crawl on dry shingle along to the far end, where a willow hid him from the road. The horses trotted past; not a string of polo ponies from the stables in the next village, but a troop of Cromwell's men. He must stay hidden.

He sat on a dry boulder, watching a minnow trapped in a pool in the shallow stream. There had been no rain for weeks. The bed of the stream was thickly planted with water-mint, kingcups, cresses and water-buttercups. The current still ran fast and deep at one place under the bank. Eating a piece of

gingerbread, he heard a sound that made him turn his head
—a "cloop" like a stone dropping into the water. But he was
alone. Then he caught another sound: the small crunch of
sharp teeth snapping off a stalk, like the sound of Brownie
eating a milk-thistle. At the same moment, a little brown
creature nosed out of the water, landed on a gravel ridge,
shook itself and began to eat watercress. Now he traced the
first crunching noise; a foot away, another small brown
animal was feeding. The "cloop" sounded again, and a third
swam with the current and landed on the ridge. Were they
rats? Then he remembered Vole; though much bigger, these
had the same burnished coats, the same colouring—darker
than baby rabbits—the same soft furry look, rather like
bumble-bees; the same faces, bright-eyed and blunt-nosed.
He knew they must be water voles.

A car hummed nearer and nearer along the road, and he
waited for them to take cover; but they took no notice. It
zoomed past, and was gone. The voles were still nibbling in
the sunlight. One—the first he had seen—was bigger than
the rest. They were a mother and two babies, he decided; no,
three babies: another appeared from under an alder root.
More horses went by, and bicycles, and a farm cart. No one
saw him under the bridge; and the voles went on scampering,
swimming, shaking themselves in the sun, and crunching
green shoots. He watched them with the same feeling of love
which he had had for the rabbit and for Vole, for Santa and
the dormice, the trapped squirrel and Snowdrop; with the
same dream-like amazement he had felt when he saw the
deer. But in one way he had changed. A year ago, he would
have wanted to take them home and keep them as pets. He
would have been making frantic plans to move them to the
pond in the old rock garden. Now he was perfectly happy to
sit here in his water-hide and watch them. If they came

within range of his camera, he was ready to click the shutter; and some time he would get his picture. But today they remained on the other side of the stream, and he did not really mind. I'll come here often, he thought. Some day I'll see the kingfisher. He could imagine how it would dart by, bright and strange, catching the eye with its extravagance, like the golden pheasants in the forest.

The voles were not like that. They were shadowy as minnows, gentle as rabbits, as much a part of the quiet stream as the brown stones, the twisted roots, the drowned weeds like green hair, and the rich smells of mud and mint. The drone of a plane in the sky, the drone of a tractor on the downs, the nearer traffic on the road seemed to go unheard. Their ancestors had not glanced up, he guessed, when King Charles rode by; a cat might look at a king, but a water vole would not bother. He was cramped now, and midges were biting him, and he wanted his dinner badly; but he sat on without moving until the family had disappeared into its burrow under the bank.

That evening he took down his diary with a sense of celebration. Today's would not only be a good entry; it would be his best so far. The diary was kept on a shelf over his bed, with the stuffed squirrel, his camera and field glasses, the owl whistle and the dried cowslip ball which he had made after his first day at school. He glanced fondly at each of these before sitting down to write. As usual, he looked first at the inscription: "Rose Izard, from Ralph Oliver. Christmas 1926"; fingered the soft leather binding, and admired the little brilliant paintings in the margins of each gilt-edged page: a brimstone butterfly, a beetle, a partridge, a crocus. The end papers were olive green, with a design in white; a winged hour glass wreathed in roses. The words printed inside the wreath gave him a pang of deep sadness, almost of panic: "The Bird of Time has but a little way to fly, and Lo! the Bird is on the Wing."

He turned to January 1, and began to read a line here and there, in Rose Izard's clear handwriting. Her entries followed a pattern: a short note, and then a piece of poetry. He skipped the poetry, understanding that it was a kind of cipher to which he had no key. "Drove to Ballymore," he read: Ballymore was near Nine Wells; the Rose Izard who drove there on the first of January, 1927, was not yet married to Father. "Meet at Kilcraig"; "Made butter roses"; "Meet at Dooley's"; "Raining of course"; "Drove to Poolaphouka"; and, in March: "Lizzie's birthday party, sweet seventeen." Then, on successive days in early April: "Packing"; "In London, staying with Aunt Kate"; "Glorious day". And last of all: "Rollo comes today. 1/1/1 for me." And another piece of poetry, a short one: "Yet seemed it winter still, and you away."

The space was not filled; there was room, as he had thought, for his own diary to begin. He ruled a line.

Underneath he wrote, very carefully, so that the ink should not run on the glossy page: "Saw water voles."

24

Cuckoo

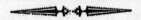

Black Lady was to be lent to Mr. Hassall; she would be one of the clocking hens in the pheasantry, and then have her coop in this year's bird-field. Mr. Hassall came to see Aunt Lizard one evening, and again they stood talking in the Dutch garden. The polyanthus, with their long red stems still carrying new buds, had been removed to the shady summer reserves under the peach walls. The beds were dull again, with small green plants; only patches of flowering wild thyme gave colour to the grey flagged garden.

Ralph brought Black Lady from the brewhouse in her basket, and stood swinging it in his hand, looking up at a broken grating in the wall above the fruit room. He knew that another clocking hen was sitting in there; a small hen, black and white: a pied wagtail.

A sudden flurry of wings at the grating made him stare. A big bird had slipped out and was flying away . . . a hawk? But Mr. Hassall cried, "See there! A cuckoo's come out of that ventilator!"

Ralph was up the wall as quickly as a cat. To find a cuckoo's egg was worth half a dozen other rarities. No one at school had ever seen one. But he was disappointed. The nest looked as usual, with its five grey-speckled eggs. If she had gone there to lay, the hen cuckoo must have thought better of it. He hoped she had not frightened off the "Polly Dishwasher" for good. It would have been a handy place for watching the baby cuckoo; and Aunt Lizard could have watched too, while he was at school. He sighed at the lost chance.

He liked school this term. Old quarrels seemed to be forgotten. It was the beginning of the new school year, and Ralph and his fellows had been moved from Mrs. Duffel's class, to sit under the eye of Governess. Mellowed, perhaps, by the fine weather, Governess was amiable. There were other changes. Several of the older children had left; Katy among them. Everyone was given new notebooks, new pens and pencils. New projects were begun. In Scripture, they had reached the story of Moses; Governess, with her sense of drama, told it as a stirring serial. Then Ralph's group were given runner beans to plant in pots; they were supposed to study the growth of the seedlings, but for the children this nature lesson had become a simple bean race. The beans were luckier than their owners: Governess allowed them a water ration, brought from her own kitchen in a milk can. They took it in turns to water the pots.

One day Ralph had stayed behind, after midday Grace, to take his turn with the watering. He knew the whole of the Grace now; like the Lord's Prayer, it was never taught, but left to infiltrate. The verse ended:

> *"These creatures bless, and grant that we*
> *May feast in Paradise with Thee."*

The "creatures" he took to be himself and the other children. Feasting in Paradise sounded gay; he pictured somewhere high and breezy, with brilliant sunshine and blue air: somewhere, in fact, very like the downland crest where he and the big boys gathered at noon; but with Christmas food instead of sandwiches. Aunt Lizard's bright invention flagged over the eleven weekly sandwich packets. Today it would be cheese and mustard again; or "tar sandwiches", as the others called his bread and butter spread with Bovril. But when he ran out to the porch, his peg was empty. No satchel hung there. He must have forgotten it.

In dismay, he thought he remembered why. Breakfast had ended with a prickly exchange between Aunt Lizard in the kitchen and himself at Brownie's hutch; he had taken out his toast crusts and was feeding Brownie through the wire.

"Hurry, Ralph. It's time you went."

"Pardon?"

"And don't say 'Pardon?', say 'What-did-you-say-please?' "

"Governess says we have to say 'Pardon?' "

"Well, you can say that to Governess, and 'What?' to me."

"Pardon?"

Then she had called him "sir" and hustled him off. It was all her fault; he would tell her so. Should he run home, and fetch the sandwiches? Once, long before, last summer, he had forgotten his satchel, and had run home; Aunt Lizard had made him stay to dinner, and Uncle Laurie had sent him back in the float, which was going to Hurst Castle. He had felt very leisurely, drinking coffee, and arriving back at half past two, with a perfectly good excuse, and only an hour of raffia-work to go. But this was painting afternoon; he did not really want to miss any of it. As he hesitated, Governess looked through the door and asked why he was still there. When he explained, she took out a leather purse and gave him sixpence. "Run and buy something at the shop. That will be quicker."

He thanked her and ran out. For sixpence you could buy a large bag of mixed biscuits. Then he had a surprise. Nat was waiting at the gate, dangling two satchels. He shouted, "Come on. I've got yours here."

"I thought I'd forgotten it!" Then Ralph showed the

sixpence. "Look, Gov'ness lent me this—I'll get some biscuits, shall I?"

The village shop was half a mile away by road, but he took a short cut through the wood and over a field. Breathless, he was soon back with the others. They had finished eating. They watched his approach in silence, and shook their heads when he offered the bag of biscuits. No one took any. They looked at him stonily.

Nat burst out suddenly, "I think it's a dirty twick, so there! Spending Govvy's money!"

"Mean, I call it," said another.

"Governess, she'd have something to say."

"So would your aunty."

"My Dad would hit *me*," said Vincent piously.

Once, in a wrestling match, someone had let go of Ralph suddenly, and he had fallen flat, knocking the breath from his body. He felt the same sensation now. He gasped, "But—she lent it to me! I'm paying her back! What do you mean?" Blank accusing faces silenced him.

"It's *stealing*," they said.

Furious now, he countered, "I've got five sixpences at home. It was only a loan . . . wasn't it?"

They went away. Left to himself, his defence began to crumble. The phrase "false pretence" was years beyond any of them; but no child taught by Governess could have been long in doubt. He saw that they were right. He should have taken back the sixpence at once, as soon as he met Nat. He had thought only that it would be nice to have some biscuits, as well as dry bread, and that he could pay it back tomorrow just the same. What a cuckoo he was! No, worse; he saw his action now through the eyes of Governess: stealing, lying and gluttony. Hell gaped for him.

He tried defiantly to choke down a biscuit; then stuffed the whole lot into a burrow, and his sandwiches after them. Nothing was right now; his painting of a dog-rose got smudged, and there were blotches on the page. Governess scolded him for carelessness with the paint water. It was not paint water, but tears. He scrubbed his eyes furtively on his cuff, and scowled at the others.

Next day brought a deadlock which he had not foreseen. Governess refused his sixpence. "No, thank you, Ralph. That's quite all right. I'm glad you told me."

He was aghast. Her kindness made his crime far worse. His classmates nodded at him with grim smiles that meant: *See? You haven't paid it back, have you?* In his misery, even raffia afternoon seemed welcome. It was no use trying to enjoy anything. The sixpence remained in his shorts pocket. How on earth could he get it into Governess's purse? He knew every hateful detail of its acorn design.

Saturday at least meant that he could stay at home. But as he wandered about, looking at nests, the truth struck him: he would have to explain to Governess what he had done, and *make* her take the sixpence. The thought made him shudder. How in the world could he face her? It was not fear he felt, exactly, but a kind of sick distaste for the scene that would follow: probably she would give the whole school a lecture on dishonesty. Couldn't he post the wretched thing to her? Or just leave it on her desk? But he knew that would only make matters worse. He would have to go through with it. And now he must wait until Monday. It never occurred to him that he might have gone to High Forest at once, and knocked on the schoolhouse door, and ended his suffering there and then. Somehow he felt as though school was a place that vanished on Friday afternoon, at the joyful moment of release, and reappeared only on Monday morning.

On Sundays, Uncle Laurie's newspaper was left at the

Cuckoo

Hurst Castle lodge two miles away, to be fetched by Fergus or Ralph. This Sunday afternoon it was Ralph who volunteered. He set off on foot; he had decided to look for pigeons' nests in the fir thickets on the south side of the drive. He worked his way from tree to tree, struggling upward through dense brushwood, and sometimes crawling from one tree to the next through interlocking boughs. He found seventeen nests, and counted twenty-nine eggs. At four o'clock he reached the lodge and turned for home with the paper. He left it at the foot of several trees on the homeward route; one nest in an oak tree, shaped like an untidy drey, he felt sure was a magpie's. He arrived home at tea time, hot, tired and filthy, his hair full of bark and twigs, his jersey smeared with green, face and hands black with resin. He had cut his hand on a fir spike. It had not struck him that poor Uncle Laurie had been waiting in vain for his pleasant Sunday afternoon with the paper. Also, he had lost the sixpence; he would have to take another from his box. Perhaps the magpie would find the lost one. Sixpence was three weeks' pocket money; but it was worth it. For a whole afternoon he had forgotten his trouble.

Governess was funny, he thought afterwards: contrary, he might have said, if a person can be agreeably contrary. So often, when one meant no harm, one proved to be in disgrace. But on that black Monday morning, when he went to her before school, and stammered his story, and put the coin into her hand, she seemed only puzzled. She even tried to give it to him again; but when he backed away, saying in horror, "No, no," she seemed to grasp the matter. Even then she only said, "Very well. Thank you, Ralph." He fled before she could begin reprisals. He had a feeling that, in all his life, no effort would ever again be so hard. Now he had

239

got it over: she could say what she liked, and so could the others. He no longer had the sixpence.

But he heard no more. The week passed peacefully. His cut hand was still bandaged, and on Friday afternoon Governess said to him, "Better not do raffiawork with that hand. I'll find you something to read." She took out a set of new reading books, and let him choose. He spent a happy afternoon with *Black Beauty*. On the next Friday she said, "I don't think your hand is quite well yet." He finished *Black Beauty* and began *Tarka the Otter*. On the third Friday, nothing was said at all; he found the book ready on his desk. Pecky had taken over his mat, and was transforming it into a dainty basket.

Then it was time to stake the beans, and Ralph was chosen to go out and cut hazel sticks. Another morning, Governess wanted a message taken to the Vicarage; it was Ralph who was sent. The others were as surprised as Ralph himself at all this, and inclined to murmur among themselves, like the children of Israel; but to no effect. The taunt "teacher's pet" glanced off him like a feather. Besides Governess, he had other allies. A gipsy family had camped at a near-by farm, and two boys came to school while their elders worked in the fields, picking peas and singling turnips. They were a handsome pair of brothers, with flashing white teeth which, they told Ralph, they cleaned with soot and willow twigs. The forest children avoided the newcomers. Ralph was charmed by their adventurous life, their gaiety, and their nonchalance in the face of isolation. No one interfered with them. They were dangerous; nearly every day they fell out and fought each other savagely.

Ralph came in one day to find the smaller brother lying on the classroom floor, panting, soaked and speechless, while Mrs. Duffel held a cup of warm milk to his lips. They had fought until he collapsed; his brother had run away, still gibbering with rage. What was the fight about? Mrs. Duffel gently questioned. The boy grinned and shook his head. Later, he told Ralph that his brother had given him some wild strawberries, and one was "a bad thing": a cuckoo-pint berry, Ralph at length discovered. Curious, he picked one and tasted it. It burned his tongue like fire, and the burning went on, even after he had reached home and held his mouth under the cold tap.

At the time, Ralph persisted, "Then why was *he* wild with *you*?"

"I let his rabbit out."

"Oh, have you got a rabbit? So have I." Then he found that the rabbit had not been in a hutch, but in a snare. "It's easy," said little Dan, with his disarming smile, "I can show you how to set one in a minute."

Cuckoo, too, found rabbiting easy. That evening, replete from his usual kill, he was sitting beside Ralph in the Dutch garden, on a stone seat warm from the day's sun. He began to gaze intently at the grating, from which the little wagtails seemed to have flown. Ralph followed his look, and realized that some sort of commotion was going on up there; and the parent wagtails had reappeared. They ran up and down the wall, bobbing and calling. Now there was a heavy fluttering and flapping from behind the small iron lid. Padding up the slate roof, he saw a bird trapped inside: a sprawling bird, the size of a thrush, with wide-open beak and a mouth the colour of orange peel. A young cuckoo. Something about its grey-and-fawn tabby markings seemed familiar. Enlightened, he told Aunt Lizard, "*Now* I know why you called Cuckoo, Cuckoo."

"Partly that. And partly because John said, 'Choose the one you want, the way I can bucket the rest.'"

So the hen cuckoo had tricked him; either she had laid her egg at the first visit, and cunningly hidden it in the nest, or she had come back later. Now the wagtails were slaves to her chick; he was fed devotedly by them, and by the swallows from the brewhouse. But she had made a mistake: the hole in the grating was too small for the clumsy fledgeling. How it would have escaped without help, or whether the foster parents would have grown tired at last, and left it to starve, Ralph could not tell. Next day he put on a leather glove and drew it through the hole, and put it into a parrot cage borrowed from Mrs. Hassall. The cage was set on top of the wall; the young cuckoo crouched on the floor, uttering harsh cries which brought a crowd of frenzied small birds to join in feeding it. They were too intent on this task to show any fear of Ralph, who sat with his camera a few feet away. Cuckoo the cat looked on from below. Sometimes the swallows would mob him, with hostile shrieks, and he would flatten his ears and give them a piercing look. But, on the third morning, he was seen on the wall, playfully slipping a paw between the bars. Uncle Laurie was afraid that he might tip the cage through the glass roof of the peach house; so Cuckoo was locked in the Sky, and the cage door was set open. Ralph came back from school to hear that the youngster had flown, followed by his twittering retinue, and had disappeared at last among the orchard trees.

Ralph missed Nat keenly all through this episode. But their friendship seemed to be over. Nat had not borrowed the owl whistle since the day of the unlucky sixpence; Ralph never saw Snowdrop now. They went by separate ways to school, and Ralph spent his spare time with the gipsies, learning to be a poacher.

Hardly a day went by, however, without some incident

which Nat would have appreciated. A hen pheasant had
nested in the rock garden, and had laid a dozen eggs. Ralph
had betrayed her to the keepers, and seen the eggs carried
away. Then, to his delight, she had laid another four. Now
she was strutting about the orchard with her chicks. Ralph
looked on the brood as his own. He had told no one about
them; but he would have told Nat. He wanted to tell him,
too, about the wren's nest he had found, full of bumble-bees;
and about the grasshopper-warbler's nest, with its tiny rose-
pink eggs; and the clever chaffinch's nest, made of grey
lichen to match the grey notches around it; and the hawk
moth, which had hatched at long last; and of his water-
hide, and the water voles, seen three times since his first visit.
And they had meant to play bicycle bird-nesting all over the
forest, up and down the rides. He felt forlorn when he
thought of Nat.

He was thinking of him one Saturday morning, as he made
his way before breakfast to see if the water voles were about.
He pedalled quickly along the lane into the early sunlight.
The gipsies were gone; but they would be back, Dan said, for
Sloe Fair and Taro Fair, in the market towns, between harvest
and tater-picking. Perhaps he could go to the fair with Nat,
he thought. They would find chestnuts together again, and
light fires at noon to roast them. Next winter, Nat had said,
he would be allowed to go "stopping" at the pheasant shoots.
I'll make Aunt Lizard let me go, he thought. Next winter,
too, there might be a real snowfall, with tobogganing on the
downs.

He came to the stream, and rode quietly to and fro, looking
out for the voles. They were not about this morning; he did
not really expect to see them, for a lorry was unloading a
mountain of grey shingle along the roadside, just by the
bridge. All along the brink of the stream there were huge

white concrete pipes, like the tree trunks beside the forest
road last summer. He saw an old roadman whom he knew,
and asked, trying to hide his anxiety:

"Will it take long, mending the road?"

"Mending it?" The old man gave a dour look at the pipes.
"It's more than mending this time. They're making it into a
blasted race-track, that's about it."

"A race-track?"

"They're making it wider, see? See them great pipes?
They're going to turn the old stream into a drain and bury it
down under."

Aunt Lizard was reading a letter at the breakfast-table. She
said, "Well! Governess says she will miss you."

"Governess? *Miss* me?"

She put the letter down and looked across at him, saying
a little uncertainly, "I had to write, you see, and explain that
we'll be leaving here."

"Leaving?"

"Why, yes. Don't you remember? We're leaving in six
weeks."

25

Caravan

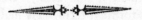

Ralph sat at the top of the warren, beside the old train. Down below he could hear the keepers calling to one another as they went round the bird-field. He could hear the steady hum of the motor mower, too, as Harry rode up and down the wide cricket lawn. Billy came after him, sweeping the mowings into a rubber-tyred cart; Sally's hooves were muffled in lawn shoes. Away to the south-west sounded the screech of the saw mill. A water cart was coming up from the home farm to the bird-field. Everyone but himself had work to do. But I could learn to do those jobs, he thought. Why do I have to go away?

Fergus and Peter were going, he knew. Both Mr. Hassall and Uncle Laurie had doubts about the future. The world had changed since Uncle Laurie sat in the daffodil wood. Forty years on, they wondered, would there be a place in England for gardeners and gamekeepers? As for the boys themselves, they wanted change and adventure. So Fergus was going into the London office of a great trading company, and then abroad, to one of the firm's estates in Africa. "Unless there's a war, of course," he told Ralph. "Then I'll be in the Army." And Peter was going to fly with the Royal Air Force.

"But it's different for me," Ralph thought. "I shall be like the Keartons. I don't want to go anywhere else."

Then he thought of the water voles; they would be going too. Anger and despair filled him.

It was true that Aunt Lizard had said, from time to time, "When you go to school at Uncle Alfred's———" "When we're together in the holidays———" Skimming strawberry jam, she had said, "I expect you may have a pot for school." Buying his new shoes, it had been, "Black, I think, then they'll still be right for next term." He had heard all this, but had, as it were, put off thinking about it. School meant High Forest, not Uncle Alfred's preparatory school. That had seemed a long way off in time, like being old enough to use the gun. Now, suddenly, it was *now*. In a few weeks, his father would be here. It was his "long leave". He would sleep in the spare room, where Peter had slept on New Year's morning. They would go to London, and then he and Father would set off together for a holiday, climbing mountains in the north: "just the two of you," Aunt Lizard had said, "before you come over to Nine Wells." Then he would go to this new school.

He thought vaguely of the north, Northumberland, Cumberland, Durham: he remembered the names from the map at High Forest school, which he had looked at every day, learning the bones of England without realizing it. Some phrase, heard once in the past, came to his mind, and he said aloud, "I don't want to go off . . . all round the moon."

Couldn't he tell Father so? Was it too late to change their plans for him? But some instinct told him that, if there had been a chance of appeal, Aunt Lizard would have taken it already. He remembered her quiet remark this morning: "Your father must be longing to see you." He knew this carried a command: "You mustn't disappoint your father."

Still, a wild idea was running in his head; a plan for turning his back on them all and taking to the forest, living as he wanted to live, like a fox cub or a hare, like Cap'n Crewe, like a gipsy. He twisted round to look at the old train. It would make a fine caravan. He might use it on winter nights, when even keepers sometimes stayed at home and would not discover him: for of course he would be hunted, a fugitive. But he could build hides; there were deep thickets in the forest where no one but himself seemed to go; sandpits in the haunted copse, yew tree and juniper spinneys on the downs, the lonely place where he had met the deer. He could lie low until he was older, like the children of the New Forest.

Then he felt his own loneliness. The New Forest children had had each other. The gipsy boys had had each other, even though they fought. Mowgli had had his wolf brothers. He would be quite alone, like old Meg Merrilies:

> *"Her Brothers were the craggy hills,*
> *Her Sisters larchen trees.*
> *Alone with her great family*
> *She lived as she did please."*

All right, he thought. That's what I'll do.

Walking through the forest, he smelt a pungent whiff of fish, and knew that Cap'n was toasting a bloater for his dinner. On Friday evenings he went to the village for his supplies, carrying them back in his knapsack. He had a cottage somewhere, but at this time of the year he seemed to live in his hazel shelter; keeping an eye on the cut timber which might otherwise have disappeared, for pea-sticks or firewood, into visiting cars. He kept an eye on other matters too. Once he had sharply accused Nat and Ralph of robbing a nest in the hazel stubs—a ground blackbird's, he called it— and then agreed reluctantly that the thief might have been a rat. His shelter was a *hide*, Ralph saw; he lived like a Kear-

ton, though he had no camera. You see, Ralph told himself
—*he* lives here. I shall too.

The old man enjoyed his hermit's life, anyone could see
that; yet he was not always unfriendly. Once, when Ralph
passed on the way to school, he had given the boy half a
bloater, sizzling between two pieces of bread. It had tasted
delicious; although later in the day, tortured by thirst, Ralph
had regretted it. The memory made him thirsty now. Skirting the clearing, he crossed the High Forest road and made
his way to the gooseberry patch by the old well. But Nat
had been there before him; the gooseberries were gone.
Sucking a grass stalk, he thought about his plan. He would
have these weeks to make a food store somewhere. Father
had sent him five shillings; he would save that for winter.
Winter, he saw, would be the problem. He wasn't a dormouse, or even a squirrel, to sleep away the cold days. There
would be blackberries at first, and then hazel nuts, and then
chestnuts. What then? Dan had shown him how to set a snare;
the thing was . . . could he eat what he caught? It would be
like eating Brownie or Santa.

He remembered one shameful day at Nine Wells, when,
prowling with bow and arrow, he had shot at a guinea fowl
chick and it had fallen. Vividly he recalled the thrill he had
felt; but when he ran to it, to receive what he took to be a
dying look of reproach—ah, that was a different story.
Bursting into tears, he had carried it to Grandmother, who
had wrapped it in a woollen shawl and nursed it by the stove.
The relief he had felt, when it hopped out of its shroud and
began to peck at the dog's dish! No, he did not believe he
could be a hunter. But he could dig a patch of ground somewhere, and grow things . . . potatoes, perhaps. He could start
with this old garden here, and bring seedlings from the
rubbish yard; onion thinnings, and carrots and cabbages. He

wished he had some young carrots now, sweet and juicy. He
wished there were some apples on the ancient tree; it was
barren this year. He thought again of poor Meg:

> *"No breakfast had she many a morn,*
> *No dinner many a noon;*
> *And 'stead of supper she would stare*
> *Full hard against the Moon."*

It seemed a bleak prospect. He walked on, and came out
on to the downs, and sat watching the little black trains in the
valley. Soon he would be in one of them, going away to
London. How could he help himself? He saw that he could
not. He lay watching small things in the grass; ants, a yellow
ladybird in a beech shuck, a burrowing mole. A cat strolled
from a cottage at the edge of the forest. That had a home, too.
They would all be here when he was gone. He wriggled
downhill into the sun, on the soft tussocky grass. I've been
up since dawn, he thought; no wonder I feel sleepy.

He woke in shadow. The sun had gone down behind the
blackthorn scrub beyond the forest. The sky looked high and
pale. It must be late. He had better go home. No, not home,
he remembered; the garden house had given him up, after
all. Trudging through a ride, among last year's leaves, he
retraced his thoughts. Surely he was not simply backing out?
He had had a plan this morning: some idea of staying away
until he was grown-up, being Mowgli, being a gipsy, living
alone in a caravan. But I can't decide now, he thought. I'll
go to my hide in the beeches, and sit there a bit, and see what
I'm going to do next. He found his way wearily through the
rides, crossed the road again and came to the beech wood
hide. Walking with bent head, scuffing the leaves, he was
almost there when he saw someone sitting on his log in front
of the door: Aunt Lizard.

She looked rather strange, he thought; or perhaps it was only the greenish light in the wood. She said, "There you are. I was just going home."

He said nothing. They walked in silence across the bird-field, between the shuttered coops. Uncle Laurie and Fergus, he remembered, were away at a cricket match. They had set off in the morning. Indoors, therefore, he was surprised to see that the dining room table still seemed to be set for the midday meal; it was untouched. A tomato salad looked dim and stale; he caught a breath of oily sweetness from it, and said at once, in a low voice:

"Oh, I do feel sick."

"What have you been eating?" Quick inevitable question.

"Nothing." He remembered, with surprise: "Just nothing."

"Better go to bed, Lord Randal, my son." She gave a queer little laugh.

She helped him into bed, as though he were three years old, and brought a sponge for his face and hands. Lying back, he heard her go to the door, and warned her in panic:

"I'm going to be sick in a minute."

"I don't think so. Go to sleep."

"I'm *far* too tired to *sleep*."

"I shan't be long."

She was gone. He lay back, breathing deeply, while tired-ness, or nausea, swept over him in waves. His feet were icy. Downstairs, he heard the whirr of an egg beater. What could she be doing? He heard Brownie thumping her hutch. Brownie would be hungry, he must tell Aunt Lizard. He opened his eyes, and found Aunt Lizard there, with a tray. She said, "I thought we might have some tea."

He was going to whisper, "I can't." But she was pouring a cup. It was China tea. The smell, dry, unsickly, faintly burnt, made him change his mind. He sat up. She moved the table and chair to sit beside him. Sipping, he saw that she had brought something to eat; a tower of small hot Welsh griddle cakes, wrapped in a napkin. Again he was ready to say, "I can't"; but the first one melted in his mouth, and he put out his hand for another. They were spread with sharp pink apple jelly. Funny, he thought; she had brought the only food in the world he could have swallowed. He remembered the Siberian crabs, and began to laugh, and to tell her about them.

Much later, but no longer feeling exhausted, he lay watching her as she stood in twilight by the dressing table. She had washed her hair, and was brushing it out. Seeing that he was not asleep, she said, "Did you know, Uncle Alfred's very clever at photography. He's got his own dark room. He'll help you a lot."

He made a small sound of assent. After a while he said, "But it'll be town, won't it? Near London?"

"Why, it's out in the country. Hertfordshire."

He thought of the names on the map. Most of them he knew only by sight. He asked at length, "Is it that one— H,e,r,t——?"

"That's the one."

It *is* near London, he told himself. Aloud he said, "There won't be any wild animals. Nor birds. Just sparrows."

Yes, there will, thought Lizard, looking into the glass. At night in London the owls go sparrow-hunting, you hear them crying over the stone forest, just like the owls here. And there are hedgehogs at Highgate and badgers at Barnet, and the Piccadilly Tube runs out among the fox holes on the edge of Hertfordshire . . . but I won't tell him that. Let him find out for himself.

26

"The Bird of Time"

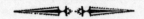

Under the trees it was dark as a cave. Chestnut fans
blotted out the sky. The beech foliage was tarnished,
almost brown in the heat of August. There was a
musty aroma of fungus. Ralph knelt on the ground, sorting
the things he had brought in Fergus's school satchel. A tin
box, string, sticking plaster, an oilskin; then the leather diary,
the owl whistle, the March copy of *Field and Forest*. He was
making a cache in the hollow tree where the owls had nested.

Like Rose Izard, he had kept the diary little more than
three months. Now he was leaving it behind; half believing
that, if he did so, he would return to finish it. He looked at
last night's entry: "Bats hanging in cricket pavilion. Ha Ha.
Gave Brownie to Nat." He had written his own name in the
book, under his parents', and hesitated over an address—"I
haven't got one," he thought—before writing: "Nine Wells,
Ballymore, Ireland."

The bats were little pipistrelles. They had littered the floor
of the pavilion with moths' wings. Yesterday morning, he
had gone there with Fergus, to return a cricket bat. Fergus,
vigorously clearing his room of ten years' ownership, had
given him the satchel, the tin box and the oilskin. In the
afternoon, Aunt Lizard and Ralph had driven with him in
the trap to Hurst Castle station. All the way they met cars

speeding towards them along the drive. Sally bucked and tossed her head. People were going to see a play in a hall at the back of the great house. The play had been running all the week. It was for some charity; and today there was a fête on the cricket outfield, and the gardens were open to visitors. When they drove back, without Fergus, the cars were ranged in ranks on the gravel sweep. A car park attendant came forward courteously to take the pony's bridle; then sprang back as Sally stared, shied and bolted. Curbing her, Aunt Lizard glanced at Ralph. The thought of Sally in a car park was diverting; but Ralph was still far away.

Fergus, on his last evening at home, had taken them to the play. It was *A Midsummer Night's Dream*. Tim Lamb was in it, a singing elf, carrying a bulrush. Tim had his wish this time; he was dressed in green from head to foot. Ralph had been out in the punt with Mr. Hassall, helping to cut the bulrushes; he had watched Ted wire them. There were real bloodhounds in the play, someone said. Apart from all this, he was only mildly interested beforehand; and the evening took him utterly by surprise. He was possessed. The grown-up scenes passed over his head; but the wood, the moonlight, the little imperious creatures pierced him. Busy Puck, Titania like a ghost moth, the beautiful boy Oberon in his silver tunic, the skipping elves—he watched them as though they were water voles or dormice. He could not bear the play to end, it should go on and on, a dream from which one need not wake. He was wrung with feeling. Next day, he could not bear to speak of it, but as the day passed, he knew he must go there again. Sent to bed, after the parting with Nat and Brownie, he climbed down the roof in dressing gown and slippers; dropped into the churchyard, and made his way, behind the yew hedges, to the shrubbery at the back of the hall. The first act was nearly over; the doors were shut, and no one was about. He stood listening. Soon he heard Puck, and another voice; then Oberon's ringing *Ill met by moonlight, proud Titania,* and her fairy mockery, *Set your heart at rest. . . .*

In the intervals, when the doors opened, he ran away to the oak tree at the end of the lawn; then stole back, thistles pricking through his slippers. The last act began; it was dark now in the shrubbery and round the hall. He crept to a door just by the stage, and leaned against it. Inside, the long speeches went on; soon the elves would return. He waited.

Then, a few feet away, came a swift movement. He saw a gleam like a raised sword; and the silence was shattered by the sound of a trumpet. The notes seemed to blaze in his ears; he leapt instantly away; then stood still. The trumpeter, awaiting his cue outside, must have been as startled as Ralph; hearing footsteps creeping in the dark, with no time to investigate. But he had stood his ground. Now, his part over, he stared towards the shadowy figure in its long robe like a boy monk. Ralph stared back. They could hear each other breathing; neither moved or spoke. The last songs began and ended. Ralph tiptoed away.

After the darkness, it seemed light as day on the lawns. Moonlight glittered in the sea creeks five miles away. Voices were piping in his head:

> *"Now it is the time of night*
> *That the graves, all gaping wide,*
> *Every one lets forth its sprite,*
> *In the church-way paths to glide . . ."*

At the churchyard gate he hesitated; then made a detour through the moonlit garden. White paper bags gleamed on the apple and pear trees, shielding the fruits from wasps and birds. The air smelled of cedars and honey. He peered, as he had done so often, through the window of the sitting room, curtained only with fronds of wistaria. No one had missed him. Uncle Laurie smoked over the crossword puzzle; Aunt Lizard was writing letters.

But, under the chestnut tree, Ralph thought: everything is different this week. It was no longer the place he had known; and he was glad, glad. Tonight, Father was coming. To-morrow they would leave. On Monday the garden would be its old self; there would be no cars on the drive and no tents on the lawn. He wanted to be gone before then.

His cache was ready, diary and whistle wrapped in the paper, parcelled in the oilskin; the parcel fitted into the tin, and the lid secured with sticking plaster. He wedged the tin inside the satchel, drawing the buckles tight. It went on his back like a rucksack, leaving his arms free. He climbed steadily to the top of the chestnut, and pulled himself into the broken crown, where three branches sloped upward. A fourth branch had rotted away, leaving the gaping hole, like a chimney, where the owls' nest had been. He slid the satchel through, and heard it drop to the floor of the chimney; like posting a letter. At once he began to regret it; quickly he climbed down, and came with relief into the sun.

People were everywhere. The garden walls echoed with voices. Music sounded through a loudspeaker: the fête was in full career. A little Moth aeroplane swooped overhead, giving five shilling flights. Groping for the two half-crowns knotted ready in his handkerchief, Ralph walked straight up the middle path between the flower borders; through the Dutch garden, where humming-bird hawk moths darted among purple verbenas and lilac-coloured dahlias; on toward the runway in the east park where the aeroplane would land. Crossing the east lawn, he met a green child: Tim Lamb, free for an hour between performances, had changed back into his own clothes, but his face and hands were still stained apple-green. Ralph looked at him with envy, thinking, "That would have been just the thing, for watching peewits in the marsh. Richard Kearton would have hit on it. Oh, well. . . ."

Tim was disconsolate. He had been given tea, but still he was faint with hunger. His home was miles away. An evening's capering and singing lay before him. The two boys walked back together to the garden, and Ralph vanished indoors. Coming out again through the front way, with a packet wrapped in sandwich paper, he was surprised to see Aunt Lizard and Uncle Laurie sitting in the shade.

"Come and have your tea!"

He called, without stopping, "I'm taking some to Tim."

"Wait. Bring Tim as well."

He stood for a second, then edged away towards the gate. "I've got this for him. He's going back——" In a moment, he knew, Aunt Lizard would notice his appearance, and send him to wash.

"Wouldn't he like a cake? What are you taking him?"

"Apricocks and dewberries," suggested Uncle Laurie.

Ralph grinned politely and fled. The hungry fairy had begged, "*Do* bring me a few cold sausages."

Aunt Lizard's voice floated after him: "Come straight back. Father——" He did not stay to hear the rest. Unless he got away now, it would be too late, he would never have his flight at all.

The Moth rested on a grass track at the top of the east park, an ancient bridle-way to the downs. No one else was waiting. The joking youths, the twittering girls were gone for a while. Even Peter was gone. The pilot sat in the bracken, smoking a pipe. He stood up and gave the breathless child a nod. He could do with this kind of passenger: mute, alert, delighted. The plane bumped along the track and rose into the air.

Ralph saw the winged shadow below, and almost screamed out, "We're like a hawk!" The wind streamed over them. Watching the park slide away underneath, he thought, "The Bird of Time"—what was that bit in the diary? "The Bird of Time has but a little way to fly, and Lo! the Bird is on the Wing." On the wing . . . but it was not sad at all. It was glorious. They were high up now, speeding over the sand-coloured park with its pools of trees, over the haunted lane, the tower, the harvest fields; heading out towards the sea. The creeks were outlined like jigsaw curves. Beyond was the steely Channel. Wheeling, they flew back over stooks and water meadows; that white thread must be all that was left of the buried stream. Here the forest began; how small and lost the roads were. He remembered the map he had drawn for homework. And there, there was High Forest school! The two playgrounds were like white pocket handkerchiefs. It seemed deserted, all of it. He gazed, longing for a last sight of Governess; he pictured her shading her eyes, frowning perhaps from her window at the plane high overhead: "the heighth of impudence," he thought, and waved his hand. The school was far away. They flew west across the forest, round over the bright links of the duck ponds, and back towards the gardens, following the black line of the Groves. Now he saw ahead the very homestead he had imagined at Nine Wells: a nutshell in a green husk. Once more they were circling. There was the chestnut where he had left his hoard; he looked down into its top. He would never see that again, until he went back for the cache.

But perhaps before then some other boy would find it. Uncle Laurie would retire. There would be new people here: Aunt Lizard had said so. One more cat would scratch the leg of the kitchen table. Another child would ride on the beech tree saddle, run along the walls, stalk mice in the harness room, spend hours in the frame yard, tight-rope walking on the narrow edges of the frames. His gooseberries in the rock garden, his secret red cowslip in the orchard, the summer-house on the roof—someone else would find them.

Suddenly, just below, he saw the garden house; four-square, tiny, planted like a tree. How quickly they were flying: only a glimpse, and then it was gone. He hoped it would stand there for a long time.